EYES ON YOU

STEVE P. VINCENT

ACT I

1

ASHLEY

A shley Wheeler walked slowly down the aisle, staring at the products on the shelves until she finally picked one at random. Staring at the soup, she read that it contained 260 calories per serving and now had 25 percent more real tomatoes. As she stared at the label with feigned interest, her ears strained, listening for that sweet voice again, but hearing nothing.

Teeth clenched and body tense, Ashley gripped the can tightly. She had to take her chance, even though she wasn't sure she had the courage to. There'd be trouble if she was caught, and she already had enough of that. After a moment's hesitation and one deep breath – a sharp, quick inhale and a long, slow exhale – she made up her mind.

The soup was still in her hand as she walked to the end of the aisle and turned the corner. Before she could make it to the next aisle, she noticed a pimply-faced boy watching her, his back to the milk he'd been stacking on the shelves. The boy glanced at the can in her hand and then his gaze returned to her face. This was the third time she'd noticed him sizing her up.

Ashley took a step towards the boy, jerking her thumb in the direction of the next aisle. "Is the pasta down here?"

The teenager gave a slow, exaggerated nod and Ashley started to move again. She'd hoped he might leave her alone if she spoke to him, but he still looked suspicious. Ashley knew she needed to move quickly. With each passing second her resolve lessened and the chances of the boy alerting security or Tom seeing her increased. A few steps down the aisle, she froze.

"Daddy, can I have some candy?" The child's voice was full of joy. "I'm going to get chocolate *and* licorice!"

It was Lucy. The voice was unmistakable. Ashley's heart swelled with happiness. Her daughter was right around the corner. She was instantly deluged with flashbacks: the smell of shampoo in her auburn hair; the way she used to tangle her fingers through Ashley's hair; the dimples on her cheeks when she got excited; her first crawl, walk and words.

Ashley shook her head. There'd be time for nostalgia later, when they were together again. A voice in the back of her brain shouted at her to turn back, but she buried the thought and pressed on. This was her chance to right the largest of so many wrongs that had occurred in her life. Ashley set aside the can of soup, balled her fists, walked around the corner and nearly cried out with joy.

Lucy was standing halfway down the aisle, her wild red hair curling down her back and a dimpled smile illuminating her face. Lucy picked up some chocolate, her face bright with excitement. The sight brought a smile to Ashley's face. Seeing Lucy up close made everything that was wrong with her life right now seem a little bit better.

Tom was searching the shelves further along the aisle, several yards from Lucy. Ashley rushed towards her daughter. Her plan was risky, but it had been a month since she'd seen Lucy, thanks to a legal system unable to look after the victims of crime, and she couldn't wait any longer. She needed her daughter back.

Lucy turned her head when Ashley was a few yards away. In an instant, that beautiful smile was replaced with a confused frown.

"Lucy." Ashley felt her voice crack as she reached for the little girl's hand. It was like reaching for some amazing treasure. "Come with me."

"Mommy?" Lucy spoke softly as her mind struggled to process seeing Ashley again. "Are you here to see Daddy and me?"

"No, baby. Just you."

Ashley gripped Lucy's hand, leading Lucy away from Tom as fast as she could. She only had a few seconds' break on her ex-husband, but she'd almost reached the end of the aisle by the time he noticed and started shouting. His negligence was further proof that Lucy needed her mother.

With the exit of the store in sight, Ashley redoubled her pace. "We're nearly there, Lucy."

Lucy finally found her voice. "Why can't Daddy come?"

Ashley had no time to argue her case or explain that Tom couldn't come with them. She reached down, scooped Lucy up and started to run. She heard Tom shout after her again, but Ashley ignored him. Her eyes were on the exit.

Then a hand clenched her shoulder.

Ashley turned to face the security guard. "We're in a hurry."

"Please don't make a scene." The guard spoke firmly. "Don't make this worse."

"She's my daughter!" Her voice was laced with months of built-up pain and grief.

Ashley was now surrounded by several members of staff. Her eyes darted around, looking for an escape, but there was nowhere to go. Her heart sank when Tom caught up with them and reached out for Lucy. Ashley squeezed Lucy tight, trying to hold on with all her strength, but the guard helped pry open her grip enough for Tom to take Lucy from her again.

Ashley cried out. "No!"

Suddenly, the flashbacks returned. But this time they were of less happy moments: fights with Tom about the trial; her struggles with her mental health; her pleas with him to help her; the sight of Lucy being driven away after the custody decision; the loneliness. With a sob, she was forced to reconcile with Tom taking her daughter from her once again.

"You're out of your mind, Ashley!" His voice was full of anger. "You need to get help."

Ashley turned her head away from him as the staff continued to grip her arms tightly. Lucy's relief at being reunited with her father was too much. Ashley had hoped to take Lucy back to Connecticut and start anew, and her failure cut even deeper than losing Lucy in the first place. She looked back to Tom and Lucy, but they were already leaving.

"Miss, you need to sit." The guard steered her towards a bench at the front of the store.

Ashley slumped down onto the bench seat with little grace or care. They'd all be judging her, thinking she was some crazy woman who'd tried to abduct a little girl. They didn't know the depth of her pain, how much she'd suffered, how damaged she was. She kept silent, and they told her not to move.

Ashley stared at the floor, her head in her hands. Her red hair fell in front of her, catching some of her tears. It was all so unfair. She'd done the right thing in the past and lost everything because of it. Nobody recognized that – not Tom, and not the legal system. She could only hope that someday there'd be justice.

Heaving sobs racked her body. Nobody comforted her or told her everything would be okay. It hadn't been for a very long time, and she'd just made things much worse.

2

DUNCAN

D uncan Rowe shook the juice box and then raised it to his mouth. With his other hand holding the binoculars to his eyes, he slurped the last of the orange juice, then threw the empty container on the ground, where it joined the other detritus from his hour-long stakeout, including a candy bar wrapper and an apple core.

"How much longer can this take?" Duncan sighed. His leg had a twitch and he was growing impatient.

He'd been watching her the whole time, never looking away in case he missed his chance. She was sitting alone on a bench in the middle of the park, waiting for her husband to arrive. Watching her cry had grown old, even if he was the architect of her sorrow, but he couldn't act yet. He hadn't put in all this work to ruin it now.

The meeting he'd engineered between the woman and her husband would be her last stand, the confrontation that would light the spark on the final conflagration of the bitch's life. She'd lost so much already, but now it was time to watch her lose it all. She deserved nothing less.

She'd come to Duncan's attention over a dating website. Her red hair had piqued his interest, but once he'd started to study her she'd lured him in even more. His grip tightened on the binoculars as he recalled her profile – the misplaced sense of entitlement, the gall to admit she had a husband at the same time she was trying to find a fuck, and the blunt statement that her career came before anything else.

It had stirred an anger in him.

Duncan had gone to work. He'd studied her, then set about taking away all the things that were important to her. Her career was ruined, her family no longer spoke to her, her husband had stormed out with their daughter. One by one, he'd kicked the struts out from beneath her life.

He'd watched her slip, from being confident and in command to out of control and grasping. Now she knew what it felt like to be powerless, humiliated, and rejected. Now that his hard work was reaching an end point, Duncan's anticipation was almost overwhelming.

The woman stood, breaking his reverie. She rubbed her eyes and offered a weak smile to someone. Duncan shifted the binoculars and saw a man approaching her. Even from this distance he looked tense. The woman tried to hug him, but he rebuffed her. Duncan couldn't blame the guy. He'd be repulsed if he were married to a lying whore, too.

Quashing the hope that her relationship could be saved had been Duncan's endgame, at least as far as her emotions were concerned. He still had more in store for her body. Duncan watched eagerly as they argued, their hand gestures animated. She was probably still saying she loved him, which Duncan knew was a lie.

He'd suffered enough pain of his own because of a woman like her and now his role was to punish those who were similar. But he was also a savior. Though he'd never met the woman's husband, Duncan knew he'd saved him. The man could begin his life anew, raising his daughter to be nothing like her mother.

The woman tried to grab her husband's hand, but he pushed her to the ground. She landed hard, clearly in pain, but this did nothing to stop her husband from leaning over and shouting at her. Duncan couldn't hear what he was saying, but that didn't matter, because his anger was clear even from this distance.

The husband turned and started to walk away. After a few steps, she said something that made him pause. Duncan wondered what promises she was making. She was on her ass in the dirt, her makeup streaking down her face as she cried, her hand outstretched. But her husband kept walking.

Duncan had her right where he wanted her. He stood and made his way down the fire escape. As he descended, his anticipation grew and his fists were balled so tightly that his fingernails cut into his palms. He reached the ground. The alley was empty. Perfect. He moved behind a dumpster and retrieved the baseball bat he'd left there.

He crossed the street to the park, sat on a bench and watched her. She was a mess, curled into a ball with her head in her hands, crying. A few passersby offered assistance, but she ignored them. Duncan waited. He had all the time in the world. He liked watching them disintegrate.

His victims went through four stages of loss. First, he took away their identity. Second, he removed the things that made them happy and successful. Third, he engineered the loss of everything that mattered to them. Then, finally, they had to reckon with him.

When the time was right, Duncan used the bat to push himself to his feet. She'd just stood and was starting to stagger deeper into the park. Her gait was unsteady, as if she was drunk, but Duncan knew it was because she was so rocked by grief and loss she could barely stand.

Duncan followed her, gripping the bat tightly. Her red hair was unkempt and messy, and her T-shirt was grimy from the grass and dirt. The sight was beautiful. Duncan wished he could read her mind; he'd love to know what she was thinking. He'd hurt her, but that was nothing compared to the pain she'd inflicted.

Or the pain he'd suffered.

Duncan quickened his pace, gaining on her rapidly. He half-expected her to turn and confront him, but she didn't seem to realize he was there at all. When he was only a few steps away, he glanced around again, then swung the bat at her head. The blow connected with a crack and she collapsed onto the grass.

Duncan smiled as he looked around again. It was late afternoon in the middle of winter and there was barely anyone around. He whistled cheerfully as he tossed the bat to the ground and hefted her up. She was a dead weight, out cold, but she didn't weigh very much. Duncan pulled her upright and wrapped an arm around her.

Although the woman had been punished for her indiscretions, there was still more to be done. Duncan whistled as he manhandled her to the edge of the park, where nature met the city. He drew a few curious glances, but nobody challenged him. He looked like a guy helping his drunk girlfriend into the car and most people didn't like getting involved in the affairs of others.

Duncan considered it his duty to do so.

3

CHRIS

FBI Special Agent Chris Horan tapped impatiently on the steering wheel. "This traffic is slower than my sister's kid. We haven't got time for this."

"What's the hurry?" His partner, Manuel Rodriguez, shook his head. "I could be three beers and six innings into the Yankees game, but instead, thanks to you, I'm here."

Chris felt a little guilty. He'd answered the dispatch call right before they'd been scheduled to finish for the night. "I just didn't want to miss the action."

Manny was unrepentant. "The action was when some dude let rip in a movie theater. The victims would be just as dead if the late crew handled the job."

Chris shrugged as he rode the horn, then reached over and flicked a switch on the dash. Though the emergency lights started to flash, they didn't help much. None of the cars could move out of the way; the traffic was bumper to bumper. Chris loved New York, but law enforcement there dealt with problems that just weren't an issue in most other places.

Chris and Manny rode in silence the rest of the way, inching closer to the movie theater where a lone gunman had killed a dozen people before turning the gun on himself. It was just another day on the job with the FBI/NYPD Extreme Homicide Joint Task Force.

Though the FBI wasn't commonly in the murder business – except for serial cases or when things crossed state lines – Chris, Manny and a half-dozen other agents from the New York field office had been working with the NYPD for the better part of two years, investigating extremely violent, mass, or serial homicides. It involved long hours and heartbreaking cases.

As they arrived at the movie theater, Chris could see a dozen other law enforcement vehicles, from NYPD cruisers to a couple of big SUVs like theirs. Chris pulled up and killed the Chevy's emergency lights. There were enough vehicles creating a disco in the street already. They climbed out of the vehicle, donned their FBI windbreakers and then headed for the scene.

When they reached the perimeter, the NYPD uniform manning it held out his hand. "I'll need some identification, guys."

"The giant fluorescent lettering on our jackets isn't enough?" Chris sighed as he flashed his badge.

The uniform studied his ID for a second and then nodded. "Okay, thanks guys, head on in."

Chris ducked under the police tape that had created an exclusion zone around the theater. Portable floodlights had been erected outside, but Chris suspected all the action was inside. That fact hadn't stopped rubberneckers being drawn to the scene, which the uniforms were trying to keep at a distance.

As he walked inside the theater with Manny, Chris felt a familiar apprehension. No matter how many times he worked a murder scene, he still got a feeling in the pit of his stomach, a primal urge to run away and let someone else deal with it. He swallowed hard as he took in the scene, his hands on his hips.

"What a fucking mess." Manny was a step in front of him, his voice laced with disgust. "I wouldn't wish this on my worst enemy."

It was hard to disagree. The gunman had sprayed the lobby. There were bodies splayed in random positions, a spark contrast to the ordered evidence markers placed next to them. Shell casings, blood splatter, and the murder weapon itself had also been marked. The JTF was fast and thorough.

"Nice of you guys to make it." The familiar voice of Captain Jane Geary, head of the JTF, broke Chris's focus on the bodies and the crime scene.

"Sorry, we got stuck in traffic." Chris fought to keep his face passive, anxious to conceal his feelings of distrust toward Geary.

"Okay, well, I appreciate you guys showing up." Geary placed a hand on Chris's shoulder. "Just take care of yourself, okay?"

"I'm fine." Chris kept his voice and face neutral, but couldn't help tensing when she touched him. "Honestly."

Chris wondered if her concern was genuine. She'd spent the last few months riding his ass for suggesting there was a link between several of the killings they'd worked. The JTF was scheduled to be shut down, so he doubted she wanted a serial killer on the books. She'd had success with the task force and was looking for her next promotion.

"Just making sure." Geary lowered her hand and then

nodded at both Chris and Manny. "I've got to get back. I just wanted to make sure things were under control here."

Chris watched Geary walk away, trying to hold it together. As soon as she was out of sight he felt the nausea in the pit of his stomach worsened. His troubles with Geary were one thing, but being reminded about the basis of her concern rocked him – the night he'd found his girlfriend murdered in her own home.

Chris pushed the door open, a bunch of flowers in one hand and the keys to his apartment in the other. The lights inside were blazing and the heat was on, which meant Tamara was home. He called out to her, but she didn't respond...

"You good, Chris?"

Chris blinked and looked up. Manny was watching him, a look of concern on his face. He was one of the few people on the JTF who knew the whole story about Tamara. He was also one of the few people who knew Chris's theory about that night and many of the other murders they were working.

"I'm good." Chris lied. He couldn't tell Manny what he was really thinking: that he was less interested in these murders than the other ones. "Let's get to work."

Chris didn't want to work this case, but he had a job to do. He'd already clocked a full day and now he was in for a long night. After that, he'd put in a few hours off the books working on his own project. His desire to find the serial killer was like an itch he desperately wanted to scratch, but couldn't right now.

His answers would have to wait.

4

ASHLEY

Ashley sat with her head in her hands and her back against the concrete wall, doing her best to ignore the other people in the holding cell. They were a noisy and chaotic mix of addicts, drunks, and minor criminals who hadn't yet been bailed out. She didn't think she belonged here, but here she was.

For the past twelve hours Ashley had kept to herself, struggling to keep it together. She had seen Lucy for only a few moments, but now it felt like she had been away from her daughter a lifetime. She didn't know what she was being charged with, but the arresting officers had accused her of trying to kidnap Lucy.

She didn't understand how that could be. She'd made a poor choice in trying to take Lucy, but she wasn't a criminal. She was Lucy's mother.

After another hour or so, a booming male voice cut through the noise of the holding cell. "I'm after Ashley Wheeler!"

Ashley looked up, squinting against the light. The other personalities in the holding cell were looking at each other, trying to work out which one of them would be back on the street shortly. Feeling self-conscious, Ashley stood and shuffled over to the police officer. She waited, and didn't speak.

"Ashley Wheeler?" The cop raised an eyebrow, looking down at his clipboard and then back up at Ashley.

"Yes." Ashley's voice was soft. "What's going to happen to me?"

"Come with me please." The cop clearly wasn't interested in her questions.

Ashley thought about pressing for information, but decided it was pointless. She kept quiet as the cop flashed a thumbs-up to a security camera. The cell door unlocked with a clunk. The cop slid it open and gestured for Ashley to exit the cell. Without looking back, she followed the police officer down the corridor.

Ashley hoped she was being escorted to freedom. Not that she deserved it. She'd reflected on her decisions and now realized she'd made a poor one. Though her motives in trying to re-unite with Lucy were pure, she'd almost lost everything. She had to make better choices.

Her hopes of freedom were short lived. The cop wasn't walking her toward the exit. Instead, he deposited her in an interview room and left without a word. She was alone, but the interview room was quieter and less frightening than the holding cell. She closed her eyes, controlled her breathing and waited for whatever came next.

The sound of the door opening woke Ashley. It was no surprise she'd fallen asleep, given she'd been awake almost twenty-four hours. She looked up as two cops walked into the room, one with a look as hard as granite, the other with a kinder face. She sat back and waited to see what they wanted from her.

The kinder-looking cop sat down first, placing a coffee cup down in front of himself and another in front of Ashley. He smiled. "Figured you could use this."

Still trying to wake up, Ashley took a sip of the coffee and savored its warmth. "Thanks for that."

"Here's the deal, Ms Wheeler," the other cop spoke for the first time. "I'm Sergeant Fasano, he's Officer Wilson, and we don't like having our time wasted."

Ashley gripped the coffee with two hands as her gaze flickered between them. She swallowed hard. "I'm sorry. I don't understand."

Fasano fixed Ashley with a hard stare. "We know you're an important witness in a bigshot mob case. We get it – witness protection is terrible, Connecticut sucks, and you miss your daughter. But you can't slip away from witness protection, catch a train to New York, try to take your girl, and put yourself in danger."

Ashley sighed. The cops had clearly spoken to the two US Marshals responsible for guarding her. They'd pieced together how she'd climbed out of a bathroom window, hitched a ride to a train station, and made it to New York. They also clearly knew about the danger she faced in the City.

"I—"

Fasano held up a hand, cutting Ashley off before she'd had a chance to speak. "No, Ms Wheeler, now is the time to listen."

"Okay." Ashley let go of the coffee cup and placed both hands on her knees. "I'm listening."

"Great." Fasano's voice suggested otherwise. "You're free to go, with a few conditions. First, poor Wilson here will take time away from his busy job and his lovely family to drive you all the way back to Connecticut. Second, you'll return to witness protection and stop trying to escape. Third, you'll turn up to court a few weeks from now and sing for the US Attorney."

Ashley breathed a sigh of relief. Though it burned her to the core that she was still separated from Lucy, being in prison wouldn't fix that. The deal on the table was the best she'd get. Though every taste she'd had of the legal system had turned to ashes in her mouth, she was glad to avoid charges. A stern talking to sure beat a cell and felony charges.

She nodded. "Okay."

Wilson spoke for the first time since handing her the coffee. "Fourth condition is that you take care of yourself once you're back in Connecticut. You're a mess, Ashley, and you're not helping anyone in this condition. We don't have a view on your family situation, but a whole lot of us want Saul Laverri put away for life."

Ashley preferred Fasano's hard-man treatment to Wilson's kind words, which pierced whatever flimsy barricades she'd put in place to protect herself. She placed a hand over her face to hide the sobs that racked her body, overwhelmed by a lack of sleep and the sheer ache of missing her daughter.

They let her cry. After a few moments Fasano excused himself, but Wilson stayed. After a while, Ashley regained her composure. She looked up at Wilson, feeling broken, but was touched to see him smiling at her. There was no hint of the judgment or the harshness she'd expected.

"Ready to go?" Wilson stood. "It's a few hours' drive, but you can sleep in the car. If you're lucky, we might catch someone speeding."

Ashley wiped her nose and offered a weak smile. "Can I shoot out his tires?"

"Don't push it." Wilson laughed. "Let's go."

Ashley followed him out of the interview room, through the station, and to Wilson's vehicle. Wilson opened the passenger door and Ashley climbed in. As soon as she was inside, she buckled up and closed her eyes. She wasn't sure what came next, but she hoped she'd make better decisions than she had in the past few days.

She was asleep before Wilson opened the driver's side door.

5

DUNCAN

Duncan removed the blindfold covering the woman's eyes. "Hello, Bridget."

He enjoyed the look in her eyes as she let out a squeal that was mostly suppressed by the gag Duncan had forced into her mouth. Her eyes widened, her nostrils flared, and her breathing became quick and shallow. Though she'd been tied to the chair for hours, this was the first time she'd seen him.

It was fun to watch the fear playing out across her face. It was like the finest art. Duncan smiled at the sight, but she couldn't see that. All she could see was a masked man inches from her face. Bound to a kitchen chair, and gagged, she had no way to escape or cry out. The effect was perfect.

"I hope you made peace with your husband, Bridget." Duncan's voice was calm, but her reaction wasn't. "Because you'll never see him again."

Her squirming and squealing grew more insistent as Duncan leaned in close and licked her on the forehead. Though the balaclava put a layer of material between them, he enjoyed the reaction his gesture elicited. She thrashed violently, her head jerking away from him as if he'd just violated her in a far more severe way. Duncan laughed as he straightened up.

He walked over to the kitchen, still getting used to the layout of her apartment. Though he'd watched her through the windows for weeks, this was his first time inside. The interior of the apartment was decorated just as he'd expected, cold and expensive. There was no warmth here, no sense of home.

"How could you?" Duncan spoke to himself, asking a question she was unable to answer. "There's no way this could be a nice place for your husband. You treated him like shit, disrespected and hurt him. You even fucked another man in his bed."

Duncan ignored the muffled screams from behind him. Even if he could understand her, there was no answer she could give that would satisfy him. He ran a gloved hand over her benchtops, opened cupboards and drawers, deciding how best to give her the justice she deserved. He wanted to take his time.

Getting her back here had gone flawlessly. The blow to her head in the park had knocked her out, but she'd started to come to in the rental car he'd bundled her into. He'd reassured her, explaining that her husband had assaulted her and he was taking her home. She'd believed him and relaxed instantly.

It had never occurred to her to ask how he knew where she lived. When they'd arrived at her place, he'd offered to walk her to her door. In the elevator on the way to her apartment, she'd thanked him and started to cry. The shock of the assault and the thought that her husband was responsible had apparently hit her hard.

Though not as hard as his fist to her face once her door was unlocked.

She'd gone out cold again and Duncan had bundled her inside, tied her to a chair with pantyhose, using another pair to stuff in her mouth. He'd left her there for hours, using the time to search the rest of her apartment, completing his mental picture of her. He was satisfied he'd got it right.

As he opened the top drawer and selected a large kitchen knife, Duncan wondered what would happen if, one day, one of his victims genuinely repented. If that ever occurred, he might consider leniency, but it never had. They usually screamed, begged, and moaned for him to leave them alone. It was wasted breath.

Duncan closed the drawer and rounded back on the frantic woman. He selected his victims carefully, then destroyed their lives meticulously. But when it came to ending them, he found simple was always best.

Duncan kept his voice soft. "Do you know how you came to my attention, Bridget?"

"Mmmm!" Her protests were muffled, indecipherable.

"Be quiet." Duncan kept the knife in hand as he started to pace. "I found you online. You said you were after some fun, that you had a husband and a kid who couldn't know. You're a whore. But that wasn't the worst of it, was it?"

"Mmmm!"

"It's to be expected, I suppose." Duncan sighed. "You were top of your class at Yale. You were in the top of your field at work. You were used to the world revolving around you. You tease, manipulate, and scheme. You show no remorse for the pain you've caused."

"Mmmm!"

"I SAID SHUT UP!" Duncan's voice boomed as he thrust the knife into her stomach.

As the woman let out a wail of pain, Duncan cursed himself for losing control. As she moaned and writhed like a fish on a hook, he let go of the knife and tried to control his breathing. It took a few moments, but he got there. He was outraged that, even when this woman was completely subdued, she still thought she could whine until she got her way.

Duncan stood, his fists clenched by his sides. "Before you die, you should know that it was all me. Your husband, your daughter, your job and your money – I took everything from you. With each strut I kicked out from under you, you had a chance to reflect and atone. But you never showed any sign of remorse."

The woman's eyes were fading now, the knife wound doing its work, but a flicker of fear and recognition crossed her eyes. Though she moaned again, Duncan was deaf to it now. He gripped the handle of the blade, which was still buried deep in the woman's stomach, and leaned in close.

Duncan was inches from her face when he pulled the knife out of her. In a movie, this would be when the captive woman freed her hands, struggled with him, somehow got hold of the knife and then killed him. That seemed unlikely, though. Her hands, feet, and torso were securely restrained.

Her eyes were extremely wide and she let out a muffled shriek as Duncan plunged the knife into her once more. Again and again he penetrated her with the blade, each strike drawing less and less reaction, until finally her eyes went dead. Even then, he dug the blade in several more times, to ensure he'd inflicted as much pain as possible.

Panting, Duncan stepped back, his chest heaving. He'd

punished and destroyed another blight on the Earth. With a smile, he stuck his index finger deep inside one of the stab wounds. After removing it again, he held up the finger and looked at the blood now covering it. He smiled as he reached out and wrote a message on her forehead.

The message wasn't something he'd done before, but he was bored with routine and wanted to add another flourish. The kill had been far less satisfying than he'd hoped. The thrill lessened each time he took a life, yet his own pain remained. No matter how much he tried to erase it, that never changed.

But he couldn't stop.

6

CHRIS

C hris sighed. "Another one."

He took his eyes off the victim and scanned the rest of the room, though he didn't spot anything that hadn't been found already. It was a simple crime scene. A red-haired woman had been tied up and stabbed a dozen times in her own home. She'd been found about four hours ago, yet Chris had only just arrived on scene. Most of the crime scene work had already been processed prior to his arrival.

The victim was a white female with red hair. That was all he needed to know.

Chris took a few steps toward the body, having delayed doing so until now. He had no official role to play at the scene, but as soon as he heard that another redhead had been found, Chris had raced to the scene. He'd known exactly what he'd find – a young, pretty, early-to-mid thirties woman who'd been brutally murdered.

It fit the pattern. Each victim had had a number of things go wrong in their lives before they ended up dead, yet Geary and the JTF refused to acknowledge the pattern. It was clear to Chris that there was a serial killer on the loose, but no one supported his theory, not even Manny.

Chris reached the body, looked down and shook his head. The woman was a mess. She was clothed, but her T-shirt was caked in blood and gore. A dozen knife wounds had torn the garment, leaving it little more than a rag. Blood had pooled on the floor, underneath the chair she'd been tied to. The killer had also written a message on the woman's head in her blood.

Whore.

Chris looked up at Detective Frank Cygnetti, one of the NYPD guys on the JTF. "Has she been identified?"

"Bridget Skinner. Age 32." He shrugged. "It's her apartment, so it was easy enough to tag her, despite the mess."

Chris nodded. He gestured at the knife on the ground next to the woman. "That's the murder weapon?"

"Looks like it." Cygnetti shrugged again. "We'll need to confirm it, but it looks like a pretty obvious conclusion."

The killer hadn't bothered to hide the body or hide the knife that was right next to the victim. It showed a complete lack of concern that he was going to be caught. All the other crime scenes Chris thought the serial killer was responsible for had been similar, yet they'd never found anything that'd let them get close to him.

This killer was clean, careful, and methodical. He always wore gloves and was never spotted on his way in or out. He was a ghost terrorizing the women of New York City.

"Do we know anything else?"

Cygnetti looked down at his notes. "The guys tell me she lost her job and her partner recently. The husband has an alibi. The kill looks random, though."

Chris doubted it. He thanked Frank, then returned to

poking around the scene. He was more certain this was the work of a serial killer targeting young, redheaded, professional females. But his superiors had dismissed his theory because of the lack of a single 'tell' – because the women were all killed in different ways.

All because they wanted to wrap up the JTF.

"What's the story, Chris?" Manny's voice jolted Chris out of his dark thoughts. "I only got a few hours' sleep after the movie theater job."

"More than me." Chris smiled weakly at his partner. "She's got red hair, Manny. She's just like the others."

"I don't want to hear it, Chris." Manny's face went from cheery to dark in less than a second. "I get it, you miss Tamara, but it was two years ago. I—"

"This has nothing to do with her!" Chris held up a hand. "It's the same killer as the others. *All* the others, not just Tamara!"

Manny shook his head and Chris knew what he was thinking. They'd discussed Chris's theory at length, many times, but his partner hadn't ever seriously considered it. Each of them was entrenched in their position. They were the perfect shadow boxers, with neither able to land a blow powerful enough to convince the other.

Chris persisted. "Manny, the victims are all successful redheads who end up dead."

"So?" Manny held his hands out, palms up, as if imploring a divine power to zap Chris with some sense. "There's no common murder weapon. There's no common time or place. There's nothing linking any of the victims except the color of their hair. The profilers don't think there's a link, but you think you're smarter than them?"

"You can't deny the physical similarities, or the fact that the victims always have a series of things go wrong in their personal lives before they're killed." Chris let that hang for a second. "Tell me I'm wrong about this, Manny. Tell me this isn't something the JTF should at least be looking at."

"Shit happens to people." Manny sighed. "You need to cool it, Chris. These murders will be investigated, but the JTF is being wound up and we've been told not to make waves."

"But—"

"Chris, for fuck's sake, just listen for once. *You've* been told not to make waves. Geary just needs an excuse to can your ass. Let it go. Let *Tamara* go."

Chris closed the door to the apartment and called out Tamara's name again. It was strange she wasn't responding. She'd never leave the house with lights on and the heat running.

Chris blinked then stared at Manny. His partner had just squeezed his shoulder.

"What?"

Manny scoffed and walked away, leaving Chris standing on his own. Chris ran a hand through his hair. There was some truth in Manny's words. He'd been warned loud and clear after his last mistake, which had badly embarrassed the Bureau and seen a dangerous criminal released.

He'd been told these murders weren't a serial case. Chris knew better. The victims' appearance and the circumstances preceding each murder were similar, and only two percent of the population had red hair, making the murder rate among that cohort in New York abnormal.

There was a serial killer on the loose. Even if others refused to believe it, he couldn't.

He wouldn't.

7

ASHLEY

"Ashley, you're okay." Simon Weltering's voice was as calm as ever. "Just focus on that, and we'll work on the rest."

A sob caught in Ashley's throat as she squeezed her eyes shut, trying to get her breathing under control. She'd broken down a few times since their counselling session had started, as she'd tried to rationalize her attempt to take Lucy. Weltering hadn't said much, just listened and made a few comments.

Ashley knew the cops in New York had only let her go because of the deal she had with the US Attorney in New York, Ben Obrist. Officer Wilson had confirmed as much on the drive back to Connecticut. But the important thing was, she was free. She had been given another chance, but she needed to get her head straight.

It was difficult – she was so torn and angry and hurt – but at least she recognized she needed help. She'd made an appointment with Weltering as soon as she'd arrived back home. He'd been her counsellor since she'd been placed in the witness protection program and moved from New York to

Wallingford, Connecticut. He'd succeeded in calming her down plenty of times before, but it didn't feel like it was happening this time. She was a mess.

The worst thing was the knowledge that she'd damaged the chances of getting her daughter back. Her actions had made her look like a madwoman, strengthening Tom's position in any future custody consideration.

"I don't feel okay." Weltering words were like white noise. "I feel like an idiot. I could've been killed, going back there, and for what? I just made things with Lucy and Tom worse!"

"It was a mistake." Weltering stared over his glasses. "And certainly not one I'd advise you to repeat. You need to be smart. Also, you need to stay away from New York until the trial."

The trial. The final act of the story that'd changed her life. Two years ago, she'd been working at a small pizza restaurant in New York, a nice place with about eight tables and a few more seats at the bar. One quiet weeknight a fat man in a sharp suit had walked in, pulled out a revolver and fired six shots into one of Ashley's regular customers. The killer had then calmly taken a slice of the man's pizza and left.

It was only later that Ashley had found out who the killer was, Saul Laverri, head of the Laverri family and number seven on the FBI's most wanted list. He'd eluded the authorities for years, until Flavio Grossi, the man he'd shot dead at the restaurant, had raped and murdered Laverri's daughter over a debt. The FBI had convinced Ashley to go into witness protection, to testify against Laverri and put one of the most dangerous men on the planet behind bars.

It had been a terrible mistake.

She hated Laverri. Not because he'd shot a mobster,

another scumbag in a parade of them to impact her life in the past few years, but because—

"Ashley!" Weltering shook her firmly, one hand on each shoulder and his face close to hers, concern painted all over it. "Ashley, it's okay."

Ashley blinked rapidly several times, struggling to focus on him. She sucked in a long breath and then let it out in ragged heaves. "This has to stop."

"What does?"

"All of it! The trial! Tom having custody of my daughter!" She slapped the arm of the sofa. "I need help, Simon! Ever since I got talked into testifying, my life has been torn apart."

"You just need to be—"

"Patient! I know!" Ashley ran a hand through her hair. "But I've lost my husband and my daughter. When does it stop? When do I get my life back?"

Weltering sighed. "Ashley, I don't know what to tell you. You've made some progress, but it's been limited. Your trip to New York was a huge setback. Even if the police didn't charge you, Tom and his lawyer will have a field day. You need to be patient. You need to be a model citizen until the trial in a few weeks."

"That's not good enough. I—"

"The best advice I can give you is the truth. Until you're through your issues and the case has been heard, you'll be apart from your daughter." Weltering smiled. "But there's hope, Ashley. Continuing to work on your issues now will give you the best chance of getting Lucy back later."

"Okay." Ashley closed her eyes. She wasn't sure she believed him, but she had no alternative. "I just want Lucy back."

Being apart from her daughter was almost unbearable. She

needed her little girl back. But she'd made a mistake, and now her chances were worse than ever. Agreeing to testify against Laverri had been her biggest mistake, but asking Tom to look after Lucy while she was struggling to cope was a close second. Tom had twisted her words and made her out to be a lunatic, leveraging the situation into sole custody. Ashley had been suffering ever since.

The attempted kidnapping would just make things worse. She'd screwed up.

She'd play it Weltering's way. What choice did she have? The only way out of her current hole was to see the court case through and then focus on getting Lucy back. It wasn't a guaranteed path, but she couldn't see any other. She just hoped she didn't end up alone, or dead, after all this was done.

8

DUNCAN

Duncan was careful to keep one hand on the top of the ladder as he reached for the bottle of wine on the top shelf. It would be a cruel twist of fate to fall off a stepladder and die, only a few days after killing Bridget Skinner. He managed to grab the bottle then climb down the ladder without meeting an untimely end.

He smiled and held out the bottle to the customer who had demanded *that* bottle of shiraz, despite there being a dozen similarly priced and comparable bottles within easy reach. Duncan let it slide, though. The guy was a regular. Duncan maintained the fake smile as he returned to the cash register, scanned the bottle and placed it on the counter.

"That'll be $13.99, Mr Bennett." Duncan held out his hand. "Would you like a bag today, sir?"

"Of course I want a bag!" Bennett placed the money in Duncan's hand. "If you make me wait forever to buy it, you should at least give me something to carry it in."

Duncan kept calm as he took the money, bagged the wine

and handed it to the customer, who snatched the bag and left without another word. Duncan gripped the counter with both hands, closed his eyes and laughed. He wouldn't let a rude customer destroy his post-kill glow.

He always felt like this for a few days afterward, like he was floating on a cloud. It was a heady mix of realized desire and satisfaction at having rid the world of another woman who thought she owned the world. He smiled, opened his eyes and had just started to wipe down the counter when the door chime rang.

Duncan turned his head toward the door. "Afternoon."

"Hi." The customer nodded at Duncan as he started to peruse the shelves.

Duncan started to whistle a tune while the customer browsed. He liked to chat with his regulars, although he'd only make small talk with unfamiliar customers if they initiated conversation. Finally, the customer picked up a mid-range bottle of bourbon and brought it to the counter. Duncan put down the cloth and scanned the bottle.

"$22.50, please." Duncan smiled as he bagged the bottle, handed it to the customer and took the man's money.

"Keep the change," the customer said. "Nice to see a man who likes his work as much as you seem to."

"It's not bad." Duncan dropped the change into the charity collection box that was chained to the counter. "Thanks. It helps sick children."

"Happy and selfless, I'll be damned." The customer smiled. "If only I could say the same about my wife."

Duncan tensed at the mention of the man's wife. He was vaguely aware of the customer laughing, then frowning, apparently confused by Duncan's silence. Here was another man in pain because of his wife. She was probably frigid, or a tease, or treated him like shit. But Duncan didn't share his thoughts. He'd learnt that his opinions weren't always welcome.

He let out a long laugh, but his attempt at camaraderie didn't work. The other man just stared at him strangely. As he opened his mouth to speak, his phone rang. As the man checked who was calling, Duncan caught a brief glimpse of the screen and sucked in a deep breath when he saw the photo of the caller.

"Speak of the devil." The customer stepped away from the counter to answer the phone. He put it to his ear. "Hi babe."

Duncan turned around to restock the cigarettes behind the counter, fighting the urge to say something to the man. The photo he'd seen on the screen was of a thirty-something redhead with a beaming smile. Clenching his teeth, Duncan listened in on the conversation. The man's voice tone hardened a few seconds into the call, which ended abruptly.

"Fucking redheads." The customer exhaled as he pulled the phone away from his ear. "She hung up on me. I've given her the world and it's still not good enough."

Duncan turned, a packet of cigarettes still in his hand, and offered a conciliatory smile. "Hope everything's okay."

"Nothing this won't fix." The customer held up the paper bag and gave a wry smile. "Thanks, pal."

As he watched the man leave, Duncan did his best to fight the urge. He knew rushed action wasn't smart, but he couldn't resist. After a few seconds, Duncan locked the cash register and fumbled in his pockets for the keys to the store. He rushed toward the front door, flipped the 'back in 15 minutes' sign over and locked up. Duncan caught sight of the man and followed him.

Five minutes ago he'd felt like he was in the clouds. Now,

he felt like he was back in the dirt. He had the itch again. His euphoria had been ruined by another red-haired woman treating her husband like shit. It was possible she needed to be punished, but first he had to confirm she fit the bill. He followed the man for three blocks to the nearest subway station.

He usually liked to research his target thoroughly before he started work. From there, he'd slowly dismantle their lives. At first, he'd cause small wounds, enough that they'd notice, but wouldn't think anything was awry. Then he'd slice deeper, until they realized there was more to the story.

That's when Duncan would strike like lightning.

Methodical preparation, controlled execution and meticulous self-preservation were key. That was the only way he could stay safe enough to continue his vital work. Despite that, sometimes targets came to him by chance and he couldn't turn away. The feeling, the urge, the need to act came as naturally as breathing. That's how he found himself on a subway platform, waiting for an uptown train, following a man he'd only met a few minutes ago.

As the train pulled up, Duncan clenched his hands into fists and boarded.

9

CHRIS

C hris eased his foot off the accelerator and brought the car to a stop a few doors down from the townhouse, a beautiful old brownstone that was very close to Columbia University. The house was on a quiet street in a relatively quiet part of Manhattan. It was the sort of place nobody working in law enforcement could ever afford. It wasn't the sort of place he'd usually have to stake out, but here he was.

Chris flicked on the interior light and glanced at the piece of paper he'd scrawled a dozen addresses on. Each was the home of a woman who fit the profile of the murder victims: red-haired, early-thirties, beautiful and successful. The brownstone was third on the list, The woman who owned it fit the profile closely. Close to making partner at a major law firm, she was a potential target of the killer Chris knew was out there.

Then again, so were the women at every other address on his list. To find them, Chris had searched the DMV database for women with red hair between the ages of twenty-five and thirty-five. He'd then dug deeper, researching them online and using that information to refine the list. Although it had taken a long time and his list wasn't perfect, it was something.

He'd made two other stops that night, adding to the dozens in the past few weeks, yet he'd seen nothing. Staking out the homes of potential victims was like shining a beam of light into an almost infinite darkness, hoping to be in the right place at the exact moment the killer struck. Though he knew the likelihood of stumbling across the killer this way was slim, it was the best he could do given that nobody else believed there was a serial killer out there.

If anyone knew what he was doing, they'd think his actions were crazy. Hell, *he* thought his actions were crazy, but he couldn't stop. As the bodies stacked up and the similarities grew, so too had his conviction that these were serial cases. His warnings had fallen on deaf ears, his superiors more interested in closing cases and winding up the JTF than admitting a serial killer was on the loose.

Chris had almost accepted it, until Tamara had died. They'd only been dating for a few months, but every moment he'd spent with her had made him feel alive. A gorgeous redhead with a career in law far more impressive than his own in law enforcement, they'd first hit it off over a cup of coffee. Their relationship had blossomed, and it was starting to feel like forever...

Until Chris had found her dead.

Chris could smell food cooking, too. Tamara must be home. He smiled, put the flowers down on the hallway stand, pocketed his keys and advanced down the hallway...

Chris blinked. A car horn had blared in the street, interrupting Chris' reverie. With a sigh and a sniff, Chris shifted in his seat and wound down the car window. The biting winter cold penetrated the car, waking him up. Chris rubbed his eyes and reached for his keys. Though he'd only been here a half-hour, he was struggling to stay awake. It was time to go home.

"Help!"

A woman's piercing scream broke the silence of the night. Chris scanned the darkness and his ears strained to hear more. After a few seconds, Chris saw someone burst from the door of the townhouse he'd been staking out, leaping down the front steps and sprinting down the street. After only a moment of consideration, Chris exited the car and gave chase.

By now the suspect was a few dozen yards ahead. They raced down well-lit streets until the suspect cut down a dark alley and out of sight. He couldn't have gone far, because there was nothing but a chain-link fence halfway down the alley. Chris looked around, wishing he had backup. This clown probably wasn't the killer, but he couldn't blow the chance if he was.

Chris drew his pistol, then pulled out his phone. He dialed the JTF and the call was answered. "This's Agent Horan. I'm chasing a murder suspect on foot and need support."

Chris explained where he wanted units sent, hung up and pocketed his phone. Raising his pistol and grabbing his flashlight, he shone the Maglite Mini down the alleyway. The suspect was nowhere to be seen. Chris advanced slowly, flashing the light into all the dark corners until the suspect emerged from behind a dumpster with a knife in his hand and a scowl on his face.

"Who the fuck are you, pal?" The suspect took a step forward. "I don't know why you're following me, but I suggest you fuck off."

"FBI." Chris flashed the light into the suspect's eyes, causing him to pause. "Don't move."

The other man turned and ran. Chris shouted at him to freeze, but the man ignored him. Chris was tempted to take the shot, but he wasn't willing to stake his career on this guy being his killer. With Manny and his superiors' warnings ringing in his mind, he gave chase. By now the man was nearly over the chain link fence, but Chris leapt after him and got a hand on the man's ankle.

"Let go of me!" The suspect kicked out at him.

Chris yanked on the ankle, nearly dislodging him. "You need to—"

The boot caught Chris right on the nose. His vision flashed with stars and pain flared in his head. He lost his grip on the man's ankle and slumped to the ground, landing heavily. Chris cursed, only vaguely aware of the suspect making it up and over the fence, and carefully felt his nose. It wasn't broken, but it hurt. Worse, the suspect was long gone. Chris had a good description, but if the kid was the killer he'd go to ground.

"Hold it there, buddy." A commanding voice boomed down the alley. "NYPD. I need you to stay calm and not make any sudden movements."

Chris held his arms out, showing he was no threat. "I'm an FBI agent, officers. I was chasing a suspect."

"Show me your identification. Slowly." The officer flashed his light in Chris's eyes, just as Chris had done to the suspect a moment ago.

Chris reached into his pocket, pulled out his badge, opened it and pointed it at the officers. The light was immediately directed away from his face and he could see the officers, weapons drawn but lowered. He took this as a sign he was free to move and got up. He reached for his flashlight and switched it off, then turned to the officers.

"I need you to call it in." Chris had second thoughts even as he said it, but he proceeded to describe the suspect. The kid had a knife, so there was a chance he was the killer.

"You got it." One of the officers reached for his radio and the call went out. Officers across the city would be on the lookout.

Chris closed his eyes tightly and took a long breath. Now that he'd initiated a manhunt, there'd be no hiding the fact that he'd been staking out the homes of potential victims. If he'd really disturbed the killer and come close to catching him, it'd be worthwhile. But he knew what the consequences would be if he'd screwed up.

His bosses wouldn't tolerate more noise from him.

10

ASHLEY

"How much longer?" Ashley asked the US Marshal sitting next to her in the back of the black SUV with tinted windows.

"Almost there." The Marshal was kind, despite the fact she'd escaped from him to go get Lucy. He was an older man with a salt-and-pepper moustache. "It'll be fine, I promise."

Ashley hoped he was right, because her nerves weren't holding up very well. She was being ferried by three US Marshals to the courthouse, where she'd be led through a back entrance. That was the plan, anyway. Ashley wasn't certain it'd work, but she hoped it would keep Saul Laverri's allies from putting a bullet in her.

She gave the kind Marshal a weak smile as she settled back into her seat. She just wanted her testimony to be over so she could get her life back. Her well-being hinged on this day. She needed to get it out of the way so she could focus on Lucy. That thought was the glue holding her together.

"Damn it." The Marshal in the front passenger seat cursed

as the car took the last turn toward the courthouse. "We're compromised."

Ashley craned her head to look out the front windshield. The back entrance to the courthouse was supposed to be cordoned off. Instead, there were dozens of people pressing against the NYPD cordon. Ashley's eyes widened as she turned to the Marshal beside her and stared at him.

"We'll get you inside, don't worry." The Marshal did his best to reassure her, but his voice was laced with doubt.

The SUV stopped, then a cop stepped forward and opened the door. The cacophony of noise that erupted felt like a shockwave. The Marshal grabbed Ashley's hand and she followed his lead, climbing out of the car and heading for the courthouse. The Marshals formed a protective ring around her. It was little comfort. Cameras flashed and journalists shouted questions at her.

Finally, she made it inside. The noise and fury from outside stopped as soon as the doors were shut. Ashley slumped into one of the benches by the door and put her head in her hands. She was shaking and her breathing was rapid as she tried to calm herself. The Marshals had timed her arrival for exactly when she was due on the stand, so she had to get it together.

"Hi Ashley, it's good to see you."

Ashley took her head out of her hands and looked up to see Manuel Rodriguez, the FBI agent who'd arrested Laverri. Ashley stood and hugged him. "Hi Manny."

Manny wrapped his arms around her. "We're finally here."

Ashley nodded. Manny was one of the few people who knew what agreeing to testify had cost her. Others, like Obrist, had done only what they'd needed to do to get her to testify. Even her own husband had cracked and walked because of the stress. Manny had been a huge support, a friend and confidant through it all.

"Ms Wheeler?" A man in a uniform interrupted them "We're ready for you. Come through."

Ashley nodded at the man and then looked at Manny. "I'll do my best in there."

"Just do what you can, Ashley." Manny gave her shoulder a squeeze. "Now go get him."

Ashley followed the uniformed man into the courtroom. Her heart rate quickened and her palms started to sweat. Whatever calm she'd felt while talking to Manny outside the courtroom shattered like glass, and now it felt like she was in a haze. As she approached the witness stand, she was aware of someone speaking, but she didn't hear the words.

Then she saw Laverri. He smiled at her and said something under his breath. She flinched, slowed to a halt and then stared at him, her mouth agape. Only when the uniformed officer placed a hand on her back and pressed her forward did her attention snap back to the courtroom.

"Thank you for agreeing to testify, Ms Wheeler." The judge looked down at her from the bench. "Please take your place on the stand."

Ashley realized the judge and the jury were staring straight at her, and felt a pang of embarrassment. In a daze, she moved to the stand, where she was sworn in. Then the US Attorney for the Eastern District of New York, Ben Obrist, stood and began the questioning they all hoped would seal Laverri's fate.

Ashley had met Obrist one other time, when he'd travelled to Connecticut to discuss the case. At that meeting, Ashley had felt like he was testing her, making sure she was reliable. He'd told Ashley how the case would work and she trusted him to protect her on the stand. She waited while he stood and gave a summary of the incident, for the benefit of the jury.

Then he asked his first question. "Ms Wheeler, can you tell us where you were and what you were doing on the evening of the incident?"

Ashley nodded. She'd rehearsed this. "I was working a noon to midnight shift at L'uccellino Pizza and Pasta on 108th Street."

The questions continued and Ashley tried her best to stay calm. They'd rehearsed this, and there were no surprises. She avoided looking at Laverri, and after a few dozen questions, Obrist was done. Once he'd established that she saw Laverri shoot Grossi dead, he told the judge he had no more questions and returned to his seat. Now came the hard part.

Paul Stoudamere – Laverri's lawyer – stood and locked eyes with her. "Miss Wheeler, what's your current occupation?"

Ashley hesitated for half a second. "I'm—"

"Objection, your honor!" Obrist called out from his seat. "I'm not sure what relevance Ms Wheeler's occupation has to this matter."

"Denied." The judge's voice boomed across the court room. "There's no harm I can see in having her answer that question, Mr Obrist."

Ashley looked at Obrist. When he nodded, she looked back at the defense lawyer. "I'm currently unemployed."

"Right." He nodded and turned to glance at the jury. "Can you tell me if you've had any trouble with the law since the night Mr Grossi was shot?"

Ashley looked to Obrist for help, but he shook his head. Clearly he thought the judge would disallow an objection. He'd also told her that if he objected too many times, the jury would think they had something to hide. She looked at

Stoudamere. "I haven't been arrested, if that's what you're asking."

"That's only a part answer." He held her gaze. "Can you elaborate on any contact you've had with the police in that time?"

Ashley sagged. Stoudamere had done his homework. "One caution for attempting to take my daughter."

"Thank you for your candor, Ms Wheeler." Stoudamere smiled like a hyena. "I'd now like to move to the night of the incident. You've stated you saw my client."

Ashley saw a chance to get one back. "I saw him shoot and kill a man, yes. He shot him lots of times, took a slice of pizza and left."

Stoudamere ignored the barb. "And can you tell me what he was wearing that evening, when you claimed to see him shoot Mr Grossi?"

Ashley made the mistake of looking at Laverri. It was almost as if he'd been waiting for her to do so. He pretended to scratch his neck, pulling his index finger across his throat as he did so. His eyes bored into hers, the message clear. Ashley flinched and looked away. She closed her eyes as her breath quickened.

"Ms Wheeler?"

Ashley blinked a few times. "What?"

Stoudamere shook his head. "Can you tell me what my client was wearing?"

"A suit. White shirt." Ashley did her best to remember.

"That's all?" Stoudamere raised an eyebrow. "No hat? No tie?"

"That's all." Ashley racked her memory, trying to recall. "Yes."

Stoudamere smiled, like she'd given him everything he

wanted. "I'd like to admit into evidence video footage from outside the restaurant, time and date stamped, that shows my client wearing both a hat and a tie as he entered that night. The footage also clearly shows him wearing a blue shirt."

Ashley gripped the edge of the box and her knuckles went white. Stoudamere had found holes in both her character and her testimony. With each additional question she struggled to hold onto her story. She shouldn't have looked at Laverri or trusted Obrist to protect her on the stand. The dogfight continued for another ten minutes.

"Ms Wheeler, you can leave the stand now." The judge's voice was insistent. He clearly wasn't impressed.

Ashley nodded, feeling like she'd been assaulted. She stood and stumbled, catching herself on the edge of the witness box. It felt like all the loss she'd endured since agreeing to testify had been for nothing. As she left the box she looked at Obrist. He had his head down and was making a point of not looking at her.

She'd blown it.

11

DUNCAN

Duncan paused outside the bar as he looked through the window. It was busier than he'd anticipated, but he decided to push ahead. He opened the door, stepped inside and was instantly assaulted by the smell of alcohol and the buzz of conversation. There was an empty stool near the bar and Duncan made a beeline for it.

The bartender spotted him within a few seconds. "What'll it be? Happy hour ends in five minutes."

"Soda and lime." Duncan smiled and put down a fifty, then nodded toward a woman seated at the end of the bar. "Plus whatever she likes."

"You got it." The bartender smiled at the sight of the fifty. "Just a heads up, though – she's got a husband."

Duncan shrugged and watched the bartender make the drinks, feeling his excitement levels rise. He'd done some research after following the customer home, and his suspicions had been correct. She needed to be punished. She was successful, popular, provocative, and a cheater. She also fit the profile: tall, lithe, and with red curls she kept in a high bun.

She'd be his next target, but this one was going to be a bit different. And the moment the bartender gave the woman her drink, he'd be committed.

"Here you go." The bartender placed a glass on the bar in front of Duncan, took the fifty and left the change on a small plate in front of him.

Duncan swallowed hard, nervous at the risk he was taking. He'd decided he wanted to get to know his latest target in person. In the past, he'd worked from afar, only revealing himself at the very end. But that had grown tiresome. The thrill had lessened each time, and he'd been unable to capture the same high. He needed more.

As the bartender handed the woman the drink, Duncan smiled at her and then looked away. Revealing himself was a risk, but he was determined to try something new. The thought of it excited him, and he hoped it would mean his targets suffered more. He was willing to try anything to maximize their pain, to help them realize their crimes, to help soothe his own hurt.

"Thanks for the drink."

Duncan turned his head, pleased by the interruption. The woman was standing next to him, one hand holding the drink and the other on her hip. This threw his plans to hell. He'd intended to buy her a drink and then approach her later. He hadn't expected her to take the initiative. He stared for just a moment too long, his mouth slightly agape as his mind raced. Her actions confirmed she was a slut, a married woman approaching a man at a bar.

"I'm Chelsea." She persisted, flashing a smile that lit up her face. "I think the bartender told you my favorite."

Duncan almost told her that he knew her name already, but caught himself. He'd have to be very careful to control what he said. "He might have. I'm Dan."

"Dan." She lifted the drink to her mouth and took a sip, then bit her lip seductively. "Why're you buying me drinks, Dan?"

Duncan forced a laugh, despite his dark mood. He wondered how fast she'd run if she knew the truth. "I like making a woman happy."

"Is that so?" She smirked, then made a show of looking him up and down. Then she placed a hand on his knee. "Well, I like being made happy."

Duncan looked down at her hand and clenched his teeth behind a tight, toothless smile. "Sounds like we're in luck, then."

As she put her purse on the bar and sat on the stool next to him, a wave of relief washed over him. There had been every chance she'd reject him, as he'd been rejected before. That would've cost him the opportunity to learn more about her. He was both excited and angered by what was to come. He was about to learn about her life in exquisite detail.

They got talking. He got to know more about her, and he fed her horse shit and lies. The drinks kept flowing, until she was struggling to sit upright on the stool. Duncan was drinking slowly, one drink for every two she consumed, and it was almost as if she was building up the courage for something. It didn't matter. He was waiting for one very particular thing.

"Excuse me for a moment. I just need to go to the bathroom." She gave him a small smile and removed her hand from his leg. "Will you mind my purse?"

Duncan nodded, and she stood and headed for the

bathroom, glad he'd built up enough trust for her to leave the purse with him. When she was out of sight, he pulled out her cell phone and pulled a SIM reader from his pocket. Working quickly, he pulled the SIM card out of her phone and ripped the contacts, messages and information from the phone. He'd also be able to clone the SIM and see any new messages she received.

As soon as it finished, he hid the SIM reader and placed the phone back in her purse.

12

CHRIS

C hris swallowed hard then knocked on the door. When the call came to enter, he pushed the door open and went inside. The office was cavernous, at least by law enforcement standards. There was one man behind the desk and two women sitting on the other side of it. The only person he didn't know, one of the women, gestured for him to sit.

That same woman spoke the moment he was in his seat. "Thanks for coming in, Agent Horan. I'm Tanya Sagan, the independent facilitator for this disciplinary panel. You know Special Agent in Charge Nowitski and Captain Geary from the NYPD. Do you have any questions before we get started?"

"Nope." Chris's voice was deadpan. "Let's get it over with."

"You're a piece of work, Horan." Nowitski got straight to business. "I don't think you appreciate the trouble you're in. That manhunt you triggered made us look like a laughing stock."

Chris winced. He regretted that. Nowitski had sent him a fairly terse email prior to the meeting, so Chris knew what was coming, but he hadn't expected Nowitski to be quite so blunt. The JTF officers had gently ribbed him about the manhunt for the last couple of days, Geary had already shouted about it, now the head of the FBI New York Field Office was joining in.

Geary gave him a small smile. "You've been involved in an inordinate number of screw-ups lately, haven't you?"

Chris leaned forward to speak. "I—"

Geary held up her hand. "I wasn't finished. We scoured the city for a college kid. When we found him and spoke to the woman you suspected he'd murdered, we found out they'd just broken up. The kid didn't have a knife, as you'd claimed, and was released without charge. Given you were off duty, I can see no basis for your chase or for the manhunt."

Chris almost knew the next line before Geary said it. He opened his mouth. "I know cooperation is very important to the work of this Joint Task Force."

Geary was slightly taken aback, but recovered well. "Correct. We asked the Bureau to join us as partners because we had a problem that's in both our interests to solve. We didn't invite the FBI and its agents on board to cause trouble, waste resources, spread panic, and freelance."

"With respect, I don't believe I'm causing trouble." Chris placed his palms flat on his knees as he spoke. "I believe many of the homicides we've been investigating and some that we claim to have solved are the work of a serial killer. He targets successful career women with partners and excellent prospects."

Nowitski groaned. "Agent Horan, you're on thin ice."

"I'm well aware of that, sir." Chris looked at each of them in turn. "Each of the victims shares that profile and each of them has red hair. Finally, each victim has every important element of her life attacked before she's killed. The killer takes away the things that make the victim happy."

Chris crossed his arms and sat back, scanning their faces. He knew what the response was going to be, but he didn't care. He was enraged by their inability to see the truth. The killer would keep offending and more women would die while they continued with their deliberate ignorance.

"Agent Horan, I know you had a personal loss some years back, just after you joined the JTF. We supported you through that tragedy, and we all felt your loss..."

Chris slowly inched down the hallway, listening hard for any sign of Tamara. He peered left into their bedroom – it was empty. Next up was their small bathroom. Empty, too. He frowned, quietly unbuckled the holster for his pistol, and tightened his hand around the grip of the weapon...

"AGENT HORAN?"

Chris blinked and stared at Geary. Her features had hardened and any hint of compassion had vanished. "Yes?"

Geary sighed. "As I said, despite your loss clearly clouding your judgement, we've had enough of your theories. We've heard them a hundred times and nothing has changed."

Chris's face twisted. He resented the implication that Tamara's death was clouding his judgement, that it was being used to discredit him. "I—"

"No." Geary held up a hand. "Let me be clear. There's no serial murderer. The cases aren't linked in any way. Any further claims of either will mean an end to your time on the JTF."

Nowitski smiled a predatory smile. "And Agent Horan, while the fine people at the NYPD may not have their hand on the leash around your neck, I sure as hell do. Let me be even clearer than Captain Geary. Any further attempt to paint these murders as a serial case will result in your termination from the FBI."

Chris opened his mouth to speak, but when Geary raised an eyebrow he kept quiet. He looked at Tanya Sagan, the supposedly independent mediator, but her face was blank. The meeting was clearly over. Chris stood and didn't look back as he left the room, slamming the door behind him.

He returned to his desk, collapsed into the chair, and tried to remain calm. He was used to being disciplined, but not to having his hands tied on an investigation or his job being threatened. And he definitely wasn't used to a personal tragedy being used to bludgeon him into submission. He placed his head in his hands and closed his eyes.

"Coffee, Chris?"

Chris looked up. Manny was standing in the doorway, a coffee cup in his hand and a worried look on his face. Chris nodded. As he reached for his own cup, a battered old FBI mug he'd had for years, he considered the logo. He used to believe in the work he did, but now he wondered if his obsession was compatible with that belief, given the views of his superiors.

There was a serial killer on the loose and nobody was doing a damn thing about it.

"Chris, come on man." Manny spoke again. "I testified at the Laverri trial yesterday. I think the bastard is going to walk. I need a coffee."

"Sorry." Chris spoke in barely more than a mumble. He clenched his hand around the mug, considered the logo, and put it back down.

He'd get a takeaway cup today.

13

ASHLEY

Ashley slammed the hotel room door shut behind her. The loud bang was music to a soul shouting at her to destroy something. Instead, she walked the five steps to the tiny kitchenette of the shittiest hotel room she'd ever stayed in and put the brown paper bag down on the counter.

A sob escaped her body and tears streaked down her face. She'd held it together just long enough to answer the door and grab the booze from one of the US Marshals watching over her. She'd smiled at him when she'd asked for a bottle of gin, then again when she'd grabbed it off him, but now she was alone again she'd reverted to the state she'd been in for days now.

A broken woman.

After her testimony, she'd walked out of the courtroom like a zombie. The media had shouted nasty and visceral questions, but she'd stayed mute as she was bundled into the SUV by the US Marshals. The Marshals had been nice to her, but she'd sensed their disappointment that Laverri was likely to walk free.

The Marshals had explained that Obrist had arranged for her to stay there for a few weeks, while measures were put in place to either extend or end her time in witness protection. Ashley had been given the chance to dispute that plan, but she'd simply nodded. Now she was a prisoner in the hotel room, with a man on the door and another in the lobby.

At least she had the booze.

She wiped her eyes and nose on her sleeve and then opened the bar fridge. She took a few cubes of ice from the small freezer section and dropped them into a wine glass, which were the only kind in the room. She poured the gin, took the glass and walked to the bathroom. As she filled a bath, she took a gulp of gin. The liquor burned her throat, but it helped calm her down a little.

As the bath filled, she pulled her cellphone out of her pocket and dialed the only man who might be able to help her. "Simon?"

"Ashley?" Weltering's voice was a mix of confusion and concern. "What's wrong? Are you okay?"

"I just needed to talk. There's nobody else." She sat on the edge of the bath, took a long pull of gin and let out a long sigh. "It's all fucked. The trial."

"I'm sorry, Ashley." Weltering sounded like he meant it. "A setback was always possible. You did your best and it's over now. You can move on."

"I just didn't think I'd crumble on the stand. I looked like a fool. I froze, I stammered, I answered questions wrong, I probably let Laverri off the hook." She took another sip. "What do I do now, Simon? I just don't see where I go from here. I've got nothing and no one, and no reason to keep on waking up."

"We can talk about it, Ashley, but not over the phone." Weltering paused, and Ashley heard a female voice in the background. She sounded angry. "Make an appointment with me for next week and we'll sort out some strategies. Until then, I'd strongly suggest you stay away from your ex-husband, your daughter, and alcohol."

"Too late." Ashley terminated the call and tossed the phone onto the tiles. She wasn't interested in an appointment.

She just wanted the hell to end.

She took another gulp of gin and then placed the glass on the tiles next to the bath. She undressed, turned the water off and climbed inside. She savored the scalding heat, hoping it might help to cauterize her emotional wounds. But as she lay there, she found it impossible to think about anything except her time in court.

Laverri would walk free and all her sacrifices would've been for nothing. She'd lived in anonymity, lost her daughter and made herself a target for nothing. After rebuilding her life following an attack in her early 20s, it had been destroyed again by her own stupidity. She should have kept her mouth shut, but instead she'd let herself be conned into testifying.

"Do the right thing." She scoffed as she imitated the cops and lawyers who'd convinced her to testify. "Look what doing the right thing got me?"

She sobbed again as she reached for the gin, disgusted by how dependent she'd become on the police, the justice system, her counselor, and her ex-husband. She'd been used by some and abused by others. Even those who'd claimed to want to help her had failed to do so, and the result was a whole lot of pain and not a lot of hope.

The wine glass started to shake in her hand and she slammed it as hard as she could into the side of the bath. The glass shattered into a dozen pieces, some landing in the bath and some landing on the floor. Ashley didn't flinch as broken glass fell over her, the jagged stem of the wine glass still in her hand.

The glass stem glimmered in the light as she rotated it in her hand. She swapped it from her right hand to her left and then back again. Settling on her right, she pressed the sharp tip against her left wrist. Gently, at first, then with more pressure. A trickle of blood mixed with the water, but she didn't stop.

She didn't want to.

14

DUNCAN

All this drinking was a bit much for Duncan. Since he'd met Chelsea in the bar, they'd had several large nights on the booze together. Her husband – the nice customer from the liquor store – hadn't been there for any of them, proving to Duncan that he'd been correct in selecting her as his next target. She was an awful woman – a flirt, a cheat, and a slut. Nearly as bad was her inane conversation. He almost wanted to kill her now, just to get some peace.

"The strangest thing happened the other day." Chelsea waved her wine glass around like it was a prop to accompany her story. "I lost my keys!"

"Oh no!" One of Chelsea's friends, Joanne, gave an exaggerated gasp. "What'd you do?"

"I had to get my super to replace them, because hubby is out of town." Chelsea took a sip of her wine. "Two hundred bucks for a key! Can you believe it?"

Duncan could, actually. "Outrageous."

"I know! That's less than I'd charge for a night in bed!"

Chelsea burst into laughter and her three friends did the same.

Duncan didn't. Not immediately. It took him a moment to process that what she'd said was a joke, rather than a statement of fact from a willing whore. When he did realize, he overcompensated with a loud guffaw that was a second or two late. The others stopped laughing and stared at him quizzically. He needed to pay more attention.

He'd been distracted by her three female friends. They'd joined them for drinks at Chelsea's place, but once again her husband was absent. She really was a horrible wife, entertaining people – including a man – without her husband. The more he learned about her, the more disgusted he was. She was far worse than he'd expected. She needed to be dealt with.

But first, he had to prune her friends from her life. They'd tried to engage him in conversation, trying to figure out who he was, but he'd ignored them and been downright rude. Now it was time to parlay that ill feeling they had toward him into hostility toward her. This would be the most challenging attempt he'd ever made to carve away an element of someone's life.

Usually, he relied on scandal, but now he was relying on his own personality.

"I wonder if your husband has the key?" Duncan laughed. "Hopefully he doesn't come home and use it tonight, just when we're starting to have some fun!"

Chelsea's eyes narrowed, but a fake smile soon lit up her face. She feigned a laugh. "Does anyone need a drink? I'm running on empty."

Before anyone could answer, she retreated to the kitchen, where three empty bottles of wine would soon be joined by a fourth. Duncan watched her go, a smile on his face, then turned back to her friends. They were glaring daggers at him, clearly more interested in protecting their friend than questioning her conduct. It was typical that a woman like Chelsea would surround herself with a pack of snakes.

"Look, I don't know who the fuck you are or whatever voodoo magic you're using to get your claws into Chelsea, but it needs to stop." One of the vipers, Joanne, struck first. "Everyone likes a little bit of fun, but you're way too noisy about it. You need to be more discreet or you'll ruin it for all of us."

Duncan's smile grew wider. "I've got nothing to hide, from you or anyone else. If you're scared, or ashamed, maybe you should take up knitting."

Duncan turned his back on them and followed Chelsea into the kitchen. She was pouring more wine, so didn't notice him until he came up behind her and wrapped his arms around her waist. As he pressed himself in close, she gave a small giggle and pushed her ass toward him. Then she turned and kissed him furiously. Duncan reciprocated, the kiss fueled by anger and devoid of passion. This was work, but it disgusted him. He felt sick.

They kissed for a minute, pressing their bodies in close. Duncan knew if he wanted her, he could have her right now. Even with her friends in the other room, there'd be no resistance from Chelsea. But Duncan was counting on a fight on another front. Letting out a low growl, he nibbled Chelsea's lower lip and squeezed her tighter, feeling her tense at his touch. After she let out a small sigh of satisfaction, Duncan released her and took a step back.

"What's wrong, Dan?" Chelsea frowned and looked at him, confusion in her eyes. "Why did you stop?"

"Well, your friends are out there..." Duncan's voice trailed off and he cast a glance over his shoulder, toward the living room. "They don't want me here."

"So?" Chelsea's tone carried a hint of outrage and disbelief. "Why do you care what they think? They all have their fun, now it's my turn!"

Duncan shrugged. "Sorry. They told me to leave you alone. I don't want to do anything while they're here. There's no rush."

"Like fuck there's not!" She exhaled forcefully, grabbed the bottle of wine and stormed past him.

Duncan smiled to himself, then followed Chelsea to the living room. No one was speaking, but Duncan could feel the hostility radiating off all of them. Duncan reached out and wrapped his arm around Chelsea from behind. She pressed into him, turned and kissed him deeply. He felt bile rise from the pit of his stomach.

He could almost feel the steam coming off Chelsea's friends. Duncan had counted on their outrage, but on its own he knew it wasn't enough. The only way to wedge Chelsea from her friends was for her to make the decision herself. Chelsea was the spark and her friends were the powder keg. All Duncan had done was prepare the fuse.

"You're an idiot, Chelsea." One of her other friends spoke up for the first time. "He's not discreet enough. He's going to blow up your marriage."

"Oh fuck off, Amber!" Chelsea's voice was full of venom. "I don't need to be judged by you! You fuck whoever you want, so why can't I?"

Duncan wanted to smile, but instead he stepped away from Chelsea. "Look, maybe it's best if I leave."

"No!" Chelsea's voice was a low rumble, a thunder that

surprised Duncan and seemed to shock her friends as well. "I've had enough of this."

There were unspoken messages beaming back and forth between the women. Duncan kept his face passive and his emotions calm as Chelsea turned, took his hand and led him in the direction of the bedroom. Behind him, he could hear her friends scoff with disgust. Duncan knew the spark had lit the fuse; he just hoped it'd be enough to ignite the powder keg. He really didn't want to have to fuck her. He needed her friends to react.

"That's it, Chels, we're done!" Joanne's shout confirmed it. "I hope this jerk fucks you like crazy, because you're not going to have a marriage at the end of it."

"You won't know!" Chelsea's shout was so loud Duncan winced, even as they both slumped onto the bed. "You're not welcome here anymore! You'll never see me again!"

Duncan almost laughed. How right she was. He squeezed Chelsea tightly until he heard the door slam, then let go and looked at her. "Sorry about that."

"Fuck them." She shook her head, clearly stunned that her best friends had just walked out. "I'm just happy to be spending more time with you."

"I have to go, unfortunately." He stood up from the bed. "It's been fun though. I'll call you."

"I just stuck up for you!" Chelsea's eyes narrowed. "Now you're going to bail for the night?"

Duncan shrugged. Turning to walk away, he flinched as a stiletto flew past his head, wondering if her aim would've been better if she wasn't drunk. He almost laughed at the beauty of it. He'd destroyed her relationship with her dearest friends. It was the first thing he'd taken from her. She deserved it, given how easy it had been to get her to betray her husband.

He doubted it was the first time, either.

The job would get harder from here on, but Duncan was confident he could pull it off. Behind him, her sobs were loud and heaving, almost irresistible, but he didn't look back. He did pause near the front door when, out of nowhere, her small dog – Kenny – barked and wagged his tail. Duncan opened the door and commanded it to come.

As he rode the elevator down and into the night, the small dog followed him.

15

CHRIS

"Goddamn it." Chris pulled his hand back. His latex glove had a cut in it and his thumb had a nasty gash.

He sucked the wound and the coppery tang of blood filled his mouth. Chris shook his head. The knife that'd cut him was now a tainted murder weapon, his own blood added to the victim's because of his own carelessness. A bit of forensic magic would take care of it, but he wasn't usually that sloppy. His mind hadn't been on the job since the meeting with his superiors, and he was struggling to focus on the current murder scene.

"Chris, come on man, can you get back to planet Earth?" Manny kicked the dirt, the disgust in his voice clear. "You need to stop fucking up the evidence?"

"Sorry." Chris looked at his partner. The displeasure on his face was clear, and Chris couldn't blame him. "I've been a shitty partner lately."

"That's an understatement." Manny sighed and jerked a

thumb toward the body. "Look, I know he hasn't got red hair, but this dead old homeless guy deserves your best effort."

Manny's words were like a slap to the face. They hurt more than the blows Chris's superiors had rained down on him at their last meeting. "Manny, I'm fine, honestly."

"No, you're not." Manny put his hands on his hips and fixed Chris with a stare. "You need to see a psychologist, or I'm telling Nowitski what you're up to."

"Wha—"

"The night stakeouts, Chris." Manny almost spat the words. "I'm not stupid. I know what you've been doing, and what led to the manhunt. You need to speak to someone."

Chris almost told Manny to shove it, but he clamped his jaw shut. There was nobody who could hurt an FBI agent like their partner. They knew all the dirt. Manny knew he'd been staking out houses of potential victims. If his superiors found out, he'd be through. They were furious about the manhunt, but they hadn't linked it to his other activity. There was only one thing Chris could say that'd satisfy Manny.

"Fine." Chris crossed his arms.

Manny smiled. "Great. I'll work this case while you do."

Chris was about to speak when someone tapped him on the shoulder. He scowled at Manny and turned to see a suited blonde woman standing behind him with a smile on her face. He knew who she was, and it was no coincidence that she was here. Manny must have planned it. There was no other reason for a psychologist to be at a murder scene. He felt like a fly that'd been swatted against a wall.

"Agent Horan?" The woman held out her hand. "I'm Catherine Williams. I'm a psych with the Bureau."

"I know who you are." Chris looked down at her hand,

ignored it, and turned to Manny. "You're going to cost me my job."

Manny scoffed. "You're doing a fine job of that yourself, Chris. Talk with her or I'm calling Nowitski right now."

"Let's walk." Chris's invitation to Williams had little warmth, and he didn't wait for her to respond. He started to walk away from the crime scene and she fell in beside him.

"Your case seems messy." Williams cut to the chase. "But I don't get the feeling that's what's on your mind."

Chris hesitated, wondering how much Manny had told her. He'd agreed to talk to the woman, not to tell her his life story. "It's tough at the moment."

She seemed to choose her words carefully. "I've been dealing with agents in difficult situations for years, Chris. Everything you say to me is private."

Chris stopped walking and turned around, looking her right in the eyes. She clearly recognized the source of his hesitation, and had a strategy to deal with it. Cops weren't the most trusting lot, but Williams knew that and came to work anyway. He needed to tell her enough to satisfy her and Manny that he was okay.

"Look," Chris finally spoke, not taking his eyes off hers. "There are some murders I believe are connected. Others don't agree. That's it."

"Sometimes people don't see what's right in front of them." Her gaze didn't shift an inch. "On the other hand, sometimes people try to connect things that aren't actually linked, to satisfy some deeper desire, or to create a narrative – a sense of order – where there's really chaos and chance. We just need to figure out where you stand, Chris."

Chris frowned at that. She had a point. It was entirely possible there was a link and he'd spotted it. But it was also possible that his bosses were right. Maybe he was searching for some greater purpose, trying to fill the hole Tamara had left...

Chris tightened his grip on the pistol as he peered into the kitchen. He'd been right, there was food cooking – some sort of soup – but there was no sign of Tamara. It was like she'd vanished from their tiny apartment, leaving all the signs of someone having been home. There was only one more place she could be, unless she had left food on the cooktop and gone out...

Chris blinked. "What?"

Williams had a hand on his shoulder. "You can trust me, Chris."

The kills were linked, he was sure of it, and bouncing his theories off someone under strict confidentiality probably wasn't a bad idea. Catherine Williams seemed a fair, neutral, and intelligent sounding board. She seemed capable of offering an expert opinion and she'd keep her mouth shut. He kept his eyes on her for several more moments, then he sighed and decided to spill it all to her.

As they strolled, he recounted it all – Tamara, all the murders of other redheads since, the links he suspected, the stakeouts, the manhunt and the latest warning he'd received. It felt as if the story had spewed out of his mouth almost involuntarily. She kept silent, merely nodding and making quiet noises of affirmation as he spoke. When he was finished he didn't look at her. He waited.

They walked a little further and then she finally spoke. "The link you see between the killings is possible, but so too is a mental construction."

"But—"

She held up a hand. "You need to be careful. I'm seeing

some of the same obsessive tendencies in you that you're chasing in a serial killer."

"You're saying I'm like the killer?" Chris flared. "Look, thanks for your time, but this was a mistake. I—"

"I didn't mean that as an insult." She smiled. "I'm not saying you're going to start murdering people. What I am saying is that you suffered incredible trauma. Your girlfriend had red hair. She was murdered. In the same city she died, more redheads have been murdered. You're an agent who investigates murders. It's only natural you see a link."

Chris gritted his teeth. "There *is* a link."

"It's possible. You're clearly hungry to catch this killer, all I'm saying is that there are many types of obsessives, Chris. It's possible for anyone to have these obsessive tendencies, you included. You just need to maintain control, be aware of your impulses, and not let them cloud your judgement or the conduct of your work."

"Okay." Chris paused. "So, if there is a serial killer, what's his story likely to be?"

She shrugged. "It's impossible to say for sure without knowing more about the cases, or being able to speak to the suspect. For some people, obsession is a positive. For some, it's not. Usually what pushes dangerous people over the line isn't their nature, but how they were nurtured or some trigger event."

"The serial killer might have something in his past?"

"I'd say it's incredibly likely, if your serial killer does indeed exist." She placed a hand on his back. "Just take it easy, keep it all in perspective, and come see me again next week."

Chris chewed on her words for a moment. "Okay."

They shook hands, then Williams headed for her car. As Chris walked back to the crime scene, he thought about their discussion. He felt better, even if talking to her hadn't changed his mind about the likelihood of a serial killer, or got him any closer to catching them. He was determined to put more effort into his other cases. It would help keep his head clear, and keep others off his back.

Manny was waiting at the edge of the crime scene. "We're done for now. The crime scene guys are scouring over it and I've done the preliminary work. Let's get out of here."

They walked to their SUV. Manny took the wheel and they drove in silence back to JTF headquarters. Either Manny was satisfied because Chris had spoken to Williams for nearly an hour, or he didn't want to bring it up. Chris saw no need to complicate that with conversation. The silence was only broken when Manny took a call, keeping one hand on the wheel while he held the phone to his ear with the other.

When the call was finished, Manny pulled over and looked at Chris. His partner looked spooked. "I need your help, Chris."

Chris frowned. They'd just finished a long shift and he wanted to get started on another set of stakeouts. "What's up?"

"A key witness in the Laverri case is gone." Manny sounded surprisingly emotional. "I worked that case. I want to find her."

16

ASHLEY

Ashley rushed down the street, weaving through pedestrians who seemed intent on getting in her way as she looked down at her cellphone. It was a third-generation out-of-date iPhone she'd picked up cheap. The map app worked, though, and it told her she was only a block away from the school. That was her only focus after spending days holed up in that awful hotel room with nothing to do except think about how badly she'd fucked up.

Ashley had thought about killing herself, but decided on another course of action. She was tired of putting her life on hold for the legal system, the same system that had removed her child. She was going to get Lucy, jump on a Greyhound bus, leave New York and set up somewhere far from here. She was meant to be meeting with Obrist to discuss a possible appeal, but she'd decided to skip it. She'd snuck past the Marshals and out of the hotel.

She knew the cops would try to find her, of course, but she'd be long gone before they knew it. She didn't care where she went, it just had to be somewhere she could get a job and send Lucy to school. Living in San Francisco and New York had severely impacted her life. Witness protection in Connecticut had been horrible. She just wanted a safe, sleepy life with Lucy somewhere out of the way. Maybe she'd head south.

Ashley stopped walking and her breath caught in her throat. She could see Lucy on a playground less than 50 yards away, going down the slide and talking to a couple of her friends. The playground was inside the school fence and there were other kids around, but all Ashley saw was her daughter. She suddenly felt thankful she hadn't killed herself. Doing so would've denied her this moment.

Ashley stood and watched for several minutes, forgetting all about her plan. Lucy was running, playing and laughing just like she used to before this disaster had afflicted their life. Ashley was suddenly torn. She didn't want to deny Lucy her happiness here in New York, her home, but she was confident her daughter could be happy wherever they ended up. Doubt raced through her mind, but she forced it away.

Ashley clenched her fists, decision made, then walked over to the playground. As she approached, the girls continued to play, oblivious. It was only when she was less than 10 yards away that Lucy looked up, squinted in confusion, and then froze in place. Her friends stopped what they were doing as well, and one of them reached out for Lucy's hand.

Ashley took another couple of steps forward and then stopped, close enough to talk but far enough away that she wasn't threatening. She smiled. "Hi, Lucy."

"Hi Mommy." Lucy beamed, her big brown eyes melting Ashley's heart. Then she started talking rapidly. "I'm sorry for getting upset at the store. I was just surprised and I—"

"Lucy, it's alright." Ashley held her arms wide. "Come here."

Lucy smiled and nodded, letting go of her friend's hand and running over to Ashley. They embraced, and as she wrapped the girl in a tight hug Ashley looked over to Lucy's friends. One was standing completely still and just staring at them, but the other had run away from the playground, back toward the school. As Lucy snuggled into her chest, alarm bells started to ring over the public-address system.

As soon as she heard the alarm Lucy tried to pull away, a look of steely determination on her face. "I have to go now, Mommy. I need to go inside and find my teacher."

Ashley squeezed Lucy tighter, pulling her head back into her chest. "Just stay with me. You're safe. Everything is alright."

"Those are the rules. I—"

Ashley inhaled sharply, spotting two security guards running from the school to the playground. "Lucy, just come with me. You need to trust me. It's okay."

Ashley gripped Lucy by the arm. Not wanting to hurt her, but aware she needed to get her away from here, Ashley pulled as hard she dared. But she wasn't fast enough. She heard shouts from behind her and turned around. Two security guards were running towards her, radios in hand and scowls on their faces. It was too late.

One of the security guards stepped toward her, holding up his hand, palm facing outwards. "You can leave that girl alone or you can end up in a cell."

"Security guards at a school." Ashley shook her head, trying her best to stay calm despite her rapidly increasing heart rate. "You'd never get that in Connecticut."

"This isn't Connecticut." The guard wasn't having any of

her small talk. He stepped forward and reached out to grab Ashley as his partner spoke into a radio. "You need to stop."

"Just leave us alone!" Ashley shouted and stepped away from him, her voice hoarse with emotion. "Mind your own business!"

The guard didn't move an inch. "The welfare of our students is our business. Now, you need to let go of her and take a few steps back."

Ashley's grip on Lucy loosened just a little bit, but it was enough for the girl to wrest herself free. She pulled away hard and fell to the ground, propelled by her own momentum. Ashley reached out to grab the girl as she fell, but Lucy started to cry and turned her head away. The gesture broke Ashley's heart, and her resolve. She looked up at the security guards, who weren't going anywhere, and then slumped onto the grass.

"Why do you keep doing this?" Lucy spoke between heaving sobs, her voice laden with accusation. "I don't like it, Mommy."

Ashley turned to face her daughter, who was looking up at her with big, sad eyes that were puffy from crying, and realized that she couldn't answer the question without sounding ridiculous. She was a grown woman who was drowning emotionally, and in scrambling to save herself by latching onto the one person she loved more than anything, she was drowning Lucy.

Ashley reached out to touch Lucy, but the girl recoiled from her touch. Ashley felt like her whole body sagged at that point, and she closed her eyes and covered her ears. One of the guards stood next to her, and she could hear police sirens in the distance, growing ever closer. It was a pattern that was becoming all too familiar, but this time the consequences could prove to be more permanent. She'd screwed up yet again.

But halfway through this screw-up she'd realized just how much things needed to change. How much *she* needed to change. As she sobbed, she hoped she'd get the opportunity to make that change.

17

DUNCAN

Duncan pushed the door open and stepped into the store. The chime that announced his arrival did nothing to rouse the bored teen staring at his phone behind the counter, who seemed unconcerned that a customer had entered the store. The internet café was empty, and the kid was probably earning seven bucks an hour working the graveyard shift, when only gamers, stoners, and those who couldn't afford a Verizon plan came in.

Or those who intended to break at least seven federal and state laws.

Duncan approached the counter and put down 20 bucks. "I just need half an hour. If you keep anyone else away from me, you can keep the change."

The attendant grunted, took the twenty and handed Duncan an access card, all without looking up. "Insert that into the card reader. And clean up after yourself."

Duncan tapped the card against his palm as he walked through the café. He chose a machine near the back, making sure the screen was visible to nobody else and there were no security cameras around. It wasn't really necessary – he'd scouted this location the day before – but caution had kept him safe over the years. He sat at the machine, inserted the access card and waited as the computer granted him access.

First he checked out a few news websites and browsed casually, careful not to log in to anything that could identify that he'd been here. After a while, once he was sure he wouldn't be disturbed, he logged into Chelsea's social media accounts. He paused for a second while he cracked his knuckles, mentally psyching himself up for the hurt he was about to inflict upon her.

Duncan was glad to find that the passwords he'd hijacked off her phone when he'd met her at the bar hadn't been changed. He'd also purchased a pre-paid cell phone and inserted a mirrored SIM of hers, which meant he'd seen every text message she'd sent or received since. He was genuinely shocked by what he'd seen. She was a far nastier woman than he'd expected.

Next, he dug around in his pocket for his USB and plugged it into the slot. The computer whirred for a moment, then a folder appeared. Duncan smiled when he saw the thumbnails of the dozens of images on the USB, a curated collection of nudes and near nudes he'd pulled off her phone. The pictures were confirmation, yet again, that what he was doing was right. As best he could tell, few of the images had made their way to her husband.

It only took a few moments to upload a selection of the nudes to her social media accounts. He even made one of the photos her profile picture on LinkedIn, even though he had never figured out what that site was for. He didn't put every shot on each site, but instead spread them widely, so as many people as possible saw her true nature.

Once the pictures had been widely circulated, he logged into her work email. He didn't bother reading anything in her inbox, though the volume of messages there suggested that plenty of people and projects relied on her. He'd learned in his time with her that Chelsea's career was more important to her than anything, even her husband.

This was Duncan's final play. He composed a new email, addressed to her boss. He took his time typing the message, in which she professed her undying shame about their affair and told him it had to end. Duncan then attached the most explicit of the nude shots, which she'd offered as a gift for him to remember her by. Once that was done, he carbon copied the entire office distribution list of 8,000 staff all across America.

Duncan licked his lips as he read over the email several times. The email would end her career, and carpet-bombing the nudes across her network would destroy her remaining professional and social links. She'd be isolated, cast aside as a crazy bitch. Already teetering from the other damage he'd caused her, this might just tip her over. Duncan was quite proud of this one. He pressed send, a malicious smile crossing his face.

It was her own fault, anyway. Every time he'd seen her, she'd dressed like she wanted it and acted as flirty as hell. She was the same as all the others he'd targeted. Ruining her was a favor to humanity, and to her husband. It was also a way to soothe Duncan's own pain. Like each one before her, she'd given Duncan something to focus on, distracting him temporarily from the gaping maw in his own heart.

But no matter who he chose and what he did, it was never

enough. No victim could ever be the same as her – the woman who'd broken his heart.

At least this time he'd mixed it up a bit. It was the first time he'd let a victim see him and interact with him before he killed her. Though it had been a risk, getting close to her had been interesting. That was vital, because recently it had been getting a bit tedious. With each new kill, the payoff was a little bit less, and never quite what he'd imagined it would be. His new approach mightn't have fully replenished the thrill, the rush, but it had certainly helped.

With a sigh, Duncan stood and wiped down everything he'd touched with the sleeve of his shirt. Although the chances of the police linking him to this crime and getting prints from this location were almost zero, he hadn't stayed free by being dumb so he took the precaution anyway. As he walked out of the internet café, his mind drifted back to Chelsea, imagining her reaction as she found out what he'd done.

He was going to enjoy killing her.

18

CHRIS

Chris pulled the Chevy Suburban over to the side of the road, right out front of the police station. He killed the engine and turned to his partner. "You sure?"

Manny frowned at him. They'd had several long days without much sleep, now both of them were short with each other. "What do you mean?"

"I'm not sure this is the right move." Chris unbuckled his seatbelt. "Maybe we should let the US Attorney handle it?"

"No." Manny's tone suggested there was little room for debate. "Laverri was found not guilty after she screwed up her testimony. If there's going to be an appeal, we need to keep her out of prison and in the right frame of mind. Obrist is already cooling on an appeal, so we need to do whatever we can do to heat up the chances."

Chris shook his head. "You're the one telling me I bend the rules too much."

Manny shrugged, the conversation clearly over.

Chris let it go. God knew he had his own issues, so who

was he to begrudge Manny this one. He knew this woman was important to him. They'd made straight for the station the minute they'd found out she was being held by the NYPD. He opened the door, climbed out of the car and followed Manny across the sidewalk to the station entrance.

Before they entered, Manny paused and looked Chris in the eye. "Let me do the talking. She trusts me."

Chris nodded. He understood. Every cop had cases that stuck with them, and suspects they wanted to put away. For Manny, it was Laverri. It had been one of his highest profile cases and he'd convinced the only witness to testify. She'd only been willing to speak to Manny, but when she did, the truth had poured out. It had been a huge scalp for a junior agent.

Once they were inside the station, Chris stayed back as Manny approached the desk and flashed his badge. "Evening."

The duty sergeant looked up from his newspaper and flashed a weary smile. "What can I do for you gentlemen?"

"We're following a rainbow and I think the pot of gold is in one of your cells." Manny pocketed his badge and rested his arms on the desk. "Her name is Ashley Wheeler."

"One second." The sergeant worked his keyboard and then tapped the monitor in front of him. "Yep, got her in here on minor stuff. She harassed her kid at school, mouthed off at some cops and was showing signs of being drunk. The boys decided she needed to cool off so we threw her in a cell."

The relief on Manny's face was clear. "She's a witness in the trial against Saul Laverri. I promised the US Attorney I'd get her to a meeting in the morning to discuss an appeal."

"Laverri? No shit?" The sergeant whistled. "If you can talk her straight and it helps keep that bastard inside, you can take her off my books. Wait, isn't she in witness protection?"

"She slipped past the Marshals guarding her in her hotel." Manny's voice was grave. "Can we speak to her?"

"On one condition." The sergeant shrugged. "She needs to agree to stay away from her daughter. She's lucky not to be facing felony attempted kidnapping. This is the second time."

"Understood." Manny smiled.

With a nod, the sergeant stood, led them to an interview room and left them to wait. A short while later the door opened and Ashley Wheeler entered. She looked like shit, dressed in jeans and a crumpled blouse. Her red hair was a mess, tied up in a rough ponytail. Chris figured she was in her mid-thirties, about the same age as...

"Tamara!" Chris screamed as he saw her body, sitting upright on the sofa but with lifeless eyes. He drew his pistol and searched the living room. Empty. He checked for a pulse. None. He let out a wail of anguish, then fumbled in his pocket for his cell phone. His hands felt like bricks and his fingers felt like stumps, but he managed to call 911...

Chris blinked. Manny had punched his arm. "What?"

Manny gave him a death glare, then stood and held his arms wide for a hug. "It's good to see you. This is my partner, Chris Horan."

The woman stepped into Manny's hug. They embraced quickly, then separated. Her eyes locked onto Chris. "Why're you both here?"

Chris tried to keep quiet, but couldn't. "You need to worry less about me and more about staying out of trouble, Ms Wheeler."

"I—"

"Take a seat." Chris knew Manny would be pissed at him. He'd promised to keep quiet, but Chris felt he had to speak. Manny was clearly compromised.

She glared daggers at him and then looked at Manny, who nodded. After a deep breath, she sat. "Fine."

Chris snorted. "Sneaking past the US Marshals and attempting to kidnap your own daughter, for starters, right after you blew a major trial. What were you thinking?"

Wheeler's face twisted in apparent fury and she leaned forward, locking eyes with Chris. "Fuck you, okay?"

"He's right, Ashley," Manny said. "I know you've had a tough time, but you need to hear some tough words. There's a chance Obrist won't launch an appeal against Laverri because you're flaky. You need to get your shit under control, or Laverri will walk. Obrist is on the edge. You already missed a meeting with him."

"I don't care!" Wheeler flared. "Ever since I saw that bastard kill the other bastard, my life has been ruined. I've lost my identity, my husband, my little girl – everything. Obrist just used me, the judge let me get smashed on the stand, my counselor is fucking useless and even the cops here harass me."

Chris raised his voice. "Ms Wheeler, you need to calm—"

She ignored Chris and spoke to Manny. "I've had enough. If the authorities won't look after my interests, I'm done helping them."

"You were lucky you weren't killed by one of Laverri's guys." Manny sighed again. "You not showing up to that meeting damages me too, Ashley."

Wheeler flared again, then paused and took a breath. It was almost as if Manny had pierced her armor. "You're the only one who hasn't screwed me, Manny."

"I appreciate you saying that." Manny placed a hand on top of hers. "Now, you've got a choice to make. You come with us to the meeting, or you go back into a cell and try your luck with this precinct. If you come with us, you need to stay away from your daughter and front up to Obrist."

It took a while, but finally she nodded. But her eyes flared again as she pointed to Chris. "I'll come with you, Manny, but Sheriff Dan over there keeps his mouth shut."

Chris raised an eyebrow and locked eyes with her. For the first time, he considered her properly. She looked like shit, but beneath the grime and the messed-up hair, he could see how beautiful she could be. Chris squinted. She actually looked a hell of a lot like some of the victims his serial killer – if there was one – had attacked. He leaned forward and looked at her closely.

"What do you want?" She scowled at him. "I just told your friend over there I'd help him and now you're getting in my face?"

"I don't suppose you've been attacked by anyone lately?" Chris said it before he had a chance to catch the words.

Her eyes went wide. "What? I—"

"Chris." Manny's voice was abrasive. He knew exactly what Chris was thinking. "Go sort out the release with the desk sergeant."

Chris sighed and nodded. He stood, walked to the door and then turned back to Wheeler. After another glance at her, which sent all sorts of questions racing through his mind, he left the room. A quick conversation with the desk sergeant was all it took. As the other man filled out the paperwork, a sharp pain bit into Chris's jaw, and he realized he'd been clenching his teeth.

It wasn't just that she looked like a potential victim. It was also the reminder that if he dropped the ball and ignored what was so clear to him, there'd be more victims. He'd tried to stay on the safe path, but he couldn't do it. He knew then that no combination of psychologists and busy work would mask the urge inside him. He couldn't ignore it.

He knew what was happening and he was the only one who could stop it. The longer he tried to deny that, the more likely it was that another woman would end up dead. Even though he'd been ordered to stop, he couldn't turn his back on it.

19

ASHLEY

Ashley looked down at the carpet, wondering how many times Obrist had walked over it since last having it replaced. "You need some new carpet."

Obrist let out a long sigh, his anger barely restrained. He'd been that way for the last thirty minutes, during which he'd been talking and she'd been looking anywhere but at him. He'd shared his thoughts on her breakdown on the stand, which had led to the not-guilty verdict and put Laverri back on the streets. Then he'd moved on to her decision to skip their meeting. Then he'd scalded her for getting arrested. It was a tour de force of Ashley's recent screw-ups.

"I don't think you appreciate how bad this is, Ashley." Obrist placed his coffee cup down on the table. "Best we can tell, Laverri has had a hand in at least eighteen murders. But this was the first we had a chance to get him on. Others will end up dead now that he's back on the street."

Ashley kept her eyes on the floor. She wanted to stand up and walk out, but she didn't. She knew he was right. After her first attempt to snatch Lucy, she'd started to get back on track. But her failure on the stand had destroyed her fragile progress, leading to her current situation. Manny's words at the police station had rammed it home. She was further away than ever from getting Lucy back, and she'd hurt others.

Manny had convinced her to front up to Obrist and face the consequences. She'd promised to leave her daughter alone. That hadn't been much of a concession, given that Ashley had already decided to do that. Her daughter deserved more than a mother who tried to snatch her out of the playground. She needed to get her head straight, and then try to get Lucy back the right way.

"I think you should appeal." Ashley's voice was soft as she looked up at him for the first time. His face showed a mix of anger and fatigue. "I'll do better next time."

Obrist sighed and leaned back in his chair. "Falling apart on the stand is one thing. I can deal with that. But disappearing when I have to decide whether to appeal or not, and then getting picked up by the police? Your continued focus on your daughter has made my position almost impossible."

His words stung. "I just miss her. I need her back. If the courts hadn't taken my daughter while I was under pressure for agreeing to help you, I might've performed better!"

Obrist's eyes narrowed. "There isn't one giant justice system that works toward one goal, Ashley. Your role in my case is completely unrelated to your family law matters."

Ashley looked down at the carpet, cheeks burning and trying to calm herself. "What now?"

"There's no way you could have damaged my case more, which makes an appeal unlikely to succeed. The defense had a field day last time you were on the stand, and now you've given them more shots to fire at you. Without you, there's definitely no case, but I'm not sure there's one with you anymore either. Our time together is at an end."

"Okay." Ashley sagged. She wasn't sure what to say now that he'd rejected her offer of support. "I understand."

"I don't think you do." Obrist's voice had a softer tone now. He stood and walked around to her side of the desk, then leaned against the edge of it. "If there's no appeal, the witness protection for you, your ex-husband and your daughter will end. For you, that means no more payments, counseling, or US Marshal protection."

Ashley looked up from the carpet and her mind raced. They had only remained safe because of the program. They'd had their names changed and been moved out of New York. Though Ashley and Tom had later separated, he and Lucy had kept their fake names when they'd moved back to New York.

Ashley would still have the new name if pulled out of the program, but she'd lose everything else, including access to the meager allowances that had kept her afloat financially. Worse, she'd no longer have free access to Simon Weltering's counseling. Despite all her criticisms of her time in the loving embrace of the Federal Government, she'd come to rely on the support.

"You can't do that." Ashley's eyes searched his for any hint of uncertainty, but his gaze was granite. "Please, I need to remain in witness protection. So do Tom and Lucy."

"Laverri has been found not guilty and your part is done." Obrist's tone was somber. "Keep your head down and focus on getting your daughter back. You should be safe."

"My daughter..."

Obrist's eyes narrowed slightly, then his features softened and he let out a long sigh. "I'll see if I can help with that. Call it a parting gift for trying to help me put Laverri away. Let me call a friend and see if he'll help gain you some access. He's a family friend and a damn good lawyer, specializing in family law."

Ashley was a little shocked by Obrist's offer. He was extending an olive branch of his own. She watched as he picked up his phone and dialed. She couldn't help wondering if he was doing this in order to soothe his own guilt, providing a kindness to a woman he'd soon forget about. She wouldn't say no to the help, though, as much as it rankled that it was only now being provided.

As he spoke, she thought. It sickened her that powerful people such as Obrist conducted business like this. They have conversations their clients never hear, but are heavily impacted by. And as quickly as deals are done, the subjects of those deals are forgotten. It was a system of justice only for those who could afford it. For everyone else, it was best to simply stay out of the way.

Ashley leaned forward as Obrist ended the call. She balled her fists by her sides and spoke louder than she intended. "Another no?"

Obrist shook his head. "No, quite the opposite. My friend will try to help you gain some access to your daughter. It's a good opportunity."

Ashley clenched her teeth. She didn't want to accept his help. She was sure it'd mean more torment at the hands of the legal system, more empty offers of assistance, more false concern. She almost told him to shove it, but the overriding desire to get things right with Lucy trumped everything else. She had to accept any help that was offered, because everything she'd tried had failed.

She held her tongue and smiled at Obrist.

20

DUNCAN

D uncan strode confidently down the hallway of the apartment building, jingling the keys until he reached Chelsea's place. After glancing around to make sure he was alone, he used the newest key in his collection to unlock the door. As he did, he remembered the story Chelsea had told about having lost her key and laughed. Pretty soon she'd be wishing she'd changed the locks.

He stepped inside and closed the door quietly behind him. The apartment was dark, but he had no need for any light. An unexpected advantage of getting close to his victims before killing them was learning the layout of their apartments well enough to walk around in the dark. He listened for a moment, to make sure his entry hadn't woken Chelsea, but he heard nothing.

As he pulled the balaclava over his head, Duncan reflected on how perfectly everything had gone. After his broadcast of her nude photographs, Chelsea's personal life had entered freefall. Her professional life had taken an even bigger hit.

He'd logged into her emails again to find dozens of messages from across her company, scolding her for sending the email. There'd been three emails that were particularly interesting.

One, from her boss, had denied all knowledge of the affair, which was quite right given Duncan had made it up. The second, from human resources, informed her that her employment had been terminated. The final email had been from her husband – who worked at the same company – told her he was on his way home from a business trip in Los Angeles and that there'd be a reckoning.

The timing couldn't be more perfect. Duncan would kill her in the hours to come and be long gone by the time Chelsea's husband walked through the door. The image of him returning home, finding his dead wife, and realizing he was free of her was sweet. Duncan smiled as he used the light on his burner cell phone to find her phone, purse, and keys. He hid them in her freezer, to make sure he had control over the apartment for the time he was here.

Knowing he wouldn't be interrupted, he walked carefully through her apartment. When he reached the door to her bedroom, he paused and put his backpack on the floor. He'd come back for it in a second, but first he needed to secure her. He removed a single item from the bag and opened the door to her room.

Chelsea was asleep, covered only with a crumpled top sheet, an empty bottle lying next to her. Typical. He detested her and what she was forcing him to do, but it needed to be done. Duncan frowned and stepped forward, with less caution now that he knew she was drunk. He locked one half of the handcuffs around the pole of the bed frame and then, as quickly as he could, secured her wrist with the other.

"Mmmm!" She started to stir as he locked the cuffs, but her mumbles were muted, because he'd covered her mouth with his hand. She flailed.

"Stay still and keep quiet" Duncan's voice was filled with menace. "Or I'll cut your heart out."

His words had no impact. Chelsea thrashed and kicked out at him, until Duncan cocked a fist and punched her in the face. She let out a scream as the blow landed. Though he cursed, both at the pain in his hand and the scream she'd let out, he raised his fist and hit her twice more. The blows knocked her out and she was quiet again.

Duncan returned to his bag and carried it into the room. Within moments she was restrained by another set of cuffs, and had a gag in her mouth. As she started to regain consciousness, he flicked on the lamp beside the bed and stood over her. Her eyes widened and she thrashed against her restraints, her attempts to speak or scream more desperate now – primal and frenzied.

Duncan ignored her and simply spoke over her. "I don't know why you're so intent on struggling and screaming. Your actions have led to this."

He reached up and pulled off his balaclava, savoring the recognition and fear in her eyes. He grabbed her by her messy red hair and yanked on it hard, ignoring her cries and lifting her head until her face was inches from his. He searched her eyes for any sign of remorse at the things she'd done. It was said that people gain insight and clarity when faced with danger or death, but all he saw was fear.

He sighed. He was going to have to explain it to her, just like most of his victims. "You were powerful. You had control over your life, your husband, everything. A puppet master, doing and taking whatever you wanted, but impervious to the damage you caused. You're a slut and an abuser. Now it's time to pay."

Letting her hair go, he watched as her head fell back onto the pillow. Then he gripped the top sheet and pulled it off her. She wore a matching underwear set that typified her attitude. Clearly she thought she could make up with her husband by greeting him in a lacy bra and thong, doing the bare minimum required to keep him under her spell. With a snarl, he ripped off the bra and pulled down her panties so she was as naked as the day she was born.

By now her moans and muffled screams had become background noise. He whistled softly as he rifled through his bag and pulled out a claw hammer. The hammer was the type of weapon Duncan preferred. It was simple and strong and honest, as opposed to her attitude. She sought to control others and inflict pain in complex and dishonest ways. He liked to mete out justice with blunt force.

He raised the hammer above his head and savored the look of fear in her eyes. Her cries became increasingly frantic, but there was nothing she could do to change his mind. He took a couple of deep breaths as he decided where to start, her thrashing and shaking making him more intent. Then his mouth formed into a snarl. He settled on her knee. It was as good a place as any.

21
CHRIS

C hris sighed as he unwrapped the hamburger and bit into it with no pleasure, having long grown tired of a diet of fast food and takeout coffee. As he chewed, he kept his eyes on the front of the apartment building he was staking out. He knew he shouldn't be here – the run-in with the college kid and the subsequent rebuke from his superiors still fresh in his mind – yet here he was.

The encounter with Ashley Wheeler had jolted him into action. Though he'd promised both Manny and the psychologist that he'd try to stop, seeing Wheeler and her red hair had made him realize he couldn't stop. The killer would continue to prey on women until he was caught. Chris couldn't turn away from the danger. Not after Tamara. He'd continue to work to find the killer, hopefully before the killer found another victim.

After finishing the burger, he started on the coffee. He was bunkered in for a long night of boredom, talk radio, and NYPD dispatch. Like usual, he didn't know exactly what he was looking for. Maybe he'd see the potential victim who lived at this address, or someone who might be the killer, but most likely he'd see nothing. He was searching for a needle in a haystack in a field full of haystacks.

"All units." The NYPD radio squawked. "We have reports of a domestic disturbance at 17 East 207th Street in Norwood."

Chris took another sip of his coffee, then realization hit him. He rummaged through a mess of papers on the passenger seat until he found the document he was looking for. He flicked on the Chevy's interior light and checked the address that had come over the radio against the one on his list. They were the same. The domestic disturbance was inside the place Chris was staking out.

Chris considered going in alone, but decided against it. He grabbed his radio. "This is FBI Special Agent Chris Horan with the Extreme Homicide JTF. I'm in the area. I'll check it out."

"Confirmed, Agent Horan."

Chris now had a reason to be here. He put the radio down and picked up his cellphone. He hesitated for just a second, but knew he needed help. If this was the killer, Chris needed someone else there when he caught him. He dialed Manny's number and put the phone to his ear. The phone rang and rang. He almost thought Manny might not pick up, given the hour, but eventually the call connected.

"Can't I even get an hour of sleep at my desk?" Manny's voice was groggy and he didn't sound impressed by the phone call. "What is it, Chris?"

Chris struggled to hide his excitement. "I'm at the house of a potential victim and a call just came over the radio. There's a domestic disturbance at the same address."

"A potential vic…" Manny's voice trailed off. "Oh, come on, Chris. Do yourself a favor and walk away."

"Can't." Chris kept the phone in his hand and opened the door of his car with the other. "I'm heading in."

The silence wasn't a good sign. Usually Manny and Chris would wade into any amount of shit for each other, but it seemed Manny might've reached his limit. Chris put his phone on speaker and rested it on the car. As he waited, he opened the trunk and dressed in his FBI raid jacket. He put on the belt holster that held his firearm and grabbed his mini-Maglite. Now he'd responded to the job and dressed the part, he had some legitimacy being here.

"Fucking hell you're asking a lot of me, Chris." Manny finally spoke, just as Chris closed the trunk. "You're asking me to skate onto the thin ice with you."

"Pretty much." Chris picked up the phone again and put it to his ear. "But at least there's a call to investigate."

"What's the address?"

"17 East 207ᵗʰ Street in Norwood."

There was another brief pause. "I'll be there in five."

The phone went dead. Chris pocketed it, locked the car and crossed the street. He buzzed a different apartment to the one he was interested in and flashed his badge in front of the video intercom. The resident opened the door and Chris took the elevator to the ninth floor. As he walked down the hallway and got closer to the woman's apartment, the more anxious he felt about what he'd find inside.

No light escaped from beneath the door. Chris paused and listened for a minute, but heard nothing. He didn't want to knock, in case the killer was inside, but he couldn't barge in unless there were exigent circumstances, where *not* barging in could lead to loss of evidence or danger to people. It was a nice little end around the Fourth Amendment that Chris had used in the past.

The bang and muffled scream Chris heard was good enough.

"FBI!" Chris shouted as loudly as he could. If enough people in the building heard his scream, he might get away with kicking the door in.

Chris drew his sidearm and held it out in front of him, together with his mini-Maglite. He gave the door a solid kick, and as it swung inward he stepped into darkness. Moving as quickly as he dared, Chris searched the apartment corner by corner, flashing the light rapidly, his finger on the trigger of the pistol. He cleared the living room and kitchen quickly – they were both empty, though it was strange to see an open window in the living room, given the time of night.

Finally, he moved to the bedroom, where a woman lay naked on the bed, her hands cuffed to the headboard and a gag stuffed into her mouth. Her body was covered in wounds, and blood covered the sheets. Her eyes were closed and she made only soft moans. She was alive. Barely...

With the cops and the ambulance on the way, Chris simply hugged Tamara. Her white singlet top was stained crimson, with clear stab wounds. Her arms had cuts all over them, probably from where she'd tried to fight off her attacker. But the way she was sitting was unnatural. She'd been cooking, then fought off an attacker, now she was sitting on the sofa? No. She'd been put there by the murderer...

Chris blinked. The loud boom of a gunshot had pierced the silence of the night and pulled him back into the present. Chris swept the room with his pistol, but whoever had done this was gone. He must've come so close to catching him.

The window.

Chris half turned, but stopped. He needed to help the woman.

She moaned softly once more. Her hair was as red as the blood covering her, and he'd managed to save her, though that wouldn't do any good unless he got some help here soon. He holstered his pistol, pulled out his cell phone and dialed it in. Within a moment an ambulance and an army of back-up was on the way. Chris ended the call and dialed Manny's number. It rang and rang, but this time nobody answered.

Chris ran to the living room window and moved the small curtain aside. Though the street was still dark, the figure splayed out in the middle of the road was unmistakable. Chris felt a lump in his throat and he froze for a split second, staring down at his partner. Then his training kicked in. He knew an ambulance was on the way, but he faced an impossible choice: try to help the victim or try to help Manny.

The woman had been stabbed. Manny might've been shot. The killer might be down there.

Chris made his decision. He drew his pistol again, climbed out of the window and rushed down the fire escape, scanning for threats as he went. But whoever had put his friend on the ground was long gone. He reached ground level and scrambled over to Manny, shining his flashlight over his partner. Manny was lying on his back with several stab wounds to his stomach. He hadn't been shot, from what Chris could tell. Had he pegged the killer?

"Manny!" Chris assessed his partner. He had a pulse and was breathing, but he was barely conscious. Chris pressed against the wounds. "Manny! Hold on!"

"He got the jump on me... took my phone..." Manny's voice was soft, almost silent. "I got a shot off... missed..."

"It's okay, buddy, we'll get him next time." Chris kept his

hands pressing down on the wound as the sound of sirens came toward them. "We might've saved a woman's life."

"That's good..." Manny's voice trailed off and his eyes closed.

22

ASHLEY

Ashley was seated in the trendiest café in Manhattan, feeling like everyone in the place was staring at her. It made her feel uncomfortable. She wanted to flip over every rustic board of food. She hated the place. Seated across from her and dressed in his business suit, her ex-husband Tom was the picture of calm detachment as he waited for her to speak. It was clear he expected Ashley to break the ice.

"They don't even have eggs benedict." Ashley looked up over the menu and was relieved when he cracked a small smirk. "Can you believe it?"

"I've seen worse." Tom's smirk turned into a cautious smile, which was understandable given the last time they'd seen each other Ashley had tried to snatch Lucy from him.

"Thanks for coming, Tom. I appreciate it." Ashley placed the menu down and took a long, slow breath. "I know it hasn't been easy."

His smile disappeared and was replaced with a darker

look. "At least if you're here with me I know Lucy is safe at school."

"I deserve that." Ashley swallowed hard. She was determined to get this right. Ashley reached out for his hand, but he pulled it away. "I'm sorry, Tom."

It seemed he was alternating between kindness and firm resolve, as if he was fighting an internal battle. "What do you want, Ashley?"

Ashley didn't hesitate. She'd rehearsed the line, over and over, until it sounded just right. Though she meant it, she still had to make sure it came out perfect. "I want to make things right, Tom. I know I've been a mess lately. That's caused issues for you and for Lucy. I wanted to say I'm sorry and I want to work out a way forward."

She'd said what she wanted to say, exactly as she wanted to say it. That was a rarity for her lately. She hoped this was the next in a series of good decisions that might lead her back to Lucy. After her close call with the police, the meeting with Obrist and a few chats with his lawyer friend, it was time to set things right. The lawyer had advised her to reach out to Tom, to rebuild something of a relationship, and to stabilize things between her, Tom, and Lucy.

Everything hinged on that.

"Tom." Ashley couldn't resist filling the silence. Her next words were totally unscripted. "I know I made mistakes. I know you've got custody of Lucy and that's the best thing for right now. All I want is hope that I can see her in the short-term and, maybe, we could work something else out in the long term."

Conceding custody of her daughter for the immediate future hurt her more than any physical pain could. Lucy was Ashley's greatest achievement, the best thing in her life and the best thing in her future. Nothing made her happy like Lucy could, but Ashley knew that, for the time being, her daughter was better off with Tom. Until she sorted her life out, there was no other way.

Finally, Tom exhaled through clenched teeth, shook his head and leaned forward. "It doesn't have to be this hard, Ashley."

She beamed. "I—"

"Let me finish." His voice was stern now. "I know what you witnessed was hard. I know the trial was difficult. Okay?

"Okay."

He nodded. "It led to the drinking, the depression, and the self-harm. I get those things. They're understandable, given the circumstances. But I can't allow you to put Lucy in danger."

"I understand." Ashley felt her resolve start to waver under his withering testimony.

"Good, because you need to." He leaned forward, animated now. "I didn't apply to take Lucy because of the trial or the witness protection. I understood all of that. I knew we'd make the right decisions for our family together. But you got paranoid, you saw evil around every corner, and you fell apart. I took Lucy for her own good."

Ashley closed her eyes and shook her head. She'd tried so hard to keep it together and follow the lawyer's advice, to take more positive steps, but she could feel herself falling apart again. Tom was right. Though at the time she'd felt her actions were justified, the counseling with Weltering had shown her there was some truth in Tom's accusations. Still, it was hard to avoid feeling that he'd abandoned her and then stolen her daughter.

"I just want her back!" Ashley stood suddenly, and her

chair fell over and clattered onto the floor. "I just want her back, Tom!"

He surprised her by reaching out to grab her hand, stalling her retreat. "And you can achieve that, Ashley, but not right now."

She relaxed a little bit and squeezed his hand, then fell to her knees in front of him, exhausted. "Tell me what to do! I just want to see Lucy. I just want my little girl."

Tom slid out of his seat and joined her on the floor. He wrapped his arms around her and rested her head on his shoulder. Neither of them paid any attention to the other patrons or café staff looking at them. "I love you, Ashley. And Lucy loves you. There's a place for you in both of our lives. But first, you need to go back to Wallingford and get help."

She looked up at him, eyes wide, searching for answers. "And then what?"

He smiled sadly. "Then we can negotiate. Until then, I can't let you see her."

Ashley nodded and nuzzled into his shoulder for the first time since their divorce. She cried. An ocean of emotions flooded out of her. Pain. Desperation. Frustration. Anger. She felt like they'd made progress, but the idea of being away from Lucy for even longer still hurt. She had a plan, and it didn't involve doing anything stupid, illegal, or harmful. As she cried, she hoped that, she could do what was necessary, and that Tom would be true to his word.

It was her only hope.

23

DUNCAN

Duncan's breath came in ragged heaves as he slammed his apartment door, leaned his back against it and slid to the floor. He hugged his knees to his chest, trying to catch his breath. He'd run all the way from Chelsea's apartment – a distance of thirty blocks. Not the fittest guy in the world, his run had been powered by fear and adrenalin, but now that was starting to wear off. That the sun had risen in that time seemed to make it worse.

"I'm alive." Nobody had seen him. Nobody had captured him. That was all that mattered. "I'm alive."

Or so he kept telling himself. In truth, things couldn't have gone much worse. He'd been halfway through his date with Chelsea when he'd been interrupted. The second he'd heard "FBI" shouted from outside the apartment, Duncan had moved quickly. There'd been no time to do anything except grab his backpack and rush down the fire escape. At least there hadn't been a bunch of cops waiting at street level. Whoever kicked in the door must've been alone.

It was no consolation for having to leave Chelsea alive.

Just when Duncan had thought he was safe, he'd seen a tired-looking Hispanic FBI agent. The agent had approached Duncan, spotted the blood, and started yelling. The agent had fired his pistol just before Duncan plunged his knife into the man's stomach, but the shot had missed. Duncan had left him alive, simply kicking his gun away and taking his phone, then he'd started running and never looked back.

It wasn't supposed to have gone like that. Chelsea should be dead by now.

Duncan snarled and stood, his breathing slowing but his mind still racing. All of his effort had been wasted. He'd never be able to finish the job now. There'd be too much heat on her. She'd heal from her wounds and rebuild her life. Worse, he was exposed. He pulled a suitcase from under his bed, cursing his stupidity. He'd revealed more of himself to her than he had to all his other victims combined. And now he'd been cheated, robbed.

This was worse than the very first time he'd been humiliated by a woman, when she'd run from his car and left him sitting there like a fool, alone and heartbroken and confused. He hated when things were out of his control, hated being at the mercy of others. He hadn't felt this way for a long time, but now the feelings had returned with a vengeance. All because some cop had stumbled across him. Duncan had no idea how, but it didn't matter. His plan was in tatters.

"Fuck." He turned on his small bedroom TV.

He flicked to the local news station and pounded the dresser. There were already reports about the woman who'd been saved and the agent who'd been stabbed. It wouldn't be long before his profile was circulating. Lucky for him, there were plenty of white males of medium height and medium build in their early-thirties in New York City. He couldn't rely on that to keep him safe, though. He had to get out of the city.

He tossed a few basics into his suitcase, closed it, and then wheeled it to the front door. He reached underneath the dining table and found the false identification and cash he'd taped to the bottom. It was his stash, in case he had to disappear. He couldn't rely on his bank accounts and cell phone remaining secure, so he'd need the stash to keep him going until he got established somewhere new. He'd done it before.

He had one more job to do. He moved to the laundry and pulled out several large bottles of chemicals, including bleach and rubbing alcohol. He poured chemicals on his way to the front door. Once the bottles were empty, he tossed them down the hallway, opened the door, and wheeled his case outside. He lit a zippo lighter, threw it inside the apartment and closed the door behind him.

He headed down the elevator and reached the street just as the fire alarm in his building sounded. Pedestrians looked up at the building curiously, but ignored the man hailing a cab out front. It was only a minute before he was in a cab and making small talk with the driver, trying to calm himself on the ride to Penn Station. He was startled to notice that there was still some blood on his hands. He licked it and then rubbed at it, trying to remove the traces.

He was sad to be leaving New York City behind. It had been one of the most fertile hunting grounds on the planet, full of women who stalked men like beasts who he'd hunted in turn. But it was time. The minute he arrived in a new city he began counting down the time until he was forced to leave. Only by being smart and agile had he managed to stay ahead of the authorities for so long. His hubris had almost cost him. He wouldn't make that mistake again.

Duncan closed his eyes in the back of the cab, trying to relax a little, when the phone he'd stolen from the agent started to ring. Duncan pulled it from his pocket and stared at the screen. Someone named Chris Horan was trying to reach the man Duncan had stabbed. He terminated the call and put the phone back in his pocket, but a moment later the phone beeped and a message appeared on the screen.

The caller had left a voicemail.

With a sigh, Duncan tapped the screen and the line to voicemail started to dial. He put the phone to his ear and listened.

"I'm going to get you, you fuck." The caller's male voice was filled with hate and malice. "I'm going to find you."

Duncan gave a slight smile and exhaled loudly. The voicemail had cheered him up a little. None of his kills had yet led the cops to his door, and although he'd almost been busted at Chelsea's house, he'd made it out. Once he was away from New York and in some other part of the vast United States, he'd be invisible again – one person in a country with several hundred million of them. The message was all bluster.

He looked down at the phone, momentarily curious about the business of the man he'd stabbed. He deleted the angry agent's message and put the phone to his ear again. The phone told him the message was from a day earlier.

"Hi Manny." The female voice sounded unsure. "It's Ashley. I wanted to say thanks for helping me the other day. Call me back if you'd like to catch up before I go back to Wallingford."

Duncan removed the phone from his ear and gripped it tight. He'd known the caller's voice from the first word, but it had taken his brain a few moments to process the amazing new piece into an already frighteningly complex puzzle. His kill being interrupted was now the second most remarkable thing to happen that day.

Hearing the voice of the woman who'd spurned him so long ago and set him on his path of vengeance wasn't something he'd ever expected to happen.

He'd left his apartment not knowing where to go, not really caring. Since a terrible date a decade ago, he'd been a nomad in search of something unattainable. He'd killed. He'd taken his revenge on others. Yet those feeling paled in comparison to the fury burning inside of him. A spark of anger had lit a conflagration of vengeance deep down in the pit of his stomach. The woman who'd started it all was within his grasp again.

Suddenly, Duncan knew exactly where he had to go.

24

CHRIS

"Good morning." Chris spoke the only words he'd been permitted to say to the sea of hungry reporters.

"Right," Geary cut in, clearly wanting to divert any attempt Chris might make to broadcast his theories to the media. "Agent in Charge Nowitski will give a statement."

Nowitski was sitting one seat down from Geary. He began reading his statement. Chris had read it already, so tuned out as Nowitski praised Manny as a great agent, gave an update on his status – critical – and passed on the Bureau's best wishes to Manny's loved ones. Chris spent the time wallowing in self-pity, much as he'd done for the day or so, blaming himself for the attack on his friend and hoping Manny would live.

He didn't want to be here. He'd been hauled in to Geary's office and told that he was being hung out to dry. He'd attend the press conference, listen while both of his superiors gave their statements, then be a willing and compliant victim as they let the press pack feast on him. They wanted someone to blame, and they told him that if he complied, he'd still lose his job, but might avoid charges. Chris was too shell-shocked to do much but nod.

After Nowitski was done, Geary took over. Chris sighed as she started to explain exactly what had happened that night. Chris kept his face completely passive, but he felt empty and broken. The explanation Geary gave wasn't necessarily untrue, but it was designed to be as damning as possible. She said that after Chris had illegally broken into the victim's house, the killer had fled, Manny had ended up in intensive care, and the victim wasn't much better off.

Finally, after what felt like a lifetime, Geary finished her statement and let out a long sigh for the cameras. "We'll now take questions."

Chris winced as hands shot into the air. He muttered under his breath. "Time for the witch hunt to begin."

Geary pointed at one of the reporters. "You."

The reporter shot to her feet. "Can you explain how Agent Horan saved the woman?"

Geary sighed. "Though Agent Horan did save her, a killer escaped and an agent ended up in hospital. I don't consider the outcome a positive one, because law enforcement has to act within the law. We've recently become aware of some deeply troubling personal circumstances that have impacted on Agent Horan's performance lately. He suffered a loss some years ago..."

The paramedics were the first to arrive, which was a little surprising. They pounded on the door and Chris stood to let them in. He had to stand in the bedroom as they pushed past, the little apartment not really built for so many people to be inside at once. He left the door unlocked, because the cops wouldn't be far away. Then he returned to the living room – to Tamara – where the paramedics were going through the motions. For the first time, he saw it. He frowned. He felt a lump in the pit of his stomach. He bent over, threw up, and then looked back at Tamara. On her forehead, the killer had written 'whore' in her own blood...

Chris blinked. The reporters were shouting his name, trying to get his attention. "Sorry, what?"

"Agent Horan." Another questioner looked straight at Chris. "How does it feel to be a hero?"

Chris looked sideways at Geary, who nodded. He swallowed hard. "I don't think I'm a hero at all. All my thoughts and prayers are with the victim and my partner."

Chris's mind flashed again to Manny. Whatever kudos he was getting from the media, he'd had none from his fellow agents or officers. Chris could deal with the insults and outward expressions of disgust, of which there had been plenty, but it was the colleagues who looked past him that made the loudest point. Although the treatment upset him, he wasn't surprised by it. Manny was in critical condition at St Jude's because Chris had freelanced.

The fact he'd found the killer after all this time was bittersweet. Chris felt vindicated. He'd been proven right. But it mattered for nothing when Manny was in the hospital and his superiors still didn't believe him. In blind anger, Chris had called Manny's phone, but the call had gone unanswered. Since cooling down a little, Chris simply felt empty. He hadn't even caught the killer. The man was on the loose and he could end up anywhere.

Chris sighed. The questions continued in a similar vein for another quarter hour. Though his superiors had wheeled Chris out to take the blame, the show hadn't gone as planned. Chris was being hailed as a hero. Chelsea Butler would almost certainly be dead if not for him. The press was lapping it up. They kept asking how he'd known. Despite Geary and

Nowitski's warnings, Chris decided to give them what they wanted.

He leaned forward, to make sure the microphone picked up his words. "It's my belief there's a serial killer targeting redheads. These claims are being ignored by the Bureau, the NYPD and the Extreme Homicide Joint Task Force. I think I almost caught him. Chelsea Butler survived, but the next victim might not."

The press pack exploded. Beside him, Geary stood and turned to exit. Nowitski was scowling at him. Though he wanted to stay longer and push harder, Chris was ushered out of the room by the media minders. Less than a minute after he'd swung for the fences, he was standing in a quiet hallway with his superiors. Geary and Nowitski both had clenched fists and flushed faces, neither of which seemed promising, but Chris had made his choice.

"Agent Horan." Nowitski spoke slowly, his anger threatening to boil over at any second. "You knew the consequences if you went off script."

"I—"

"No, Agent Horan." Nowitski shook his head and held up a hand. "I don't want to hear it. You're going to listen. You were warned that your behavior was unacceptable. You were warned to work your assigned cases, and to remain quiet about your insane theory. Instead, you doubled down. Your actions have left me with an agent in hospital and a media shitstorm."

"And one woman still breathing."

Nowitski stared at him for a good ten seconds. The silence was almost unbearable, but neither man looked away. Finally, Nowitski spoke. "Let me be clear. If I had my way, I'd be firing you right now. You're a disgrace to the Bureau. The only thing that saved your career is the media branding you a hero cop."

Chris broke into a wide smile, feeling triumph where a second ago there'd been ruin. "Thank you, sir."

"I said your career, Horan." Now it was Nowitski's turn to smile, wide and vicious. "But not your job. I'll not tolerate agents who disobey me. You're done in New York. I'm going to have you transferred to the shittiest office I can find. If Alaska has no vacancies, I'll work back from there. And I'll take great pleasure in doing so. Now get out of my sight."

Chris's turned his back on both of them and walked down the hall, away from the briefing room they'd used for the press conference and back to his desk. An already cold office, made worse by Manny's absence and the frostiness of his colleagues, was now completely arctic. He knew what he had to do: pack up his things and get out of there. You didn't get to stick around once you'd been bounced out.

Chris swung back in his chair for a moment, taking in the blow. He'd worked in the New York field office his entire career. It was the premier posting in the Bureau – the largest office with the best cases. Going anywhere else was like a baseballer being sent from the Yankees to some scrub minor league team. Any hope he had of further progression was gone. The fact he even had a job was a miracle. The media attention had done him some good.

With a sigh, he started to clear his desk, packing the few belongings he wanted to take with him into a box. As he rifled through old case files, he reflected on how much good he'd done here. He felt a brief pang of regret, but the more he thought about it the more he believed he'd done the right thing. He'd saved a woman's life, come within inches of catching the killer, and come closer to identifying the man.

He'd been ready to roll over in order to avoid criminal charges, but he'd taken his chances and still avoided that fate. It was the only thing he had left to hang onto. On his way out, nobody said goodbye. It was as if he had Ebola. It felt like his career was ending with the saddest whimper. It felt as if the downward spiral he'd fallen into when Tamara had died had finally planted him on his ass, right at rock bottom.

He didn't know if he could to pull himself up again, but he was about to find out.

ACT II

25

ASHLEY

Ashley dropped down onto her haunches and hugged Lucy as tight as she thought the little girl could handle. She watched Tom approach from a few dozen yards away, knowing that in a few minutes he would take Lucy away again. For the first time in a long time, though, Ashley was okay with that.

"Your dad is coming." Ashley relaxed her grip on Lucy, backed away slightly and looked her in the eyes. "I hope you had a good time at breakfast."

"It was great." Lucy beamed, her cheeks dimpling. "I really wanted pancakes with bacon, though. Can I have that next time?"

Ashley laughed. "I'll make sure they order more so they don't run out. We'll get you a double order, if you like."

"I'm not that big yet!" Lucy laughed at the thought, then turned to face her father. "Hi Daddy."

"Hi munchkin." Tom hugged Lucy briefly and then turned to Ashley. "Was breakfast good?"

The question was a loaded one and they both knew it. This was the first time Ashley had seen her daughter in months and he wanted to know that it hadn't gone off the rails. For once, Ashley was able to say she'd kept to the plan. They'd had a nice breakfast and a play in the park.

"It was perfect." Ashley smiled. Spending so much time with Lucy had been the best thing to happen in a long time. "We had a great time."

"I'm glad." Tom smiled at Ashley and then grabbed Lucy's hand tight. "Are you ready to go?"

"Yep!" Lucy beamed, oblivious to the fragile truce between her parents.

"Go get in the car and buckle up then." Tom unlocked the vehicle, which was parked a few yards away. "I just want to speak with your mom for a second."

"Okay!" Lucy let go of his hand, turned and ran to the car without another word.

Tom waited until she was in the car and out of earshot before he spoke. "Anything you need to tell me?"

A lump caught in Ashley's throat when she tried to answer the question. She swallowed hard and smiled. "It went perfect. It just feels too soon to be saying goodbye."

Tom nodded. "This was a trial run. We'll see if we can sort out something more regular soon. I just need to be sure I can trust you, Ashley."

He had every right to doubt her. It hadn't been easy for Ashley to admit she'd been out of control. She'd only been saved by the counseling and the leniency granted to her by the police. She was determined to make the most of this second chance. She needed to show Tom and Lucy and everyone else that she'd healed.

"You can." Ashley reached out and grabbed his hand. "I hate what I became, and I hate that I lost you and Lucy."

"Ashley, I—"

She locked her eyes onto Tom. "Let me finish!"

"Okay." He pursed his lips, clearly concerned.

Ashley closed her eyes. "I hated all of those things. I thought everyone else was to blame. But now I recognize that my actions were the problem. I shouldn't have tried to take Lucy, I shouldn't have tried to take my own life, and I should've focused on meeting my responsibilities."

Ashley paused, expecting Tom to say something. When he didn't, she continued. "I think I saw Lucy as my salvation. I love her more than anything, but it was about more than wanting to be with my daughter. I wanted some stability when there was nothing but uncertainty and chaos."

"And now?"

"Now?" Ashley shrugged. "You can trust me to do the right thing, Tom."

Tom gave her a hard look, sizing her up, then nodded and made his way to the car. They'd established some sort of understanding. It had taken several months for Ashley to build up enough trust for Tom to allow breakfast, so it would probably take a while to get more than that. Ashley didn't care. Seeing Lucy was worth it.

The trial, the decision by Obrist not to appeal, and the loss of her place in witness protection had nearly toppled her over the edge, especially when combined with the despair she felt at being apart from Lucy for so long. But after Manny had pulled her out of the cop station, Ashley had realized she needed to change, and things had started to improve.

Slowly, she'd fumbled her way through making those

changes, now things were starting to go right. She'd gone some way toward getting her shit together. She'd found a house to rent, she was working and she seemed to be safe. Yet all that paled against the small amount of access that Tom had granted her. It wasn't much of a life, but it was good for her right now.

"Bye!" Lucy shouted and waved as Tom drove off. "Bye Mommy!"

Ashley held up her hand in farewell, waving until the car was out of sight. With a sigh, Ashley turned and headed for the clothing store where she worked. Her shift began soon and she'd squeezed every last second out of the visit from Lucy. The thought of going weeks without seeing her daughter again was hard. The job helped keep her mind off it all.

Ashley reached the store, paused to compose herself, then entered. Her boss, Jana, waved from behind the counter and Ashley smiled at her. "Morning."

"Early!" Jana looked down at her watch, then back up at Ashley with a smile. "At this rate I'm going to have to give you a pay rise, Ashley."

"I had an appointment nearby that finished early, so I thought I'd come straight in. But I wouldn't say no to a pay rise!" Ashley laughed. She kept the appointment details vague out of habit. She was used to living in secret and compartmentalizing her life. Trust was something else she'd lost.

Jana nodded as Ashley made her way to the room at the back of the store. She closed the door, removed the t-shirt she was wearing and put on a blouse more appropriate for work. There was no way she could afford anything in the store, so Jana was kind enough to let Ashley borrow some older stock to wear during her shifts.

As she changed, she smiled, thinking about her breakfast with Lucy. Things weren't perfect, but they were definitely looking up.

26

DUNCAN

"I'll take anything, really." Duncan placed his resume on the counter. "I can do whatever you need."

The owner of the takeout chicken store looked at Duncan and then down at his resume. "I'm sorry, buddy. I like your initiative, but I just can't take anyone on right now."

"Can I at least leave my resume?" Duncan hated how pathetic his voice sounded, but he was desperate. "In case something becomes available?"

"You can if you like." The owner looked back up at Duncan and shrugged. It was clear there'd be no job coming up anytime soon. "Now, I need to get back to work."

Duncan nodded, walked away from the counter and out of the store. Once he was out front, he gripped the few resumes left in his possession tightly, but tried to force down the anger that was welling up inside of him. At least this guy had been nice about the rejection. Plenty of store owners had just stared at him. The females in particular seemed to regard him as something they'd scraped off a shoe.

Finding a job was proving tough, but it was necessary.

Since travelling to Wallingford from New York, Duncan's furious anger and desire to find Ashley again had not subsided at all. His failure to kill Chelsea Butler was as significant as a speck of dust when put alongside the chance to kill the woman who'd started it all. From the minute he'd arrived, he'd searched high and low for Ashley. But he didn't know the surname she was using, he hadn't managed to locate her and nobody in town he'd asked knew who she was.

As the months had ticked by, reality had started to bite. Though he wanted to spend every waking moment searching for her, he had no money and needed to find work. Despite applying for jobs and handing out resumes in every store he could find, he'd had no luck. He was living in a trailer and had almost burned through his stash of cash. A lifelong nomad, he was used to change, but not to living so desperately.

But one thing was working in his favor. In the months he'd been searching for Ashley and for work, he'd gone off the radar. Though there was a rough likeness of him in circulation, he'd grown a beard and nobody in Wallingford cared enough to recognize him. Beyond that, it appeared the cops in New York had no clue who he was. The news outlets had lost interest, so Duncan felt safer with each passing day. His mistake had cost him the right to take Chelsea's life, his job, and the apartment he'd been living in, but the damage stopped there.

The fact he'd taken a step closer to Ashley made it feel like a win.

Now he just wanted to find her.

With a sigh, he kept walking, looking for stores where he hadn't yet applied for work. At first he'd been picky about the jobs he applied for, but his standards had been steadily forced downward. This street was mostly a waste of time, full of stores he'd already tried, but there was one he'd bypassed previously. There was no chance a ladies' fashion store would employ him, but he had to try.

"Hang in there! Keep your chin up and life can't hurt you."

Duncan paused and looked around for the source of the voice. Then he spotted a homeless guy sitting in an alley that ran off the street. The man was wrapped up in a sleeping bag and had a wide-brimmed hat on, a ridiculous but effective way to avoid the weather. Duncan smiled at the man. "Thanks, pal."

The other man cracked a toothless smile. "We've all been there. I know the look of a man down on his luck. You'll be okay."

Duncan felt his face starting to burn red. Having a bum try to perk him up felt like a new low. He fumbled through his pockets for some change and put it into the man's empty coffee cup. It was only a few bucks, but the man's toothless smile grew into a grin and he issued a stream of thanks. Duncan walked away, his fists clenched by his sides as a fury burned inside him. He was pathetic. It had taken a homeless guy to show Duncan how far he'd fallen.

He had to find a job, then he could redouble his effort on his real work.

Finding her.

He reached the clothing boutique, determined to try. As he reached for the door, a member of staff caught his eye through the window. His face brightened, but hers darkened as she saw the paper he was carrying. The message was clear. His fury was white-hot now. He swallowed hard, pushed the door open and stepped inside. The woman greeted him with a fake smile.

Duncan forced a smile of his own. "I'd like to apply for a job here, if you've got any available."

"Do you have any work history you can share with me?" The woman's reaction was one Duncan knew well. "Any experience in ladies' fashion?"

Duncan sighed. He had no experience he could share. That was a consequence of changing your identity. "No, none."

"Then there's not much I can offer you." The woman gave a sympathetic smile. "I've got enough staff, and I need to be careful before I take more on."

"I understand." Duncan felt his face go red again. He just wanted to get out of the store. All his drive and motivation from a minute ago had vanished.

"I hope so." The manager turned and gestured toward another staff member, who was checking the stock levels on the clothing racks. "I've a hard enough time giving Ashley shifts, and I've only just taken her on. It would be unfair to take someone else on, given the circumstances..."

"I under—"

A breath caught in Duncan's throat and his eyes widened. He'd seen the glance of red hair when the manager had gestured at the staff member, but she'd just turned, and he'd caught sight of her face. He felt a tingle all over. She looked a little bit rough, but it was unmistakably her. He was frozen in place, watching her. She was the entire reason he'd come to Wallingford, his chance to turn a defeat into a victory.

She was the one who'd started it all, the bitch who'd shown him the true nature of women. She was the woman who'd stolen his heart, ripped it out, and then vanished. Though he'd searched, he'd never found her. Until now. She looked different, older, but there was no doubt it was her. She still had the hair, the face, and the curves that had excited him so many years ago.

His mind screamed at him.

As if on cue, the woman glanced sideways, straight at him. Duncan waited for a spark, of fear or recognition, but she was oblivious. Though he'd aged and he'd grown a beard since arriving in Wallingford, she should still recognize him. Yet she merely smiled at him and got back to work. A flood of pain and anger coursed through him and he wanted desperately to strangle her. Duncan's head hurt. All he could see was the red-haired woman.

"Sir?"

Duncan cried out as someone touched his shoulder from behind, snapping him back to the present. He turned, pushing the store manager's hand away. She was still speaking as Duncan exited the shop. He broke into a run, his mind racing his body as it tried to process what he'd seen.

Everything had just changed.

27

CHRIS

"Thanks for visiting us here at the Omaha field office." Chris held his arms wide while forcing a smile. "I hope you now know more about the work of the Bureau."

The smiles he received almost made it worthwhile. Almost. He made small talk with a few of the citizens of Omaha, Nebraska as they made their way out. They'd been glued to their seats during his session, and Chris had no doubt he'd entertained them. He'd shared some interesting cases from the history of the Omaha field office, his new professional home, then explained how the Bureau worked.

The briefing was one of many Chris had conducted over the past few months. The aim was to explain the role of the local FBI division to citizens who applied to be a part of the sessions. Although he considered the work to be a sort of penance for his mistakes in New York, it was starting to get tiresome.

After the attendees had left, Chris returned to his office and collapsed into the chair. Nowitski had been true to his word. Chris had been handed the equivalent of latrine duty in the hope that he'd quit. Though he'd arrived in Omaha with some hope of getting a fresh start, that hope had ebbed away. As the months passed, the number of briefings had grown, and real work had continued to evade him.

"Hope the briefing went well." His boss, Agent Tony Harvey, was leaning against the doorframe of his office with a manila folder in his hand. "Got a job for you."

"Not a problem, sir." Chris forced a smile as he stood, crossed the room, and took the folder. "Thanks."

"Keep up the good work." Harvey gave him a thin smile, making it clear he'd handed Chris another shit sandwich, then turned and walked out of the office.

Chris closed the door and returned to his seat. He didn't have to open the folder to know what was inside, another community briefing, and a half-hearted glance confirmed his hunch. At this rate, Chris felt like he'd be doing community briefings until the projector clicker was pried out of his cold dead hands. He tossed the folder on his desk and watched, numb, as the papers scattered.

He stared at the ceiling and closed his eyes, trying to calm his breathing as the wave of regrets hit him again. The damage he'd caused to Manny was the main one. Though Manny had survived the stabbing, his career had taken a hit as a result. Chris knew their friendship was ruined. Although he'd tried to make contact with Manny a few times, both to check on Manny and also to check the progress of the investigation, each time he'd been rebuffed.

Chris also regretted failing to catch the serial killer. Though there'd been no further kills in New York City that fit the profile, that was the only small silver lining. Chris had disturbed the killer in action, and obviously spooked him enough to make him stop for a while, but he would strike again sooner or later. The chances of catching him were remote now. The Bureau wasn't interested and Chris had lost any ability to investigate effectively.

Now, exiled to Nebraska, he'd refrained from telling anyone about his serial killer theory. Chris had been marked as damaged goods, and everyone was wary of him already. His superiors had kept him away from any real work, and his colleagues would barely speak to him. He still felt the burning urge to catch the killer, he still had flashbacks to Tamara's death every single day, although he was trying hard to focus on other things.

The last thing he wanted to do was make it worse.

Then again, could things really be any worse?

He opened his eyes and stared at the laptop on his desk, which gave him access to a trove of information gathered from all facets of law enforcement. The urge was overwhelming. All it would take was to log in, define some search terms, and away he'd go. Ironically, he had more time to investigate the killer now than ever, given that he was cooling his heels in Nebraska.

His mind flashed briefly back to the words of the psychologist. She had said that Chris had some obsessive tendencies, and now he was on the verge of proving her right. He knew he should leave it alone. The obsession had already cost him plenty, including his relationship with Manny and his career. But he couldn't resist. He logged into his computer, opened up the database and stared at the search screen. It promised limitless information he could use to find the killer.

Over the next fifteen minutes, Chris printed the profiles of all the woman killed in New York who matched his theory, starting with Tamara and ending with the victim before

Chelsea Butler. Then he accessed Butler's statement, the woman he'd saved. There was a wealth of information including a physical description of the killer, information about his interactions with the victim prior to the attack, and details about the attack itself.

It was clear the killer had revealed himself to Chelsea Butler. He'd learnt all about her, then set about damaging the various parts of her life with the same brutality he'd later shown in the attack on her body. Unfortunately, the killer had not let her into his life. Chris had to assume the name he'd used, Dan Rafferty, was a false one, and that anything he'd said about himself was a lie. Once he'd finished reading the document, he printed that, too.

A small cough near the door interrupted his search. Justine Hopkins was standing in the door, with an eyebrow raised and a coffee in each hand. She was the one agent who hadn't totally avoided him since he'd been posted to Omaha. She was young and new to the Bureau, so probably hadn't got the memo that he was a pariah. Or perhaps Hopkins had decided to make up her own mind.

He raised an eyebrow. "What do you want, Hopkins? Make a habit of lurking quietly while others are working?"

"What are you doing?" She took a step inside, passing him a coffee, then glanced at his printer. "That's a lot of printing for someone doing community briefings."

"I like to take some handouts along with me." Chris didn't even believe his own lie as he took the coffee.

"The admin staff take care of that." Hopkins smiled. "I used to run the briefings before you got here and took them off my hands."

Chris was going to deny it further, then paused. While it was a risk to let her in on his theory, if he wanted any chance of getting out of his current predicament, he needed to start collecting some allies. He sighed, turned his laptop around and showed her. He swung back on his chair and sipped his coffee as he watched her, peering in closely at the screen and then looking up at him. Her eyes narrowed.

"I'm chasing a hunch." Chris shrugged. "Running the community briefings takes up precisely none of my time."

"More than a hunch, from the looks of it." She placed her coffee down on the desk and sat in the chair opposite him. "I've heard the stories about you: a rogue agent from the New York field office who got his partner stabbed and let a nasty dude get away. I heard you have some pretty crazy theories."

"I know what I know." Chris was surprised at how much her words upset him. "I saw a bunch of bodies. I know there's a link between them."

She considered his words for a second. "Even so, are you sure you should start digging into murders in New York City from your desk in Omaha? You're on thin ice, and it sounds a lot like you're trying to shoehorn a theory into a poorly fitting shoe. I'd leave it alone and focus on your work here."

"I'll live my own life and you live yours, but I bet mine is more interesting." Chris raised an eyebrow and kept his eyes locked on hers. "What're you working on?"

She hesitated. After a second, her eyes glanced back down to the screen. "I don't want to get in trouble."

Chris nodded. He could understand her hesitation. "Any risk is mine. I'll take the fall if we get caught, but I could use some help."

28

ASHLEY

Ashley stroked her cat and sipped her tea, wishing briefly that it was gin before shaking the thought off. She'd now gone several months without a drink, and she wasn't going to start again while sitting at home watching romantic comedies. She put the cup on the coffee table and then relaxed back on the sofa, feeling her eyes grow heavy. She wasn't sure she'd be able to stay awake until the end of the movie.

The main character was a bit too pathetic for her liking. She was chasing after a man, desperate to marry him, even though he wasn't interested in her at all. As she watched, Ashley wondered if there were parallels with her own life. Only in her case, she chased after her daughter instead of a man. She wondered if everyone obsessed about something, in one way or another.

"What the hell?" Ashley woke with a start to a loud rattling sound outside her house. She must have dozed off at some point. The cat shot off her lap, spooked by the sudden movement.

A quick glance at the television told her the noise hadn't come from there, because the credits were rolling with nothing but background music to accompany them. Ashley muted the television. Now sitting in silence, her ears strained to hear the sound again. She waited, frozen in place, for several tense moments.

When she heard the sound again, her heart started to pound. There was something outside, making regular, unusual sounds Ashley had never heard at this house before. She'd moved here a few months ago, when her time in witness protection had come to an end and she'd been forced to find a smaller place. She could afford it with her income from the clothing store, and it was starting to feel like home.

"Fucking hell." Ashley spoke to herself.

The police had told her it was possible that Laverri or his men might try to get to her, despite the fact she still had her new name and that it had been months since the trial. With each passing day she'd felt safer. The noise outside could be innocent, and she didn't want to overreact, but she couldn't be sure. She tried to calm her breathing, keeping still and silent, while she waited.

But when she heard the noise a third time her nerves broke. She jumped up from the sofa, ran to the kitchen and grabbed the largest knife she owned. Once she had it in her hands she felt a bit safer. Leaning against the bench with her back to the wall, she stared at the door closest to the sound. She thought about calling the police, but if there was someone outside, it would take too long for them to arrive. And if there wasn't, she'd feel like an idiot.

She moved toward the door. She wasn't sure she should go

out there, but she refused to run, or cower. As she stalked toward the door, her mind flashed back to an event a decade ago, when she'd run away from danger, out of a car and along a beach. Alone and afraid in the dark, she'd run and then hidden. Though he'd never found her hiding in the high grass, she'd never forget the fear.

The man who'd entered the clothing store and stared at her a few weeks earlier had reminded her of him. Since that day she'd had the most horrible nightmares about that night. Her sleep had been plagued by strange variations of it – running away, hiding, and being frightened for her life. She'd never been as afraid as she had been that night, not even when she'd seen Saul Laverri shoot Flavio Grossi.

Ashley reached the door and paused. With the knife in one hand, she used the other to flick the switch that turned on the outside light. The light was faint, the result of a low-wattage globe, but it was enough for her to see within a few feet of the house. She couldn't see anything obvious, so she faced a choice: stay inside the locked house, not knowing what was outside, or charge out and confront it.

She made her decision. As she turned the handle slowly, the knife ready, she heard the rattling sound again. This time it felt like it was further away. She opened the door and stepped outside. The light cast by the weak outdoor globe didn't do much to make her feel better, but she was glad to have something to see by. Now that she was outside, Ashley could hear nothing else. It was just a quiet night in a suburban neighborhood.

Ashley's heart was pounding, and her mouth was as dry as the Nevada desert. She stalked forward, trying to step quietly. She searched around the entrance, but didn't see anything that could have made the noise. As she turned down the side of the house, the same rattle sounded from behind her. Ashley squealed and turned, thrusting the knife out in front of her and then dropping it quickly, overcome with laughter.

A raccoon looked up at her, eyes wide, as surprised by her as she was by it. Ashley let out another nervous laugh, then shooed the animal away. It ran off, trailing a piece of metal detritus behind it. The metal was attached to some string caught on its leg. In seconds, the animal had disappeared, the rattling sound growing faint as it got further away.

Ashley smiled. She was just being paranoid. If Laverri wanted to get to her, it would have happened already. The police warnings and the nightmares had made her jumpy. She couldn't afford to be brought undone by irrational fears.

Still, if the fright had proven anything, it was that she needed better home security. The cat wasn't much good, and she couldn't afford to keep a dog, but she'd go out tomorrow and buy some stronger globes for the outdoor lights. Ashley walked back inside the house, locked the door behind her and then moved to the kitchen. With a long sigh, she put the knife back in the block.

29

DUNCAN

Duncan clenched his teeth so hard his jaw hurt, adding to his headache and his heaving breaths. He ignored the pain, focused only on the photo on the laptop in front of him and the fist squeezed around his penis, which pumped up and down like a piston. As he stared at the photo, which was dark and blurry, and yet perfect, his nostrils flared from anger and effort, the rhythm of his movements automatic and rapid.

As he drew closer, he felt no pleasure. He worked harder, until he reached the edge, and let out a furious scream as he came. It was loud and visceral, a noise that even surprised Duncan, and would surely see him reported to the trailer park manager. He was left in a mess and panting hard. Duncan stayed still, eyes locked on the photo and penis still in hand, until his breathing returned to normal. Only then did his mind start to clear.

Duncan cleaned up, had a drink of water and returned to the computer. Now he'd calmed down a bit, he spent some time searching through the folder of photos on the desktop.

His collection was growing rapidly since he'd seen Ashley inside the clothing store. He'd taken shots of her there, on her way to and from work, at the grocery store and in other relatively normal situations.

The shots he was proudest of, and the ones that had got him so worked up, were from the previous evening. He'd been watching her home, hoping to see something interesting, but all he'd seen was her falling asleep while watching a movie, curtains open and lights blazing. Duncan had stayed for over an hour, watching her sleep. He'd been ready to leave when he'd hit the jackpot.

She'd sat up in alarm and thrown off the blanket. Duncan had almost cried out with rage at the discovery that she was only wearing underwear. It proved so much. After another second she'd rushed out of Duncan's view. At first he'd been worried that she'd somehow been alerted to his presence, at the same time almost hoping she'd see him, but when she'd rushed outside with a knife in her hand, she'd moved away from him and never looked in his direction.

Duncan had managed to get one decent shot on his cell phone out of the dozens he'd taken, most of which were blurry or too dark. He'd snapped a shot of her looking terrified, wearing nothing but her underwear, right at the moment she'd turned around, raised the knife and confronted the raccoon. The light had been good enough, and his timing had been perfect. He added it to the photos of all his targets from over the years, neatly organized into folders.

This would become *the* photo of *the* victim.

He still couldn't believe he'd found her in the ass end of Connecticut, despite the message on the phone. Being forced out of New York City and unable to find work suddenly seemed like a positive.. He'd thought of nothing but her since the moment he saw her. The fatigue he'd felt recently was now a distant memory. His vengeance would be slow, brutal, and soul crushing.

"Mr Ellington?" Someone pounded on the door of his trailer, interrupting Duncan's thoughts.

Duncan's face twisted into a snarl. He closed the lid of the laptop, stood, and put some pants on. Only then did he unlock the door. "Yes?"

The trailer park manager, a middle-aged man with ample chins and little hair, wore a weaselly smile. "Mr Ellington? There have been complaints."

Duncan stepped down from his trailer, keeping his features impassive. "Complaints about what?"

"Complaints about..." The manager took a step back, obviously uncomfortable with Duncan's lack of a shirt. "Well, uh, you see, this is a family park, Mr Ellington. What you do inside your trailer is your business, unless it's loud enough to make it everyone's business. I need you to stop with that."

Duncan laughed, short and mean. "I thought in a place like this people would keep to themselves and mind their own business, like I do mine."

The manager shook his head. "Afraid not, when you're that loud. Now, there's also the matter of this month's fees we need to—"

"You'll get your money when it's due." Duncan stepped back into the trailer and slammed the door behind him.

Duncan hated that his mind had drifted back to money when all he wanted to think about was her. All thoughts of a job, the investigation in New York or the future had vanished from his mind. She was everything. Everything else could wait.

He'd found out a lot about her: where she worked, where she lived, what car she drove. But he hadn't yet managed to penetrate below that. He needed to know about her friends, family, love interests, hobbies, and pets. But Duncan was happy to take it slowly, to learn all he could before making any move against her. His experience in New York had reminded him of the value of patience. He didn't want to make any mistakes this time – especially not with her.

He wanted to enjoy this one. Once this was done, he'd have slain his unicorn: the woman who'd eluded him years ago, who no other woman had measured up to. She'd be dealt with slowly. He'd savor it, taking his time, making sure he'd ground everything important to her into dust before taking her life. And he'd take his time deciding how to end it. It would have to be something commensurate to the pain she'd caused him.

He lay down on the bed and stared at the ceiling, the trailer now lit by nothing but the light that managed to bleed in from outside. He hadn't slept in days. He knew he probably should, but doubted he could, knowing she was so close. If he wanted to, he could go to her house right now, force his way in and end it. But he wouldn't do that. There wasn't a woman in the world who deserved more pain than she did, and she had that pain coming to her.

A whole lot of pain.

30

CHRIS

C hris rubbed his eyes, opened them as wide as he could and blinked a few times. It wasn't as good as sleep, or coffee, but neither was at hand so it was the best he could do. He hadn't slept well for several days and the coffee pot had run out of the good stuff a few hours ago. But a few seconds later, he found himself reading back over a sentence he'd read six times already. If his mind had a fatigue limit, Chris had hit it.

It had been worth it, though. Working with Agent Hopkins in secret whenever gaps in his schedule and her caseload allowed, they'd spent hours trawling through records, case notes, interviews and media reports of kills in New York. It was a lot of effort, but it had yielded far greater results than Chris had found on his own.

They now had a solid physical profile of the killer, a detailed chronology of his likely victims in New York City, and knowledge of the damage he'd inflicted on those victims' personal, social and professional lives prior to their murders. More importantly, with Hopkins' help, Chris had found kills from all over America that may have links to the killer, starting in California and moving on to Florida, Illinois, Massachusetts and, finally, New York.

Chris had thought the killer was only striking in New York. The truth seemed far worse.

That might also explain why the killer had gone silent since almost being caught. To Chris, it had seemed strange that a killer who'd struck so regularly would suddenly stop, especially after what the psychologist had told him. No, such a man was driven by compulsion and he wouldn't be able to stop even if he wanted to. It seemed far more likely that the killer had simply moved again, finding a new city after escaping a close call in New York.

"You okay, Chris?" Hopkins walked into his office, breaking his chain of thought as she closed the door and perched on the edge of his desk. "You look like hell."

Chris looked up at her. "Just tired, that's all. I'm just trying to get a few more hours in while I've got the chance. I'm busy with community briefings for the next few days."

"Damn job getting in the way of our side project." Hopkins laughed. "Go home, relax, sleep, get drunk. You're useless like this."

Chris shook his head. "No, I—"

She held up a hand, her face serious now. "I'm not joking, Chris. If you keep working like this, you'll make mistakes. What we're doing is dangerous enough without you being overtired and fucking something up. I'll keep working on it, but you need to go home. You can start fresh tomorrow."

Chris didn't want to tell her he didn't really have a home in Omaha. He had an apartment with a bed and some other odd pieces of furniture, but he hated it and barely spent any time there. It wasn't a place of rest or warmth. He spent most of his free time and his salary at the bar next to his house, only going home for a quick sleep, a shower, a shave, and a change of clothes. Between the work and the drinking he was slowly coming apart.

"Chris." Hopkins broke his reverie, now standing with her hands on her hips. "If you agree to go home, I'll tell you what I just found."

"Fine." Chris raised an eyebrow. He saved the document he was working on, shut down his laptop and started to gather his things. "I'm listening."

"I think I've found a survivor."

Chris stopped what he was doing. His mouth fell open. The ramifications were enormous. Though Chelsea Butler had survived, and provided a wealth of information, it was limited. Chris also knew there was no way he could make contact with her, because Nowitski would find out and he'd be busted. This was huge.

"You found a survivor?"

"You're so tired you're repeating what I'm saying." She smiled. "Look, no promises, but it adds up. I spent a bunch of time on the National Crime Information Center database, and also dug into some case reports. It took some work, but I think it fits. She's a woman in Boston who I think survived a run-in with our killer."

"You're sure?" Chris was hanging on her every word.

"No, but she fits the profile, except for the hair. She's a natural blonde, but she had red hair at the time of the attack. Her attacker fits the profile. The attempted murder fits the chronology of when we think our guy was in the state, and she had nasty things happen right before it. It's worth looking at. It's the best lead I've found."

Chris couldn't believe it. His mistake in New York City had

been focusing on potential victims, rather than on the big picture. Though he'd come close to getting his man, he wondered if he might've actually caught the killer if he'd taken a different approach. He should've been focusing on linking the kills in New York to those in other places.

"I want to speak with her."

She shook her head. "Hold your horses. First we need to see if she's willing to talk. I'll follow it up tonight while you're at home trying to get some sleep. Once I've done that, we'll figure out how to speak to her without raising any red flags. Getting from Omaha to Boston without tripping the alarm is going to be hard."

Chris nodded. She was right. "We can't let anyone else get wind of what we're doing. Do the legwork and then I'll see if I can get out to Boston to talk to her."

"Fat chance!" She laughed. "I found her, and I'm going to prep her. I'm not going to let you walk in there and take the glory!"

"I was hoping—"

"Keep dreaming, Chris. I'm only doing this with you because it's interesting. There's no way I'm going to miss the chance to speak with this woman. Let me see if there's any substance, then we'll figure out a pretext to head out there. Both of us. Those are my conditions, in addition to you getting some sleep."

Chris wanted to protest, to stay in the office and help her chase down this fresh new lead, but she seemed adamant. "Fine. I'll go straight home."

She smiled. "Great."

Chris didn't tell her that the chances of him getting any sleep were slight.

31

ASHLEY

A shley gripped her coffee cup in one hand, while fumbling with the keys to the store in the other. Finally, she got the door unlocked. Putting the keys back in her purse, she picked up the mail that had been slipped underneath the door, walked to the counter and put her coffee down. A flick through the mail showed that it was all junk, so she threw it in the trash.

Ashley whistled a nameless tune as she readied the store, still pleased that Jana had entrusted her to do so. She unlocked the cash register, turned on the lights, opened the curtains, put on a coffee pot and wiped down the counter. In less than fifteen minutes, the store was ready for the day's business. Ashley had been working there long enough now that Jana had started rostering her to open up in the morning.

For most people it wouldn't be a big deal. For Ashley it was a huge sign of progress.

Jana walked through the door about an hour later, looking

tired and a little worse for wear. Another thing Ashley had learned was that her boss liked to party. Ashley was well past hanging out in bars until past midnight, but Jana seemed able to drink herself into oblivion and still show up for work the next day. Today, she wore dark sunglasses, even inside the store.

"Morning!" Ashley was deliberately chirpy, amused by the sight of someone else in a mess for once. "There's some coffee in the pot."

Jana's response came in the form of a mumble. "Thanks, Ashley. I appreciate you opening up."

Ashley smiled and resumed her work. The morning passed uneventfully, with Ashley handling the few customers that came in and Jana doing her best to stay upright. Slowly, the coffee kicked in and Ashley managed to engage in an actual conversation with Jana. The other woman's exploits were way outside of Ashley's comfort zone, and it sounded like the previous night was no exception. Ashley smiled and nodded, but was glad when a customer walked in.

Ashley greeted the customer. "Good morning. Is there anything in particular you're after today?"

The elderly woman took a few more steps inside the shop and spoke. "Yes, yes. I'm after a dress for my daughter. It's her birthday next month. Could you show me a selection?"

"Of course." Ashley smiled. "We've got a good range. Let me gather up a few that might suit."

Ashley chose half a dozen dresses for the woman to look at. She considered it practice for when Lucy grew up. The thought of Lucy made her smile. The previous evening, Ashley had spent the whole night with her. Tom had driven her to Ashley's house, and then found a local sports bar to watch football at while Ashley cooked a meal for Lucy. It was the first time she'd had Lucy in her house. It had felt good, especially after the scare she'd had a few weeks ago. Ashley felt like her little girl's laughter had been her version of a housewarming.

It took around twenty minutes to find something the woman was happy with. Ashley suggested that she bring her daughter in to try it on, but the woman insisted that what she'd selected would be fine. The woman paid, Ashley bagged up the dress and the customer left the store.

Ashley turned to check with Jana, only to realize she wasn't there. Ashley double checked, but the store was totally empty. Jana's absence was strange. She glanced into the back room and realized what had happened. The back door was ajar, meaning Jana had used the back door to go out to her car, which she usually parked in the alley beside the store. With a sigh of relief, Ashley glanced outside, then her alarm bells started to ring again.

Jana was nowhere to be seen and her car was still parked in the space. Ashley walked down the alley to the street at the front of the store, which was virtually empty. She waited there for several moments, looking up and down the street and scratching her head. She watched one car drive past, then a guy ride past on his bike, but nothing she saw helped her figure out what had happened. It was unusual for Jana to disappear from the store without a word.

The last thing Ashley thought to try was dialing Jana's cell phone. She went inside, found her phone behind the counter and dialed. The call went straight to voicemail. Ashley leaned on the counter and put her chin in her hands. She had no idea what had happened to Jana. It was the first time she had ever vanished without telling Ashley where she was going, but she was the boss. She could come and go as she pleased.

Ashley thought about calling the cops, but knew they'd

laugh it off and accuse her of overreacting. With a shrug, she walked back inside the store and got back to work. It wouldn't be long until Jana returned, anyway. She'd probably just gone to the grocery store.

32

DUNCAN

Duncan pressed his finger against the cylinder of the revolver and gave it a firm spin. It made a slight whirring sound as it turned, and Duncan watched it until it stopped. Only then did he look up at his prisoner, sucking in a breath through his teeth. She was still out cold. He let the breath out slowly in the form of a long sigh that escaped between pressed together lips. He had a lot of patience, but this woman was testing it. She'd been out cold for a couple of hours now.

"Who knew chloroform could be so effective?" He sighed again. He'd probably used too much. Or not used it correctly. He'd never had to bother with that sort of thing, because he rarely came into contact with his targets. Instead, he dismantled them from a distance, only moving in for the final kill. Chelsea Butler had been the only exception, and look how that had ended.

He'd promised himself he'd revert to form, to being methodical and calculating and smart. And so Duncan had tried to resist scooping up Ashley's boss. He'd had every intention of taking his time as he researched Ashley, quietly and carefully constructing a picture of her life before finally moving to destroy it. But his promise hadn't lasted long. This one was different, because she was different.

Emotion had gotten the better of him, and when he'd seen the opportunity he'd taken it.

Ashley's boss had emerged from the back of the store and stepped out into the alley. He'd been watching the front of the store from inside his car, focused on Ashley, when he'd noticed the manager making repeat trips to her car. Something had snapped inside of him. He'd fumbled around in the back of his car for the rag and the chloroform, got out, and crossed the road. He'd snuck up behind her and forced the rag over her mouth.

She hadn't seen him coming, and it hadn't taken long to subdue her. Duncan didn't think anyone had seen him pull his car around the other end of the alley and put her into the trunk.

Duncan smiled as the woman finally started to stir. He was itching to get on with this, because he had a shift at his new job later in the day. Having to split his time with a job was frustrating, but he needed the money. He walked over to the woman, removed the cloth he'd tied over her eyes and then took a step back. It took a few minutes for her to come around. She opened her eyes, blinked a few times and then panicked as she realized her situation.

"Mmmm!" She screamed, but the gag muffled the noise.

Duncan tapped the revolver against his leg as he leaned in, getting ever closer. He enjoyed watching as her eyes widened, her terror clear. He stopped an inch from her face and brought the revolver up under her chin. He smiled, and she let out a squeal. "I thought you'd never wake up."

"Mmmm!"

"You need to be quiet while I explain what's going to happen here." Duncan spoke slowly, calmly. "If you promise to be quiet, I'll ungag you. If you tell me who you are, I'll give you some water. If you tell me what I want, you'll live. Those are the only things you need to think about right now. Okay?"

"Mmmm!" This time she nodded insistently. "Mmmm! Mmmm!"

"Okay. Remember, if you scream, you'll die in the next fifteen seconds." He reached out and untied the gag, then pulled it away and smiled. "Better?"

"Thank you." She spoke in only a whisper, but the tremor in her voice was clear. She opened her mouth widely and licked her lips. "Who are you?"

"I'm the person who'll decide whether you live or die." Duncan took a step back, dragged his chair over and sat opposite her. "Tell me who you are."

"I'm Jana Greenham."

Duncan smiled. As she squirmed and waited for him to continue, Duncan took a second to calm himself. The prospect of finally learning more about the woman who'd damaged him so profoundly was tantalizing. This was his first chance for him to strike back after waiting for so many years. It was the first spark of a fire that would consume her life, if he had his way. She had been his singular focus so many years ago, and now Duncan could feel it happening again.

He had a brief moment of doubt as he considered what would happen after he'd finished with her. He'd spent a decade fantasizing about finding her, but never expected he'd actually do so. He'd tried, and failed, for years. But after hearing the message on the phone and travelling to Wallingford, it had actually happened. He'd found her. Now he feared no high would ever be greater than the moment he saw the spark in her eyes go out.

But that was a question for another day.

First he needed to learn all about her life for the last decade. He gave Jana a sip of water, which she sucked down greedily. He'd read on the internet that the key to a successful interrogation was to establish trust, boundaries, and consequences. He'd killed plenty of women, but he'd never had to torture one before. Duncan liked learning new skills, but not when their application was so important.

"Tell me everything you know about Ashley." He moved the water bottle away from her mouth.

"Ashley?" Jana's face screwed up in confusion. "My staff member? Why do you want to know about her?"

"You need to stop asking questions." Duncan walked over to the table where he'd assembled his collection of torture implements. "And start answering them."

"Please, just let me go." The woman's voice grew urgent, and desperate, as she watched Duncan caress the objects on the table. "I barely know her."

Duncan sighed. He picked up one of the screwdrivers and spun it in his fingers as he walked back to the woman. He locked eyes with her, held her gaze for a few seconds, then drove the screwdriver down into her leg as hard as he could. She let out an ear-splitting scream as her eyes bulged and stared at the screwdriver now sticking out of her upper thigh. Duncan didn't mind that she'd screamed. He'd only wanted her quiet earlier for his own comfort.

"Please!" Her nostrils were flaring as she screamed. Spittle came from her mouth and snot escaped her nose. "Let me go!"

EYES ON YOU | 163

"Nobody will hear you scream. We're miles from anyone who can help you." He smiled at her. "Now, you need to start paying attention. Answer my question."

Her eyes flickered between Duncan and the screwdriver protruding from her thigh. Her breath came in short bursts. "Okay."

Duncan exhaled with relief. He was glad he didn't have to totally break this woman to get her to talk. He'd searched for Ashley for years, and always found it strange that she had no internet profile, had left so little mark on the world. She was all but invisible, and he intended to find out why. Ashley's manager was the first key to finding out where Ashley had been for the last decade.

Since she'd run away from him.

33

CHRIS

"Day release is nice." Chris laughed, enjoying the fresh air blowing in through the car window. "We should've just flown to Boston, though."

"Try explaining that to Tony." Hopkins scoffed. "I told him I needed to go to DC, and he thinks that's where we are right now, working diligently."

Chris grunted, knowing he was travelling at Hopkins' pleasure. That she'd managed to negotiate a trip to the northeast at all was incredible, but somehow she had also convinced their boss that she needed Chris along for support. It hadn't taken much for him to agree. None of the other agents in the office had offered to go with Hopkins, too busy with their own caseloads, so begrudgingly, Harvey had agreed to Chris doing so.

They'd flown Washington DC with five days to get their work done. In that time, Chris and Hopkins had three things to do: speak to the woman who'd escaped their killer, test Chris's theory with a trip to the National Center for the

Analysis of Violent Crime – an FBI resource – and, finally, make some solid progress on the case Hopkins was working. At Dulles they'd jumped straight into a rental car and started the seven-hour drive to Boston.

"We're here." Hopkins exhaled slowly as she signaled and pulled the car over to the curb.

Chris looked at the house, thinking about the woman who lived there. By all rights she should be dead, another victim of a serial killer nobody except Chris and Hopkins wanted to believe existed. Instead, six years ago, she'd escaped, before moving overseas for a short while. She hadn't shown up in any of Chris's searches because a cop had input her hair color incorrectly. Hopkins had found her when looking for crime reports with similar but not exact profiles to the other victims.

"Let me handle the conversation to start with." Hopkins' voice was insistent. "You're too close to this. We don't want to spook her."

Chris wanted to protest, but he knew she had a point. He would be like a kid with a new toy, whereas she'd be more measured. "Okay. Let's go."

They exited the car and approached the house. Chris inhaled slowly through his nose and then out again, trying to stay calm, hoping desperately that the next few minutes might give them something to help break open the case. They needed it. He needed it. He knocked on the front door of the nondescript family home and waited. From inside came the deep barks of a dog, then footsteps as someone approached the door.

The door opened and a middle-aged man greeted them, suspicion on his face and the dog beside him. "Yes?"

"Mr Jenkins?" Hopkins smiled and flashed her badge. "I'm Agent Hopkins and this is Agent Horan. We're with the FBI."

John Jenkins nodded, opened the door further and stood aside, allowing them to enter. "Come on in."

Hopkins nodded and Chris followed her inside, lapping up detail as they walked through the house to the kitchen. The photos on the walls showed a pretty, red-haired woman smiling at her college graduation and in various locations around the world. At some point, she'd changed her hair color, reverting to her natural blonde.

When they entered the kitchen, Chris saw that same woman, sitting with a cigarette in one hand and her chin in the other. She looked a lot like the other victims, except she was alive.

"Sarah? Those FBI agents are here." Jenkins flashed a sad smile at his wife, then turned to Chris and Hopkins, his voice harder. "Take it easy on her."

Hopkins nodded and they took a seat. She smiled. "I can't thank you enough for talking to us, Ms Jenkins. We believe the man who attacked you has struck again. Any information you can share with us will go a long way toward catching him."

"It didn't last time." She placed her cigarette in an ashtray, lifted her chin and then undid the top few buttons on her blouse, revealing scarring from severe burns. "See?"

Chris gave a small gasp, then composed himself when Hopkins glared at him. He spoke for the first time. "What happened?"

"I told the cops all of this already. Don't you guys share notes?" She sighed, took another drag of her cigarette and then blew the smoke out slowly. "That prick tormented me for weeks and I never even knew it. All I knew was that a whole bunch of things started to go wrong and I couldn't explain it."

Hopkins leaned in closer. "Can you tell us about that?"

Another sigh. "Sure. He sent a letter to my boyfriend at the time, purporting to be my lover. I lost my boyfriend. He threw steak laced with fishhooks over my fence. I lost my dog. He sabotaged my mother's car. She crashed it, and I was lucky not to lose her too. All of this happened within a few weeks."

Chris shook his head. It was exactly the same as the other victims. They'd all had their lives destroyed in the weeks leading up to their deaths. It was never very elaborate. The killer didn't seem to relish in complicated plots, nor did he have a calling card that would make it easy to detect him, or that they could warn potential victims about. But he was brutally effective. He seemed to find as much pleasure in destroying a victim's life as he did in taking it.

"And that's when he attacked you?" Chris recoiled from the look Sarah Jenkins flashed him. He deserved it. "Sorry, I mean physically attacked you."

"Yes. He broke into my home and attacked me. I struggled, but he was too strong. After he'd knocked me out and restrained me, he stripped me naked." She paused for a moment, a small sob escaping her as her husband placed his hand on her shoulder. "I'm sorry. It's not something I like to think about."

"It's fine." Hopkins gave a sympathetic smile. "Take your time. Please, this is all a great help. We don't want it to be more difficult than it needs to be."

Jenkins nodded, wiped her eyes and continued. "As I said, he stripped me. I thought he was going to rape me and kill me. It was strange, though. It's almost like he saw my pubic hair and recoiled. He ran to the bathroom for a minute, then came back and just started shouting at me."

Chris knew what had happened, but he needed to be sure. "I notice that in some photos you're a redhead and in some you're blonde. Which is your natural color?"

"Blonde."

"Right." Chris nodded. "So when he saw that your pubic hair wasn't red, he lost interest?"

Jenkins nodded. "He left me bound on the bed and knocked a candle over as he rushed out the door. I don't think he meant to, but it set the bedding on fire. I made it out with third-degree burns across 30 percent of my body. But I made it out alive. I didn't think I was going to get out at all."

"That's awful." Hopkins offered her best reassuring gesture, placing her hand on Jenkins' arm. "Could you tell us what he looked like?"

Chris prayed silently for a break, a lead they didn't have already. He wanted a more detailed physical description, a trait or a solid detail that would distinguish the man from the other two hundred million men in America. At the moment, they knew he was in his early or mid-thirties, with brown hair and brown eyes. The search was hopeless, because there was nothing specific to search for. He needed something else.

"I gave the police the description, six years ago." Jenkins shook her head. "I told them his height, weight, and hair color. I even told them the name he kept saying. I—"

"Wait a minute, what name?" Chris leaned forward. There'd been no mention of any name on the police report about this case. Or any of the others. He'd have remembered something like that. "Would you mind sharing it with us?"

Jenkins shrugged. "Even as he was attacking me, violently, it was almost like he was distant. There was a name he kept saying, over and over again, every time he hit me or looked at me. He was muttering it under his breath. The guy was crazy."

Chris rushed the words out. "What was the name?"

"Ashley."

34

ASHLEY

shley slapped her palm on the table. "How many times do I have to tell you? I don't know where she went and you're not going to find her by talking to me!"

"We're not so sure." The detective investigating Jana's disappearance tapped his pen. "You're the last person who saw her before she disappeared."

Ashley sighed. This was the second time she'd been questioned about Jana's disappearance. While Ashley may have been the last person to see Jana, she had no idea where she'd gone. The cops hadn't brought her in to discuss any new leads, they were just desperate to get answers and clear the case. It seemed like a spectacular waste of everyone's time.

"Plus, there's the small detail of your past to consider, Ms Wheeler." The other, younger case detective chimed in. "You came to the attention of the police in New York for several abduction attempts a few months back, and now your boss has just flat-out disappeared..."

Ashley flared. "Plus I was a witness in a high-profile murder case, which failed, so I must be a suspect, right?"

"Ms Wheeler, I—"

"No." Ashley shook her head. "I had nothing to do with this. I don't know where Jana went or where she is. I'm not the scab you pick to break this open."

The older detective picked up his pen and exhaled through clenched teeth. "Okay, Ms Wheeler, I'll level with you. We don't know what happened to your boss. There's no evidence in the store, in the alleyway, in her car, or on any camera footage we have available."

"Okay then." Ashley leaned forward, placed her elbows on the table and steepled her fingers in front of her. "Ask what you have to ask."

The younger detective smiled. "Do you know what happened to Jana Greenham or where she's gone?"

"No."

The detective nodded and scribbled on his pad. "Had she mentioned anything to you about leaving town? Going to see a friend or family member, perhaps?"

"No."

"Okay, finally, did you have anything to do with the disappearance of Ms Greenham, either deliberately or accidentally?"

"No. I thought she'd gone down to the grocery store or something." Ashley leaned back. "There's no help I can provide. I don't know anything. I've answered all your questions, some of them several times. I know you're trying to catch me out with a lie, but there's nothing to catch. I like Jana, I miss her, and I'm scared. That's it."

"Okay, Ms Wheeler." The older detective closed his notebook and looked at his partner, seemingly unsatisfied.

"We're just going to take a couple minutes. Will you wait here?"

Ashley shrugged as they stood and walked out of the room. It was tiring to spend so much time at the police station, especially since she'd done nothing wrong, but at least the police were taking Jana's disappearance seriously. It was just a shame they'd done little more than question her repeatedly. Ashley knew the first 24 hours were crucial in missing persons cases, which meant the chances of finding Jana were now slim and getting worse.

After a while, the door swung open and Ashley raised an eyebrow at the detectives. "Well? Satisfied I'm not the arch kidnapper?"

The older detective winced at her words and ran a hand through his thinning hair. He rested his palms on the table. "There's been a development."

"That's great! Do you know where Jana is?" Ashley smiled and started to stand, then sat again when it was clear they didn't. "What is it?"

"Someone's come forward with a cell phone video of the kidnapping. He kept quiet at first because he thought it was a domestic issue." The older detective didn't seem very happy about the last point. "Unfortunately, it's grainy. The old man who took it has a camera phone that's older than time. Still, it proves she was taken, and it might give us something."

"Want me to take a look?" Ashley saw doubt flash across the older detective's face. "I've worked at the store for a while now. I might recognize whoever did it."

The detective weighed up her words, then turned and nodded at his younger partner. The other man left the room as the detective looked back at Ashley. "Okay."

Ashley smiled, and they sat in silence while they waited for the other detective to return. Ashley tapped on the table softly with her thumb, glad they finally had something to chase after. With each passing hour she grew more fearful for Jana's well-being. The woman wasn't her friend, but she'd become something more than a boss or an acquaintance. The abduction had also rammed home to Ashley just how vulnerable she was.

The younger detective returned to the room and put a laptop down on the table in front of her. She watched intently as he hit play and a ridiculously grainy video started up. It showed a man moving close to Jana, walking up behind her. His features were barely discernable. Ashley gasped and leaned closer as he placed something over Jana's mouth, then caught her weight when she stopped struggling and collapsed. The video stopped.

The older detective sighed. "The guy who was filming it got spooked, stopped filming, and walked the other way. This is all we've got."

"It's not much. Average height, average build, brown hair." The younger detective sat down opposite Ashley with a long sigh. "Recognize him?"

Ashley stared at the screen for a few moments, not speaking as she tried her hardest to place the man. He looked vaguely familiar, but as the younger detective had said, the guy looked like hundred others Ashley saw in any given week. The man could be anyone – a friend of Jana's, someone she'd met during one of her late-night bar hops, or even a complete stranger. Ashley had told the police everything she knew and, though this video proved Jana had been taken, she had nothing to offer that could help them track down her abductor.

Finally, Ashley shook her head and looked up at the

officers. "Nobody I could place. But, as you say, he looks quite common."

"Yeah..." The older detective's voice trailed off. "There's probably a thousand guys in the city with those exact features. But if you remember anything, please give us a call."

Ashley nodded. "What now? Am I safe? Should I do anything?"

"Nothing out of the ordinary. Just keep your doors locked, Ms Wheeler."

35

DUNCAN

Duncan screwed up his nose at the stench as he stepped into the room. He'd held Jana Greenham captive for several days now, using that time to interrogate her. The results had been mixed, for both of them. Duncan now had some of the information he craved, but not as much as he'd hoped. Greenham had cooperated, but not nearly enough. Because of that, he'd been forced to cut her, bruise her, and abuse her.

Unfortunately for Duncan's nose, this had resulted in a mess he wasn't overly fond of.

He walked to the wall and grabbed the hose. Thankfully, he was able to wash away the worst of the mess. He turned on the water and started to spray the blood, piss, and shit down the drain, never taking his eyes off Greenham. She whimpered. He smiled and turned the hose on her. She gasped as the cold water sprayed her.

He turned off the hose, tossed it onto the floor and moved toward her, stopping a few inches away. To his surprise,

Duncan had discovered he didn't actually like inflicting physical torture. His targets suffered mental and emotional scars, which helped Duncan keep his hands clean until their death. And in this case, he wasn't even overly interested in the woman. The pain he'd inflicted upon Greenham wasn't personal, it was simply a means to an end. If she had never employed the woman he *was* interested in, they'd never have come in contact.

He needed information, this was one way to get it. The results had been positive, but insufficient. He grabbed a bunch of her hair, squeezed tightly and lifted his arm. Greenham gave an ear-curdling scream as she was lifted up off the chair. He held her there for nearly a minute, watching as she squirmed like a fish on a hook. Then he dropped her back into the chair, cocked his fist and smashed it into her face. As her head snapped back, Duncan cursed and shook his hand.

He removed her gag and the mask over her eyes. "Back for another day." Duncan's voice was still laced with pain from the blow. "Ready?"

Her head was slumped forward. After a second, she started to sob. "I've told you everything I know."

"Jana Greenham. Forty years old. Hired Ashley Wheeler almost two months ago." Duncan sighed. "I don't know how her surname became Wheeler."

"I—"

Duncan didn't let her speak. "In the time she's worked for you, you claim to have learned little more than that about her. Let me make it clear. I don't believe you. I need to know about her family, friends, love interests, pets, hobbies – everything. If you don't give me more, you're going to die."

"I'm telling the truth!" She gave a loud sob. "She came in

searching for work and I gave her a shot. That's all I know! She seemed like she had a kind heart, just down on her luck!"

"That's why you're a fucking idiot!" Duncan shouted, as loudly as he could, spittle flying from his mouth. He clenched his fists and thrust his face forward until it was just an inch from hers. "You can't trust her! She'll screw you over! She's the reason you're here, broken and bleeding and shitting all over the floor!"

Greenham jerked her head forward, the headbutt catching Duncan right on the chin. He staggered back, and as he did, she spat blood at him. His grimace must've looked terrifying, because her eyes went wide. He could taste blood in his mouth as he moved toward her. He lifted his foot and kicked her hard in the chest. She grunted at the blow, and then squealed as the chair fell back and she landed hard on the concrete floor, still strapped in tight.

Duncan stood over her. She gave a gargling sound as Duncan's boot pressed into her throat. "Did that feel good?"

Unable to dislodge him, her hands tethered tightly to the chair, she could only thrash and struggle, her efforts futile. Duncan didn't take his eyes off hers, watching as her face turned a dark color. Her eyes bulged, filled with fear and desperation and the realization that she was about to die. He usually enjoyed the moment when his targets lost all hope, when they realized their own behavior had led to their death. But in this case, all he felt was frustration.

He'd hoped for so much from her.

"Tell me something I can use!" he shouted, easing the pressure of his boot just a little, allowing her to breathe.

Greenham sucked in several long breaths, then coughed them out just as fast as quickly. She tried to speak, several times, but it took her a moment. "A daughter."

"What?" Duncan's mind was clouded with rage and frustration. He'd tortured this woman to within an inch of her life and she had still revealed nothing.

"She has a daughter!" The woman sobbed, closing her eyes. "Please, let me go. She has a daughter. I saw a photo in her purse."

Duncan's mouth fell open. A daughter. That meant Ashley Wheeler had lured some poor bastard into a relationship. Was she married? Was it a one-night stand? His mind was racing with even more questions, and he had precious few answers. Another mystery, one more lock to be unpicked to gain access to the information he needed to destroy her.

"Will you let me go now?" Her voice sounded pathetic, desperate. "Was that information good enough?"

"Good enough." Duncan rolled the words around in his mouth. "A lot of this mess could have been avoided if you'd just told me that."

"You promised!"

Duncan smiled and turned away from the woman. His boots sloshed in the water as he walked toward the door. The hose he'd tossed to the ground had kept running, and the woman's shit had blocked the drain. They were both ankle-deep in water, but only one of them could escape. He exited the room and stepped up onto a rubber mat he'd put in place. The same drill he'd used on her the previous day would end her life now.

He tested the drill to see if it was on and then threw it into the water.

36

CHRIS

C hris broke away from the embrace. "It was good to see you, Tina. I think you've given Agent Hopkins here plenty to think about."

Hopkins glared at Chris, then smiled as she shook the other woman's hand. "Don't mind him, he's just sore he's riding shotgun on this case."

"I thought that was strange. No offense, Justine." Tina Fuller grimaced. "So it's true you got punted out of the New York office, Chris?"

Chris nodded. Though he'd worked with Fuller years ago in the New York field office, she clearly didn't know why he'd been run out of town. She was now the chief profiler at the National Center for the Analysis of Violent Crime, a resource available to law enforcement dealing with serial or complex violent crimes. They'd spent the last few hours picking Fuller's brain about possible suspects for the serious assault Hopkins was investigating. Chris needed their help in pursuing his killer, too, but he couldn't exactly make an official request.

"I'm sad to hear that, Chris." Fuller gripped his shoulder. "You're a good agent. You'll get back on your feet. Just hang in there and stay out of trouble."

"Thanks Tina." Chris placed a hand on top of hers and gave it a squeeze. "Just trying to keep busy and let things take their course. Thanks again."

Fuller smiled at both of them and then headed back to her office. Chris and Hopkins were left standing alone outside the meeting room. With a nod, Chris started down the hallway, Hopkins by his side.

"How do you know her, anyway?" Hopkins spoke softly. "You two seemed friendly."

"We worked together for a while." Chris shrugged. "That's all."

"So you weren't always the office pariah?" Hopkins laughed. "Did you ever date her?"

"No." Chris's tone made it clear he didn't want to talk about his dating history. After Tamara, he'd lost all interest in dating. He shook off the thought. "Okay, let's go find James Miles. If anyone can find a suspect or spot something we've missed, it's him."

They reached the exit of the main building and Chris pushed open the door. He was excited by the prospect of meeting with Miles again. They'd worked one case together, a decade ago, and now Miles worked some of the most difficult cases in America. If there was one man able to spot a pattern, observe signals, and help to develop both a working theory and a plan of attack, it was Miles.

They reached a smaller building and Chris paused out the front. "Are you sure you want to come inside? I can take care of this if you want."

Hopkins frowned. "Why wouldn't I? I came all the way

here on a thin pretext just so you could have this meeting. There's no way I'm going to miss it."

"Okay." Chris shrugged. "But listen, this place is full of geniuses and he's the most talented of them all. I'm sure he'll see something we've missed all along, but he's sensitive. He's not going to be too happy taking the risk we're about to ask him to take."

Hopkins reached out to open the door, then paused. "Why did he agree to help us at all if he's so touchy?"

"He owes me a favor."

Miles was an extreme introvert, whose profiling genius more than compensated for his social issues. He kept to himself unless it was absolutely necessary to speak to others. Once they were outside Miles's office, Chris knocked on the door. He smiled as he heard footfalls from inside the office, then silence as Miles checked the peephole.

"Yes?" The voice from the other side of the door was muffled, but easily understandable.

"James?" Chris spoke louder than he'd like to. "It's Chris Horan."

The door opened an inch, an eyeball appeared. "You can come in. She can't."

Chris shook his head. "No deal. She's my new partner. You can trust her."

"Wrong." The door started to close.

Chris managed to get his foot in the doorway. "James, remember Brooklyn."

"I—" The eyeball widened and the voice stuttered.

"Exactly." Chris pushed on the door firmly, forcing his way into Miles' office.

"Fine, fine." Miles moved into the office, which was a mess of paper and books. "Sit."

Chris smiled, gestured for Hopkins to come inside and then closed the door behind her. They both took a seat and Chris looked Miles directly in the eye. "Now, let's try this again. Thank you for meeting with us. We're square now. I hope you've had a chance to look over the files I sent you?"

"Yes, yes, I did. And you have my thanks for clearing our debt. I'll do my best to help you with your particular problem." Miles smiled and his eyes lit up. He stood suddenly and started to rush around the office. "Just let me find the file."

Chris smiled. He'd been the investigating agent on a minor cybercrime case a decade or so ago, and had chased it down to Miles. Chris had let it go, choosing not to ruin a career over something minor. Miles had kept his job and been squeaky clean ever since. In return, he'd told Chris that if he ever needed anything, he just needed to ask. Miles had risen to become one of the Center's most brilliant profilers. Chris hoped he'd used the favor well.

"So what do you think of the profile, James?" Hopkins spoke for the first time. "We're in a bit of a hurry."

Hopkins was right. They couldn't stay here any longer than they absolutely needed to. He nodded. "Any light you can shine on the situation would help."

"Ha, found it." Miles laughed as he sat and flicked rapidly through some papers. "Okay. I reviewed what you sent through. It might be a serial case. If so, it's likely your killer has been wronged in the past by a woman or women who look like his victims. It's likely they damaged him, and he either felt like dying or tried suicide."

Chris nodded. "That's interesting, I—"

Miles held up a hand. "Your killer is unsatisfied by the simple prospect of killing his victims. He destroys them first. To answer your next question, yes, I think the killings are linked – including your girlfriend – and there's a long history. Now, in answer to your *next* question, I don't have any clue about who it might be. I ran the check on the database. It came up empty."

Chris felt a red haze overcome him. The smartest profiler in the country had just confirmed what he'd long known, that it was highly likely that Tamara had been murdered by the same killer as all the others. Chris wasn't insane. He wasn't letting personal circumstances impact his judgement. He wasn't a bad agent.

He was right.

There was a monster out there.

"We need to get this guy. *I* need to get this guy." Chris locked eyes on Miles. "We're desperate for a lead, but it needs to be discreet."

"Investigating illegally, I understand." Miles nodded. "If I had the time before you head back to Nebraska, I'd cross-reference the profile against crimes other than murder, hoping to find either your killer or victims who are still alive. But such a complex query would take several days. You have to get back, and I have other work."

"Let's do that." Chris smiled.

"Chris..." The warning in Hopkins' voice was clear. "We need to get back by tomorrow. We don't have any more time to spend here."

"That's fine." Chris smiled. "We can just call you or Skype you in a couple of days and—"

"No." Miles held up a hand. "If you want me to do this, you stick around. I'll run the query, give you the hard copy documents, and then destroy all the records."

Chris hesitated. He was supposed to return to Nebraska with Hopkins. But how could he pass up an opportunity to get valuable new information from one of the most talented profilers in the country? He mightn't have this chance again. Without new information, there was no chance of a breakthrough on the case. He risked setting what remained of his career on fire for the chance at an identity.

It was a shot he was willing to take.

He leaned forward and smiled. "Run the query, including a cross-reference for victims named Ashley. I'll stick around for a few days."

37

ASHLEY

Ashley leaned on the broom and ran a hand through her hair as she surveyed the store. It looked a hell of a lot better than it had an hour ago.

Ashley had spent some time cleaning the store after opening up. There'd been few customers, leaving her plenty of time to get things in order, but the store still felt strange. Empty. The quick clean-up had helped a little, but it still felt strange to be here. It was hard not to think of Jana, missing or captive or dead, while she stood among party dresses and blouses. The police still hadn't found Jana, despite the cell phone video.

The police had advised Ashley that they were done with the scene, and it was up to her whether she wanted to open the store or not. It wasn't ideal, given Ashley had only worked there a few months and was the only other member of staff. Ashley had decided to open, though she'd changed her mind at least five times in the process. If nothing else, keeping the store going felt like a show of faith that Jana was alive.

Ashley also felt like keeping the store in operation was an investment in herself. Since she'd been working there, she'd started getting her life together. She had a bit of money, and a small amount of access to Lucy. To be honest, Jana's disappearance scared her for another reason, too. Ashley feared that another shock in her life would destabilize her, undoing all of the progress she'd made. This job had become an important piece of her own jigsaw, which felt like it was being put together for the first time in ages.

If Jana wasn't okay...

The phone started to ring. With a sigh, Ashley walked back to the counter, propped the broom against it and answered the phone. It was a simple customer query. As she spoke, she flicked through the mail. None of it seemed overly urgent. Also on the counter was the CV she'd found earlier, which had been dropped underneath a clothes rack. She screwed it up and tossed it in the bin by her feet.

The minute she placed the phone down, there was a loud knocking on the back door. Ashley froze. The pounding went on for several seconds and then stopped suddenly. Her mind screamed at her as she realized she was alone in the store. Nobody came to the back, not even couriers. Whoever had abducted Jana could easily have come back for Ashley. Her heartbeat quickened, her mouth went dry, she gripped the counter tightly. Although she wanted to ignore the knock, she knew she couldn't. She had to find out who was out there.

Ashley sucked in a deep breath, then exhaled quickly. She thought about calling the police, then had a flashback to the raccoon at her house. If she called the cops every time she heard a noise, she'd need them on speed dial. No, she had to handle this herself. Steeling herself, she reached under the counter and grabbed the baseball bat that was kept there in case of moments just like this. Though the weapon didn't make Ashley feel any safer, it was better than nothing. She felt confident she could swing it hard enough to cause some pain.

She walked to the front door and locked it, then slowly inched toward the back door, gripping the bat tightly. Her legs felt shaky and her ears strained for any sound, but there was nothing. She told herself it had just been a courier, or some kids playing a prank. Or maybe it was Jana, her abductor having finished with her, in bad shape but alive. Or maybe it was Jana's abductor, on the lookout for another victim.

Ashley didn't care. It had been a mistake coming to the store on her own. She was terrified. No matter how much she tried to live a quiet life, it seemed like trouble followed her. She was tired of feeling afraid, but she had to know what was on the other side of the door. Once she reached the door she braced her foot against the bottom of it, paused for a few short breaths, then peered through the peephole. All she could see was the grey brick wall on the other side of the alley.

Ashley made her decision. Time seemed to slow as she inched open the door with one hand and gripped the bat with the other. Her eyes widened. Jana was lying on her back with unseeing eyes staring at the sky. She was clearly dead, and her body looked like it had been badly abused. There were cuts, burns, and bruises all over her. Ashley closed the door and locked it as fast as she could.

Ashley leaned against the door, gripping the bat tightly. She fumbled for her cell phone and dialed 911. Ashley spoke with the dispatcher on autopilot, her mind racing. Whoever had abducted and killed Jana had returned the body. Why? Ashley wondered if it was some sort of fetish, or if there was a deeper meaning. Either way, she didn't feel safe. She wasn't going to move an inch until the police got here, and then she was going to go home.

She'd never return to this store again.

38

DUNCAN

"It's good to be back." Duncan spoke softly to himself as he approached his target.

The last time he'd been here, he'd taken dozens of photographs of Ashley while she chased after a raccoon. Now it was time for another visit to her house. A closer visit. He looked around, alert for anyone else, or any sign he was being watched, but there was nothing. The street was quiet, but still he was careful. He walked down the drive. Once he reached the backyard, which was little more than a patch of grass and a small patio table, Duncan paused to look around. The moon provided enough illumination that he could see a small window, which looked like it led to a bathroom.

Duncan looked around one more time as he approached the window. As quietly as he could, he jimmied it in its frame. It was no good. The window was stuck tight. Short of breaking the glass, which would be too noisy, he couldn't pull it out of the frame. Not unless he dealt with the frame, anyway.

Smiling, he grabbed a screwdriver from his pocket and used it to pry the frame away. Then he removed the glass.

He quickly climbed inside the window, laughing at the fallacy that anyone could be safe in their home. He'd always wondered how anyone could believe that, when it was so easy for a predator like him to break in.

He'd half expected to arrive here and find the house empty, Ashley having fled after finding her dead manager in the alleyway outside her work. But here she was, waiting like a dumb hen as the fox drew closer. The thought made him smile. This time, he had the control.

His feet landed on the tiles and he caught his breath, using the light on his cell phone to illuminate the room. It turned out to be a laundry room, not a bathroom. Ashley's dirty clothing was scattered around the washing machine. The dryer was similarly covered. All up, there was probably a full week's worth of dirty laundry scattered around, which Duncan took his time picking through. He'd been right about her bra size, but wrong about her other measurements.

"Oh, Ashley." He scolded her as he picked up the skimpiest thong he'd ever seen. It confirmed all his beliefs about her.

He opened the door, then used the light from his cell phone to begin the search of her house. He started in the living room. He rifled through drawers, but there was nothing worth his time. On the coffee table he found a stack of bills, some other mail, and a photo album. He lifted the album and stuffed it into his backpack. He found little of use in Ashley's dining room, bathroom, or in the spare bedrooms.

With only the room she was sleeping in left to search, Duncan was very disappointed. Though he hadn't expected to find a great trove of information lying around, he had hoped for more. He paused outside of her bedroom for just a moment, killed the light on his phone, took a deep breath, and then slowly turned the doorknob. Thankfully, the door opened silently. His night vision was shot, thanks to the light on his phone, but the fluorescent numbers on her alarm clock projected just enough light for him to see her.

"Bitch." Duncan hissed the words in a soft whisper, then clenched his teeth hard to keep from saying any more.

Thankfully, Ashley didn't stir, despite Duncan's momentary lapse. She stayed in exactly the same position, curled into a small ball in the far corner of the bed, only her legs covered by the sheets. He could see the top half of her body clearly. He became both enraged and aroused by the sight of her naked breasts in the dim green fluorescent light. He shook his head to clear the thought that shouted in his head: it'd be all too easy to just end her right now. He'd known he'd be tempted, but he needed to show some self-control.

That self-control didn't stop him from creeping around to the other side of her bed, crouching down, and inhaling her scent. He devoured her with his eyes, every poorly lit inch of her better than any photo. Most thrilling of all was the soft snore she emitted, completely oblivious to the predator just inches from her.

He allowed himself this moment of indulgence, and then got back to work. He picked up her cell phone from the table beside her, making sure it was on silent, then he grabbed her purse. He quietly stuffed both into his backpack and left the room, closing the door behind him.

He'd finished his search, but wasn't ready to leave just yet. He stood in the middle of the living room for several minutes, thinking. Torturing and killing her boss was the first step, a way to scare Ashley while also getting more information about her. He needed to strike again, to make her feel even less sure.

He wanted her so traumatized that she trusted nobody and believed in nothing. Only then would she feel the pain she deserved. The pain she, more than all the other women, truly deserved.

Shaking his head to get his mind back in the game, Duncan dug through his backpack for the half gallon bottle he'd packed. Then he hefted the backpack, opened the bottle, and started pouring its contents slowly around the living room – on the floor, the furniture, and the curtains. When the bottle was empty he tossed it on the floor. With a quick glance at Ashley's bedroom door, he walked into the kitchen, washed his hands carefully, then walked back to the living room.

He dug through his pockets for the zippo lighter, flicked it open, and then walked slowly across the room to the window. It seemed fitting to start the fire using the curtains she'd installed after her scare with the raccoon. She'd obviously felt like someone was watching her.

He held the lighter to the curtain. The flame caught the accelerant he'd poured over it and rushed quickly toward the ceiling. Duncan smiled as he walked to the front door, tossing the zippo on the floor on his way out. He could already feel the heat from the flames as they started to roar behind him.

As he unlocked the front door and walked outside, he reached for his cell phone.

39

CHRIS

"Thanks, pal." Chris paid the barista, stuffed his wallet back in his pocket, picked up the two coffees and then walked away from the cart.

He took a sip of the coffee, then cursed. It felt like his mouth was losing a battle with liquid magma. As the pain receded, Chris shook his head and headed for James Miles' office, where the promise of something even hotter than the coffee awaited. Miles had called Chris earlier in the day, telling him that the analysis was complete, that it had turned up some interesting results.

Chris hoped so. He needed a break. Staying in D.C. had been a huge risk. He'd called in sick for the last few days, but if his bosses in Omaha asked Hopkins too many questions, his flimsy cover wouldn't hold up for long. Hopefully his gamble had paid off.

Once he reached the office, he didn't even bother to knock. Chris had figured out the man didn't even lock the door, making all the theatrics a waste of time. He watched Miles for a few moments, the profiler apparently too enthralled by whatever was on his computer to realize Chris was there. Chris didn't have time to wait for Miles to notice him. After a few more minutes, he cleared his throat.

Miles jumped slightly, then locked eyes on Chris, nodding approvingly at the coffees. "Sorry, didn't hear you come in. Thanks for the coffee. I definitely need it."

Chris handed him a coffee and sat. Chris waited patiently while Miles took a few large gulps of coffee, apparently not bothered by its scalding temperature. The man really was an enigma. He was also a brilliant profiler, so Chris hoped he had worked some magic on his behalf.

"How's it looking, James?" Chris tapped the lid of his coffee cup, eager for some news. "Was it worth me staying on here?"

"That's for you to evaluate, but the query is complete." Miles set his cup down, then handed Chris a manila folder. "I was able to find eleven crimes with a similar victim, perpetrator, and case profile. They're not all murders, but most are murder, serious violence, or serious sexual assault."

Chris's eyes widened. "Over what period of time?"

"A decade."

"So what does this give me?" Chris flicked through the papers as he spoke. "I really need something big to break open this case."

"It means I can give you a small list of women who've probably had a run-in with the man you're chasing." Miles smiled. "Or as best as I can predict, anyway."

"More living victims?" Chris smiled. "Excellent. Speaking to them could help me narrow down the hunt. Thanks, James. If anything else comes up, I—"

"Something else came up." Miles' voice was flat, as if he

were reporting on the weather. "I have some potential suspects."

Chris dropped his coffee. The lid came off and the contents started spilling all over the floor. He cursed loudly and started to mop at it with a few napkins. As he did, Chris looked up at the profiler. "What do you mean, you have potential suspects? How? None of the murders has ever had a solid suspect attached to it."

"No, but there are several men who were either suspected or arrested for the more minor crimes who also fit the physical and psychological profile we've developed." Miles shrugged, looking at the spill with disdain while making no move to help. "I started with seven possibilities, but when I line it up with previous kills and other known point-in-time locations of these men, it brings it to two."

"Who?" Chris's voice was more aggressive than he intended. He wasn't sure he could believe Miles had found his killer, but the hope was irresistible.

"All the details are in your folder." Miles paused and glanced at the manila folder while Chris cleaned the coffee. "Please treat those pages like gold. I've worked very hard to hide my activity, as you requested, so there's no electronic record of my search."

"Understood." Chris stood, having cleaned up the coffee as best he could. He gripped the folder, then held out his hand to Miles. "I appreciate what you've done for me. You've helped me prove something I've been working on for a long time now. You may have helped save lives."

"Of course." Miles shook Chris's hand briefly, softly. "I consider my debt paid in full. Please don't contact me again. I never helped you."

Chris nodded. "We're square. And I don't have the slightest idea who you are."

Chris left the office, returned to his car and drove back to the motel. He'd grab his things and check out, then start the long drive back to Nebraska. He couldn't wait to start searching through the information Miles had given him. It was quite possible he'd just broken the case wide open.

He'd already known there were kills that fit the mold in California, Florida, Illinois, Massachusetts and New York over the past decade. The problem had been accounting for gaps in the timeline, but it sounded like Miles had uncovered more crimes that fit the bill, as well as some other survivors Chris could talk to. Best of all, he had potential suspects. He was holding a folder that very possibly contained the name of the man who'd killed them all. The name of the man who'd killed Tamara. The stalker was now being stalked.

Though he knew he was still a long way off from catching the serial killer, Chris had never been surer that he was on the right track. Once he was back in Omaha, he'd fill Hopkins in so they could get back to work. After they'd connected all the dots, Chris would need to decide when to inform his superiors about what he'd been doing. He could develop profiles and identify potential suspects, but without the resources of the Bureau there was no chance of catching the man.

Chris wondered if the killer knew he was being hunted, or if he even cared.

40

ASHLEY

The noises were confusing. She could hear heels on tiles, machines beeping, people talking and loudspeaker announcements. The cacophony of sound overwhelmed Ashley's senses, making her feel like she was in some sort of black, hazy, exhausting dream. The noises sounded distant, as if she were underwater. She'd listen for a few moments before falling asleep again. Each time she woke, the process would repeat. She lived it for what felt like an eternity.

Her vision was no help. A few times, she tried to blink but saw only black. It felt like there was a set of heavy weights sitting on top of each eyelid, locking them shut. She tried to speak, but her mouth was so dry she could only produce a strange, scratchy sound. The sum effect was that she felt drunk, insane, mute, deaf, and blind all at the same time.

Finally, Ashley managed to flick her eyes open briefly. The light felt like a spear to her skull and she quickly closed her eyes again. After a few more attempts, she eventually managed to keep them open, squinting painfully. Ashley still didn't know where she was, but the ceiling was white, and harsh fluorescent light beamed down on her. That narrowed down the options significantly. A hospital. Probably a hospital.

As she lay there, she grew certain that she was in a hospital. It felt like reaching that conclusion had taken an eternity. The next challenge was figuring how she'd gotten there. She remembered waking in confusion. Heat. Smoke. Flames. Sirens. It had all combined into a sensory assault like no other, coalescing into the certainty she was going to die.

"Ah, you're awake, Miss Wheeler." A nurse with a kind smile leaned over the bed and looked into Ashley's eyes. "How do you feel?"

Ashley tried to speak, but the same scratchy sound came out. She pointed a thumb toward her mouth. "Water?"

"Of course." The nurse smiled and reached for a cup next to the table. She handed it to Ashley and waited patiently as she sipped eagerly at the water.

"Thanks." The water was the best thing she'd ever tasted. Ashley swallowed a few more times, her mouth was still dry.

The nurse placed one hand on Ashley's forehead and the other on her hand. "You need to take it slowly. You're safe. It's okay."

Ashley's brow furrowed. "I remember a fire, but I don't remember escaping. How'd I get here?"

The nurse smiled. "Someone called 911. The firefighters got you out just in time. You're very lucky. You have minor burns, smoke inhalation, and a nasty head wound. We think you fell over and hit it on something. We've dosed you up with painkillers, dressed your wounds and treated the smoke inhalation. You're okay."

Tears began to streak down Ashley's cheeks. The nurse sat with her for several minutes, not speaking, just holding Ashley's hand. Ashley reached up and felt her face, careful not to dislodge the tubes feeding into her arm. Half her face was covered in gauze, and some of it in bandages. It seemed fitting, given that Ashley felt like she'd been smashed in the face by everything that had happened recently.

When Ashley's crying slowed from a torrent to a trickle, the nurse squeezed her hand. "It'll be okay," she said.

Ashley turned her head to face the nurse, embarrassed. "I just want to curl into a ball and sleep for a few days."

"This is a really expensive hotel, I'm afraid." The nurse smiled warmly. "We'll find you a cheaper one, but before that we need to do some more tests."

"Okay, I—"

"Plus, the police wanted us to call them as soon as you stirred. I'll let them know you're awake, if that's okay?"

Ashley wasn't in a hurry to speak with them, but she wanted to get it over with. She nodded at the nurse, who smiled once more as she left the room to collect the police. Once Ashley was alone again, she did her best to compose herself. She didn't mind the nurse witnessing her emotions, but the police were a different matter.

A few hours later, the detectives who'd questioned her about Jana's disappearance entered the room and approached the bed. Ashley suddenly wondered if the two things were related.

The younger detective staying back while the older one came closer and offered a sympathetic smile. "Ms Wheeler."

"Hello." Ashley didn't take her eyes off him. "Can you tell me what happened?" She was sure he knew something.

"We're almost certain the fire was deliberately lit." The older detective sat in the chair beside the bed with an exaggerated sigh. "It spread very quickly. We think some sort of accelerant was used. We should have a better idea in a day or so, when the experts tell us what happened."

Ashley felt as if someone had punched her in the stomach. Her heart was pounding. She'd preferred the feeling of helpless confusion to the complete certainty that had just hit her. "It's Laverri. It's the mob. They're getting back at me. First it was my boss, next it was my house."

The older detective shook his head. "We've no evidence of that. We know about your history and will be treating this matter seriously, but we're just not sure."

Ashley sat up in bed, a struggle with the drugs still in her system making her woozy. "I am."

"As a precaution, we've posted a uniformed officer to guard you in hospital and after you leave. It should be enough to ward off anyone who means you harm." The older detective paused, as if checking off a list in his head. "We can also have a social worker help you find you a new home, if you like."

Ashley stared at him. It was like he was mouthing the words; he didn't really seem to care about what he was saying. She knew it was the mob punishing her for being a witness. She'd been targeted for helping the cops, and now she was in danger. So was Lucy. Ashley had made a few gains, but the stability she'd gained recently was feeling shaky. She lay back down on the bed and turned her head. Eventually the detectives left.

There was only one person she could turn to for help. Most importantly, that person was close to Lucy. She reached for the hospital telephone, dialed the number from memory, and waited as it rang.

"Manny?"

"Who am I speaking to?" The voice of Special Agent Manuel Rodriguez was the most welcome sound she could imagine hearing right now.

"It's Ashley Wheeler," she sobbed. "I've been attacked. I need your help. I need you to check on Lucy."

41

DUNCAN

Duncan smiled as he flicked through Ashley Wheeler's photo album, thrilled to be sharing the intimate parts of her childhood. But the smile turned into a scowl as he pushed deeper into the album. He could tell she'd been pretty and popular at school and when she went to college, but that's where things had gone haywire. The shots showed her partying, hanging off men. They confirmed all his theories about her.

Then his eyes locked onto a photo he hadn't expected to see.

"Bitch."

He stared at the photo for almost a minute, but it felt like much longer. In it, Ashley was hanging off a man about her age, who was dressed like a bit of a loser and smiling like a cat that'd just caught a mouse. Duncan ground his teeth as he tried to imagine what the boy had been feeling. Pride? Pleasure? Fear? Disbelief? All of those, probably. He snarled as he pulled back the protective plastic that covered the photo, pulled out the shot, and stuffed it into his pocket. He'd keep it close.

He snapped the photo album shut firmly, breaking its spell. He clenched his teeth and looked at the roof of the trailer, sucking in and easing out a few deep breaths. He couldn't let himself get caught up in one item this much, given the treasure trove he'd uncovered at her house. He was still searching through it all. There was no password on her laptop or phone, so he had access to more information than he ever expected.

The early results were promising, though. The fact that she'd been in witness protection was probably the biggest surprise. The authorities had changed her name, and done everything they could to eradicate all signs of her online. That explained why Duncan's internet searches had turned up so little, a first in his experience. She'd been the witness to a mob case and until very recently had been completely off the grid. He now understood the case and her role in it, which gave him further clues about how to dismantle her.

Her lack of online presence was offset by the diary she kept, which he'd managed to swipe. It had helped him learn more about Ashley, including her family. Duncan found out that she'd been married and then divorced. The daughter – Lucy – was the product of that relationship and the subject of a custody battle. It amused him that they still shared a surname, assigned by the authorities as part of witness protection, no doubt.

What he'd learned, most of all, was how fucked in the head she was. He'd found that she was devoted to her daughter, above all else, and had done some reckless things because of that devotion. Most of all, he'd learned how unstable her mental state was, and how much work she'd put into fixing it over the past few months. This didn't change his course of action, but it did change some things.

Duncan knew he shouldn't do it. There'd been too many close calls lately – freezing in the store, almost being caught snooping near Ashley's house, hovering too long in her bedroom – and if he lost his composure, he was far more likely to make a mistake. But he couldn't help it. This woman was different. He didn't just want to take away the parts of her life that made it worth living, he wanted to become *part* of her story.

He wanted to be more than just the destroyer. He wanted her to need him.

The temptation was impossible to resist. He picked up the phone, found the number and dialed. With each ring his breath quickened and his heart beat faster. Finally, the phone stopped ringing and Duncan could hear muffled sounds from the other end.

Finally, a little girl spoke. "Hello. This's Lucy Wheeler speaking. How can I help you?"

"I—"

A lump caught in Duncan's throat. He'd gone blank. There was so much he wanted to say to this little spawn of evil, it seemed to assault his brain all at once. His face twisted into a snarl and he breathed heavily. For several seconds they shared an impasse, then the spell was broken. Another voice could be heard in the background. A man's voice. Tom Wheeler's voice, he assumed. The fool she'd sucked in.

"Daddy, they're not talking to me." The angst in Lucy Wheeler's voice was clear. Palpable. "What do I do?"

"Give the phone to me, honey." The man's voice was deep and laced with concern, becoming louder as he picked up the phone. "Who's this?"

Duncan snarled. If he'd been overwhelmed by speaking to the little girl, the second this man – this foolish imposter – picked up the phone, Duncan was blessed with singular clarity. He still didn't speak, but his teeth and lips clenched together, his breaths coming in forceful bursts. Duncan heard a sigh from the other end. Tom Wheeler kept speaking, but the words all blended into one as Duncan struggled to contain his anger. He tried to force it down, but like an untamable beast, it refused to be curtailed.

There was a sigh on the other end. "Look pal, if this is some sort of sick joke, it needs to stop. Don't call here again."

The line went dead. Duncan was breathing hard, as if he'd just gone for a brisk jog. He placed the phone down slowly on the table next to him, closed his eyes and tried to calm himself. It didn't work. His eyes shot open and he tossed the phone against the wall, smashing it into several pieces. He hadn't known much about Ashley Wheeler before, but now he knew all he needed to. She'd devastated him a decade ago, then gone on to get everything she ever wanted.

Now he was going to take it all away.

42

CHRIS

"I think it was worth calling in sick for all of this." Chris spread papers out over his desk and smiled at Hopkins.

"You sounded excited over the phone, that's for sure." Hopkins laughed, closed the door to Chris's office, then sat down opposite him. "What'd you find?"

"The Holy Grail." Chris tapped one pile of documents with his index finger. "This is the entire suspected chronology of our killer, from the first crime to the knife he put into my partner and everything in between. On top of that, we've got more potential survivors and a bunch of other leads to chase."

"Good thing you got that horrible flu." Hopkins smiled as she scanned the various piles. "What now?"

Chris crossed his arms. "Plenty. I have a list of women who may have crossed paths with the killer. Each was the victim of a lesser crime at the hands of a perp who fits the profile, was either a suspect or arrested, and has other point-in-time hits with our other cities and cases. We need to speak to the women and refine those results."

Hopkins looked up at Chris. "And figure out who has pole position in the murderer stakes?"

Chris nodded. "Precisely."

Hopkins whistled as her eyes continued to dance across the piles. "So we've at least twelve murders in California, Florida, Illinois, Massachusetts and New York locked in. Each fits the timeline and the profile. In the gaps, we've got two lesser crimes where both the victim and the attacker fit the profile."

Chris grinned. "And where a suspect was identified or arrested. If we figure out which of those more minor crimes were committed by our killer, we can link it all together."

"One sexual assault in California, a decade ago." Hopkins flicked through the relevant pages. "Another in Colorado."

"Miles was pretty sure one of those is our link and our guy." Chris let it hang in the air for a moment. "I'm thinking we might actually crack this damned thing."

Chris believed that for the first time in months. When he'd been staking out the homes of potential victims in New York City, he'd been acting blind and hoping for some luck. He'd had some, but then the killer had escaped anyway, costing Manny his health and Chris his career. With the help of Hopkins and Miles, he felt like he was finally on the cusp of catching this cockroach who'd kept a low profile and devastated women for a decade.

"In that case, Chris, I think we should tell the bosses and bring the rest of the Bureau in on this." She locked eyes with him and raised her eyebrows slightly. "I understand why you've had to freelance, and it's been great to work with you on this, but if we want to actually catch the guy and lock him up, we have to do it properly."

"Not a chance."

She frowned. "Chris, I covered for your absence and I've put my own career at risk to help you. We've done great work building a case, now we need to share it."

Chris repeated himself. "No, I—"

She held up a hand. "If you won't do it, I will. We need to rejoin the fold or else we're going to lose the killer, and probably our jobs."

Chris's mouth opened, but he bit back the words. He needed to keep her on side, and keep his superiors in the dark. He was about to respond to plead with her to keep their secret, when his cell phone started to ring. His eyes narrowed when he saw the caller ID. "I need to take this. Can you just give me a couple of days before you tell anyone?"

"A couple of days. No problem." Her look suggested there was a problem, but she stood and left the room without a word.

Chris waited until he was alone and then answered the call. He'd never really expected to hear from this person again. "Hi Manny."

"Chris." The other man's voice was cold and distant. "I hope things are going well in Nebraska?"

Chris faked a laugh. "Well, the Cornhuskers won a few days back, and I haven't been fired yet, so it's not all bad."

There was a pause. "Chris, I don't want things to stay the way they are between us. I forgive you, okay?"

Chris was stunned by his former partner's words. As he'd made his way to Nebraska, Manny had still been sedated in hospital. He hadn't seen his friend since the stabbing, nor had they spoken. In the one message they'd shared, Manny had made it clear they would never speak again, and that he blamed Chris for ruining his career. Manny still hadn't returned to active duty, so it was no surprise the man held a grudge.

"Chris, are you there?" Manny's voice was concerned now, insistent. "Look, I—"

"I'm here Manny." Chris interrupted. "I'm just surprised."

"It's time, Chris. You can't go through what we've been through and stay mad for long." Manny sighed. "Besides, I need a favor, if you're up for it."

If Manny was extending the hand of friendship, Chris was ready to take it. "You name it."

"Remember that woman we pulled out of NYPD custody and drove to the meeting with Ben Obrist?" Manny paused. "She called me up asking for help. I think she's got the mob on her ass in a pretty bad way. It looks like they torched her house. She was in hospital for a few days with minor burns."

Chris remembered the woman, though her name escaped him. She'd reminded him of his killer's victims. "Sure, I remember. She's important to you."

"I'm worried about her, Chris. She's a good lady, but the system has fucked her badly." Manny sighed. "She wants someone to talk to. I've checked on her daughter here in New York and she's fine, but I need someone to meet with her and make sure the local cops are doing all they can to keep her safe. I'd go, but I can't because of my rehab."

"I'll do it." Chris knew he'd have to take some more time off, but it was a small price for his friend's forgiveness. "What's her name, and where is she?"

"She's in Wallingford, Connecticut." Manny laughed as he said it. "Picturesque, I hear, but not much else. I'll send you her address. Her name is Ashley Wheeler."

Chris's eyes narrowed. Manny kept speaking, but Chris wasn't listening. He jammed the phone between his ear and his shoulder, then used both hands to sort through the papers on his desk. Ashley Wheeler. The name rang a bell. He searched his memory, sure he'd heard it recently. Finally, with Manny still speaking in his ear, he found it.

He tapped his index finger down on the name hard. Ashley Wheeler. She was one of the sexual assault victims Miles had suggested he track down. She'd been assaulted in California almost a decade ago. She fit the victim profile, and the man who'd attacked her matched the killer's profile. She'd had her surname changed by witness protection. Miles had noted that down, too.

Was it possible this woman could hold the key to everything?

"I'll give her a call and check it out, Manny."

43

ASHLEY

"Four bucks for a Coke, can you believe it?" Ashley held up the can to the police officer. "Damn minibars. I can get a gallon for half the price across the road."

The officer didn't smile. "I'd prefer you stayed in your room, Ms Wheeler. That includes going to the store."

Ashley nodded and cracked the can. As she took a sip, the officer turned and walked outside, his hourly check on her complete. She waved with a sigh as the door closed behind him. The routine had been completed on the hour, every hour, for the past few days. It was almost like being in the hospital, though in place of the cheery but overworked nurses she'd been given the grumpiest police officer in Connecticut. She returned to the bed to resume the terrible romantic comedy she'd been watching when the cop had interrupted her.

Still, it wasn't all bad. At least she was out of the hospital, and there was a uniformed police officer posted on the front door of her motel. She hadn't wanted to go to the motel, but she didn't have much of a choice now that her house was gone.

Thankfully, the police had spoken to a local charity and they'd picked up the bill, or else she'd be on the street. Until the insurance payment from the fire came through she'd have no money or belongings, but at least she had a roof over her head and felt safe.

Feeling safe didn't mean feeling good, however. The cops didn't seem to believe that Laverri had started the fire, so she'd called FBI Agent Manuel Rodriguez and asked for help. She'd told him what had happened and her theories about the cause, then asked him for help and to make sure Lucy was okay. Though he'd told her he'd check on Lucy, he'd sounded pained when he told her he couldn't leave the city to help her.

He'd called back a day later, telling her to expect a call from his former partner, FBI Agent Chris Horan. Ashley wasn't comfortable with the compromise, but she hadn't told Manny that. Unsure if she'd answer when Agent Horan phoned her, she'd thought hard about it for hours before the call came in. Manny vouched for Horan, but Ashley remembered the man vividly. He'd been an asshole when they'd met.

A day later, Chris Horan had called, and it had gone surprisingly well. Ashley had confided in him about her fears and her theories, and he'd offered to come to Connecticut to see her. She was meeting him in five minutes. Or now – there was a knock on the door. Ashley took another sip of her Coke, turned off the TV and stood. She ran a hand over her clothes, keeping her eyes on the door. She could hear the cop out front speaking to the new arrival and then radioing the visit in. Finally, the door opened.

"Ms Wheeler?" Horan gave a weary smile. "I'm Chris Horan. I'm not sure if you remember me."

Ashley kept her face neutral as she moved toward him and

extended her hand. "I remember you. Manny speaks highly of you."

"Manny speaks highly of everyone." Horan laughed as he reached out to shake her hand. "But I'm sorry about my behavior the last time we met."

Ashley involuntarily cracked a small smile. "Well, you were helping Manny get me out of a holding cell, so who am I to judge?"

"We'll call it even, then." He placed his bag on the ground. "I'm sorry you've been through such an ordeal. Manny told me about it. I'll do my best to help you."

Ashley nodded and gestured him over to the small table next to the television. She offered him a Coke, which he took her up on. Once they were settled, she began to detail the attacks on her boss and her house. He listened intently to her entire explanation, and didn't even interrupt when she told him who she thought was behind the attacks. It was nice to meet a cop who listened. Only once she'd finished did he speak.

"I think there's more to it than you suspect, Ashley." Horan stood, walked to his bag and pulled out a manila folder. "I'd like you to look at this."

Ashley's eyes narrowed as he opened the folder and spread its contents on the small table. He placed a photo on top. It felt like an ambush. "I don't understand."

"I've been investigating a series of crimes I believe started with an assault in California." He tapped the photo. "Did this man attack you?"

Ashley's focus narrowed, until there was nothing in the world but the man in the photo. That man had altered the course of her life. "Yes."

His eyes widened. There was a spark in them that

reminded her of the night the man had attacked her. The night she'd recognized his obsession with her, and the danger he posed. Horan wanted something, Ashley was sure, but it wasn't her. His spark seemed reserved for her attacker. "What happened?" he asked.

"That's not easy to answer." Ashley's voice was soft. "He was just a normal guy, maybe a little bit weird. We worked together and he asked me out. I felt sorry for him, so I agreed to get dinner with him."

The memories she'd suppressed for nearly a decade came flooding back. The awkward meal, spent mostly in silence. The regret she felt half-way through the meal, kicking herself for agreeing to go out with him. The tense car ride home. Her feeling of unease as his hand rested on her thigh, and her panic once she realized what he was after. He'd seemed like a normal guy, but after a few hours he'd started to make her skin crawl. He'd done nothing but stare at her. None of the signals she gave off worked – removing his hand from her leg, crossing her arms, staring out the window – and she'd started to panic.

Her face twisted into a grimace and her sobs turned to tears. "I told him I wanted to go home, but he pulled the car over anyway. He touched me. The more I pushed him away, the more aggressive he got. He grabbed my hair and pulled me closer, but I fought back and ran."

Horan placed a hand on her shoulder. "It's okay, Ashley. That's enough. I just need to know if he attacked you."

"He did more than that!" she shouted. "I ran and he chased me. I hid in the bushes while he shouted threats and abuse. He stalked me for hours. Shouting, kicking the bushes, trying to find me. I didn't move an inch. I barely breathed. When he eventually left, I called the police. They didn't help me. He kept trying to find me, so I left the state."

"And the man in the photo is the man who attacked you?" Chris pushed the photo closer to her. "You're sure?"

"That's him." Her voice was a hiss. "Why'd you bring this file here? What's that attack got to do with anything? I asked for help, not an interrogation. I'd like you to leave."

Horan stayed seated. "I'm sorry to dredge up painful memories, Ashley, but there's a fairly good chance this man is a serial killer."

"Of course he is, because my life isn't fucked up enough already." Ashley shook her head. "Look, I appreciate you coming, but I told the police everything I knew years ago. I thought you were here to talk about my safety, not dredge up the past. Things are bad enough as it is without going back over all of that. I just want to leave it alone."

Horan persisted. "I believe he's killed twelve women in the past decade. First he dismantles the lives of his victims – career, friends, family, pets, finances – and then finally, he kills them. Each victim had red hair, was about your height and weight, and had some terrible things happen to them in the weeks before their death."

"Like—" Ashley stammered.

"Like a fire at their house."

Ashley's mouth fell open. She reached for the photo in a daze. She thought hard, searching for a link between her past and her present. A second later, she dropped the Coke and it fell to the floor. "Fucking hell. That's him. I can't believe it, but that's him."

Horan leaned in, ignoring the Coke spilling across the floor. "What do you mean?"

"That's him. That's the guy who killed my boss."

44

DUNCAN

Duncan smiled as he caught a glimpse of Ashley Wheeler through the window of the motel room. Though he didn't stop driving, and she was only visible for a second, it was long enough for him to confirm she was still there. He'd done a similar check every day since she'd left the hospital. Now that he'd finally found her, he wasn't going to lose her again. The only risk was the cop standing beside her door, yet Duncan was confident a man who looked that bored wouldn't notice him.

Once he was past the motel, he sped up until it was a mile behind him. Only then did he remove his dark glasses and baseball cap and toss them onto the seat beside him. He was pleased she was still in place, that the situation was still under his control.

It took him about twenty minutes to drive back to his trailer. As usual, he checked it from end-to-end to make sure it hadn't been disturbed. Satisfied that the trailer was untouched, he mustered up some candy and then sat in the trailer's dining booth with a smile. As he snacked, he took notes on everything he'd seen at the motel, adding to those he'd already scribbled down or typed into his laptop. He found the files helped him remember details and assisted in identifying the things that needed to be taken away from his target. For some women it was obvious, but for others it was considerably less so.

Duncan had been watching Ashley for days. First in the hospital, where he'd stolen a nurse's uniform from a locker, using the disguise to get close to Ashley and check her medical charts. He was glad she hadn't been seriously injured in the fire. It hadn't been his intention to hurt her – not yet – but the fire had been necessary to scare her and to cover up the theft of the things he'd taken from her house.

He'd already taken away her job and her home, the two things she seemed to draw her sense of security from. On top of that, he'd worked hard to scare her, to make her know she was being targeted. The trap was already sprung, but she didn't even realize it yet. He wanted to take this one slowly. He wanted her to feel every ounce of pain and loss, to learn how it felt to be utterly devastated by another person. Only then would her pain be sufficient. Then it would be time to end her.

Once she'd left the hospital, he'd followed the car that had taken her to the motel, less than two blocks from the hospital. The lack of security the local police department had deployed to protect her was almost criminal. Not that he was complaining. Duncan closed his eyes, trying to think of anything he'd forgotten from his latest visit to her motel room. Even the smallest details could matter.

When he was sure he'd taken it all down, he put down the pen, picked up his cell phone and dialed a number he'd written on a scrap of paper. As it rang, he heard a meowing sound from down near his feet. Without looking, he reached down and patted Ashley's cat. It had been homeless after her place had burned down. He'd claimed it from the pound, telling them he was Ashley's boyfriend. They'd been glad to have one less animal on their hands.

"L'uccellino Pizza and Pasta." A sweet-sounding woman answered the phone. "You're speaking with Jane, would you mind holding the line?"

"Sure, I'll hold." Duncan injected as much kindness into his voice as possible. He was about to ask for something highly unusual.

Finally, after a few moments and some terrible hold music, the woman picked up the call. "Thanks for waiting, sir, how can I help you?"

Duncan smiled. "Well, you see, it's coming up on my anniversary and I was hoping to get one of your delicious chocolate cakes."

"Of course, sir, we offer pick-up or we can deliver on the Island, but there's a five-dollar surcharge."

"I was hoping for something a little bit more long-distance than that... Connecticut." Duncan winced as he waited for the response. "I'm prepared to pay."

"Hold again, please. I need to speak with the manager."

As hold music again filled his ear, Duncan hoped she would agree. He'd pay almost anything to get this particular cake delivered. Usually he focused on taking things away from his targets. In Ashley Wheeler's case, though, he'd decided on an expanded approach. Ashley's identity was so intertwined with her past, he had decided to do something he'd never done before, dredging up something from her past.

Finally, the woman on the other end of the phone spoke.

"We can send the cake, sir, but I can't guarantee it'll survive the journey, or be as fresh as we'd like."

Duncan grinned. He didn't think Ashley would eat the cake, nor did he care if she did. "That's fine. I'd also like a special message with it."

"Of course, sir. We can either include a card inside the box or write the message on the cake itself."

"Perfect."

45

CHRIS

C hris shook himself out of his trance-like focus and looked up to see Hopkins leaning against his doorframe. "What'd you say?"

She smiled and placed a hand on her hip. "I said I'm going to go get lunch, and asked if you wanted to join me."

"Oh, no. Thanks." Chris shook his head, glanced at the clock and rubbed his eyes. "Sorry, I'm just going over my notes from the meeting with Ashley Wheeler. I'm almost certain she was the first target of our killer. I don't know if he would have killed her that night if she hadn't escaped, but she was a victim. The attacker profile fits, the victim profile fits, the timing fits."

She nodded. "And it feels right, doesn't it?"

"Yep." Chris smiled and rubbed at his face. "And if it all works out we'll have him cold."

"Just remember our deal. You've got two days to tell Harvey about our progress or I will."

Chris was about to argue, but she'd already left his office.

He'd bought some extra time, which had given him the breathing space to follow up more leads, meet with Ashley Wheeler and form a working theory, but the clock was ticking. He needed more time.

With a sigh, he looked back down at his computer, still hoping he could change her mind. If management got hold of the work he'd done then it'd be wasted, disregarded in the race to jettison him. He hoped he could convince Hopkins to reconsider, or at least convince her to give him more time. He'd begun to regret letting her in on the case at all. She'd gone from being a great asset to a potential thorn in his side, but there was no way to unscramble that egg.

Chris looked up again as he heard a woman clear her throat. He was about to tell Hopkins to go get her lunch when the words caught in his mouth. "I—"

His boss, Tony Harvey, stood in his doorway alongside a woman and a man who Chris didn't recognize. They all wore serious expressions, and the woman held a clear plastic folder with some documents inside. Without being invited, they stepped inside and closed the door. Chris didn't know what was happening, but he had a fair suspicion. This felt a lot like he'd eaten his final meal and was about to be led to the galleys. Chris gestured for them to sit, and started neatening up the stacks of paper on his desk.

"Agent Horan." Harvey spoke first. "I hope we're not interrupting anything too urgent? I know you're supposed to run a briefing tonight."

"That's the plan, sir." Chris closed his laptop. "Is there some way I can help you guys?"

"This is Trish Worthington, she's from IT. And Dean Nelson, from Human Resources." Harvey gestured at his female companion. "We need to speak to you."

"Nice to meet you all," Chris lied.

Harvey sighed. "Chris, I'm afraid there have been some fairly serious accusations leveled against Agent Hopkins. Computer records show she's been accessing files related to a number of murders you worked on during your time in the New York office. We can't explain it, so we thought we'd speak to you first."

Chris's mind raced. He couldn't believe Hopkins had been so sloppy. Early on in their collaboration he'd told her the hard limits on the Bureau's IT systems, the lines she had to avoid crossing. She obviously hadn't listened and had chased something too hard, flagging her activity. Once that happened, it wouldn't have taken Harvey long to figure out what she'd been up to and, probably, whom she'd been doing it with.

She was fucked. He probably was too.

Chris had only one chance – play dumb. "What's that have to do with me, sir? I've done nothing but community briefings in my entire time here."

Harvey sighed. "Chris, we've gone back over your recent records too. You and Hopkins have both been looking through files related to murders all around the country, and particularly several you worked on during your time in New York. Though only Hopkins' searches raised flags, you're both implicated."

Chris raised his eyebrows. "Implicated in what, exactly? It's not a crime to access Bureau records relating to cases I've worked on. It's not like the community briefings keep me very busy. What do you expect me to do all day? As far as I can see, neither Hopkins or I have done anything illegal by accessing the files of any murder I've worked on."

"Wrong." The woman from IT spoke for the first time, then flicked through her papers and placed a single sheet down on his desk. "Hopkins accessed a restricted file on Ashley Wheeler, a witness in a high-profile mob case. This is a serious matter. It could cost her career, unless there's some other explanation."

Chris kept silent, staring back and forth between them. Finally, Harvey sighed and asked the others to leave. Chris kept his face impassive as they argued for a few moments then left the room in a huff.

Harvey took a seat opposite Chris. The two of them sat in silence for several moments, then Harvey reached out and started to flick through some of the documents on Chris's desk. Though he could close the lid on his laptop, Chris couldn't hide the dozens of documents that proved his ongoing interest in the killer.

"You're right in saying you've done nothing wrong, but Hopkins is in deep shit. She's got no cover on this." Harvey sighed. "Are you really going to sit here and tell me you didn't tell her to access those files, Chris? You've put me in an impossible bind."

"I've done nothing of the sort." Chris paused. He had to ask the question. "But if I were to admit to it, what would the consequences be for both of us?"

"Hopkins would be fine. You'd be canned." Harvey's voice was full of venom. "You've had a warning already, followed by a re-posting. I know it was you. Admit it, Chris, and then go away."

Chris had a choice to make. Though they knew the serial killer theory was his, he had an excuse for looking up the files, and had done nothing wrong in doing so. Hopkins had no such cover. He could either take the bullet, protecting her and accepting responsibility, or he could lie. If she wore the accusation, it'd be a terrible blot against her record, and would likely prevent her from advancing very far for the foreseeable future.

He made his decision. He'd come too close to catching the killer to blow his chances now. "I've done nothing wrong. I accessed the files of some old cases, but I haven't influenced Hopkins in any way. I'm clean."

"You're nothing of the kind." Harvey scowled and stood. "You've damaged the career of one of my best young agents. You'll need to live with that."

Chris kept silent as Harvey left the room, slamming the door behind him. He swung back on his chair and stared at the ceiling, wondering if he'd made the right decision. He'd pushed Hopkins on top of the grenade to save his own skin – and more importantly, to save any chance of catching the killer. He hated to admit it, but her threat to reveal their shadow investigation to Harvey had influenced his decision.

There was another knock on the door. Chris sighed. His breath caught in his throat, then he composed himself. "Justine, I—"

"I just saw Harvey on my way back from lunch." The tears streaked down her face as she stared at him, the food in her hand seemingly forgotten. "You make a habit of ruining those who help you, don't you Chris? I'm not sure you're any better than the killer you're chasing. The only difference is you leave your victims alive."

The words were like a blow to the stomach. He knew there was some truth to them. "I–"

"Save it, Chris. I'm done."

46

ASHLEY

"I'm fine, Lucy, I promise." Ashley placed a hand on her daughter's shoulder, crouching down so she was at Lucy's eye level. "There's no need to be upset."

Ashley hated lying to her daughter, but what else could she say? That her mommy had been home when some of the nastiest criminals in America set her house alight? That those same criminals lived in the same city as Lucy? She'd told Tom the truth and they'd agreed their daughter didn't need to know. As far as their family unit was concerned, the house fire that had nearly killed her was a terrible accident. It was easier for everyone.

Tom had finally agreed to bring Lucy for a visit after the fire and Ashley's time in hospital. The minute Ashley had opened the door, Lucy had rushed to hug her and hadn't let go for several minutes, no matter how much tickling Ashley had inflicted. Her daughter hadn't even asked about the cop standing guard out front. They'd talked about what had happened and, after Ashley had promised Lucy she was fine, the little girl had started to cry.

"Are you going to be okay now?" Lucy had stopped trembling, but she was still teary. "Is there someone trying to hurt you?"

"I'm okay." Ashley smiled, pulling Lucy in close for a hug. "Now, you need to eat that chocolate before the chocolate monster eats it all!"

Lucy giggled, but didn't move out of her arms. After another second, Ashley let go and Lucy ran over to the coffee table where she'd left the chocolate bar. Ashley watched, an indulgent smile on her face, as Lucy ripped open the wrapper and bit off far too much for a small mouth to chew. Then Ashley stalked forward with exaggerated movements, growling as she imitated the threatened chocolate monster. Lucy squealed and stuffed more chocolate into her mouth.

"The chocolate monster is going to get you!" Ashley spoke in her deepest voice. "You better watch out!"

"No!" Lucy squealed again, her laughs mixing with the last of the sobs as she tried to escape Ashley's grasp.

"Got you!" Ashley scooped Lucy up, swinging her around as they both laughed loudly. "Now, give up your chocolate!"

"No! I—"

A knock on the door penetrated their fragile bubble. Ashley looked at the door, waiting for the cop outside to enter. She stood frozen in place, until there was another knock. She placed Lucy down on the floor, walked to the door and peered through the peephole. A man who looked like a courier stood there, looking completely disinterested as he waited. Ashley assumed the cop had checked him out, so she opened the door.

"Hello," Ashley addressed the courier, then turned and looked at the cop who stood nearby. "Is it all good?"

"He checks out, Ms Wheeler." The police officer offered Ashley a nod. "I've checked his identification and the package. It's just a cake. I thought your girl could use a treat."

"Thanks." Ashley frowned, a bit unsure by what the officer meant, then turned her attention back to the courier. "How can I help you?"

The courier held out a box, which had a clipboard on top of it. "I just need you to sign there."

Ashley had no idea what the package could be, but she signed and took possession of it regardless. She thanked the courier and carried the box inside, closing the door behind her. The package was about the size of a shoebox, and wasn't overly heavy. Ashley had never been a prolific shopper, and nobody knew she was here at the motel, which made her very suspicious. As she placed the box down on the small dining table, Lucy came over, curious.

"What is it?" Lucy grabbed at Ashley's hand and squeezed it tightly, standing on her tiptoes to stare at the box.

"I don't know, honey." Ashley started opening the box with her free hand and then paused as soon as she saw what was inside. "Get us a soda while I open it?"

"Okay!" Lucy beamed. She let go of Ashley's hand and ran into the small kitchenette, where there was a bar fridge filled with expensive minibar soda.

Ashley opened the box with some trepidation. Inside the courier's box was a second box, one with a decorative pattern and a restaurant name on it. The moment she read the name, Ashley tensed up. She didn't want to open the box, but she had to find out what was inside. All the strange things in her life at the moment pointed to the mob, yet Chris Horan had a different theory. She wasn't sure which was true, but this parcel seemed to suggest the former.

The box was from the restaurant where she used to work. The restaurant where she'd seen Saul Laverri shoot Flavio Grossi.

With a shaking hand, Ashley opened the box. There was a chocolate cake inside. It didn't look very special, but the writing on it told Ashley all she needed to know. It simply said her name. Not her witness protection name, her real name.

The officer on the door had clearly felt like it was an innocent gift, but Ashley knew better. The mob had figured out where she was hiding after they'd torched her house.

"What's wrong?" Lucy returned to Ashley's side, holding out the soda for her mother to open.

"Nothing honey." Ashley reached down and scooped up Ashley in a hug. "Nothing at all. Everything is going to be great."

As she hugged her daughter, Ashley's bottom lip quivered. The man who'd attacked her a decade ago was back on the scene, and now she was faced with Laverri's revenge as well? It didn't seem fair.

She had to fight. There was no other way to make sure the threat was dealt with, and that Lucy was safe. She'd tried taking Lucy, she'd tried hiding in Wallingford, she'd tried letting the police deal with it, but none of those things had worked. Worse, some of her actions had harmed Lucy, the most important thing in her life.

Now her daughter was in danger. Ashley needed to be strong. She decided then that she wouldn't see her daughter again until it was safe. She'd help Horan find the man who'd attacked her so many years ago and deal with him, then she'd figure out what to do about Laverri.

Until then, she wouldn't see Lucy. It wasn't safe.

47

DUNCAN

"Two hundred people dead." Duncan shook his head as his eyes scanned the newspaper story. "Can you believe it?"

"It's crazy. The whole world has gone to shit." The waitress chimed in, wiping the table in front of him. "Can I get you anything else, honey?"

Duncan shook his head and looked up at her with a smile. "I'll just get the check while I finish my paper, if that's okay?"

"Take your time, we're not pressed for tables." The waitress smiled back, then moved away to collect the check.

Duncan took a sip of his coffee, then turned the page in his newspaper. He wasn't really reading it. Instead, he was imagining Ashley Wheeler's reaction when the cake he'd ordered from her old workplace arrived. It should've been delivered about an hour ago. He'd reintroduced fear into her life, now he was going to take something else away from her.

After another sip of coffee, Duncan glanced toward the stairs that led down to the bathroom, where a man had just disappeared from sight. Duncan stood, rolled the newspaper under his arm and placed a twenty on the table. He looked around, making sure everything was as it should be, then he took the stairs, rolling the newspaper carefully as he did. He folded the rolled-up newspaper in two, then clutched it tightly.

It'd hit like a brick. He was counting on it.

He stopped briefly outside the male and female bathrooms, listening for any sound from the latter. After a few seconds, he was convinced it was quiet enough to proceed. He started to whistle as he pushed open the door to the men's, moved to the urinal and stood beside the other man. Duncan didn't unzip, he just whistled and clutched the paper until the man looked sideways at him.

"Can I help you, pal?" The man spoke in a New York accent. "Are you some kind of freak?"

Duncan turned his head slowly. He clenched the newspaper tightly, then smiled at Tom Wheeler.

"Yes."

As Wheeler frowned at him and started to put his dick away, Duncan turned and brought the newspaper up in an arc, swinging it in one smooth motion. The overhand blow smashed Wheeler in the side of the head. Wheeler grunted, reeling from the blow. Staggering back, he reached up, instinctively trying to shield his head against another blow.

But Duncan didn't give him a chance to regain his composure. He pressed forward, hitting him again and again. It was only after the third blow that Wheeler put up his fists and readied himself to fight back. He'd planned to kill Tom Wheeler, but Duncan suddenly had a strong desire to fight this man. He wanted to prove he was better, more powerful. He'd prove that he was the one who should've had Ashley by besting the man she'd chosen instead.

Duncan tossed the paper onto the bathroom floor and raised his fists. He wasn't much of a fighter, but Tom Wheeler didn't look to be at his best. He was unsteady on his feet, swaying as he stepped forward. Wheeler threw a punch, a straight right jab, and Duncan flinched backward. The punch hit Duncan in the chest, but it had very little force behind it.

As Wheeler's arm drew back, Duncan stepped forward. He brought his right fist around with as much power as he could and clipped Wheeler in the jaw. His already shaky opponent's eyes went glassy and he dropped to the tiled floor. As the other man's head hit the tiles, Duncan gave him a vicious kick in the midsection. Bloodied and dazed, Wheeler tried to curl himself up to protect against the kicks Duncan was laying into him.

Duncan leaned over Wheeler, breathing heavily, until his face was only inches away from the other man's stunned, bloodied face. "I win."

"Please, take my wallet and phone, just leave me alone." Wheeler spat out the blood in his mouth. "I've got a little girl."

Duncan smiled as he gave Wheeler another vicious kick to the mid-section. "I know. Lucy is next."

Wheeler's eyes widened, despite the pain. He gave a guttural growl, struggling back to his hands and knees. Duncan smiled and took a step back as his opponent staggered to his feet. It took around fifteen seconds for him to rise. Duncan didn't think it'd take long for him to fall again. He took another step back, reaching into his pocket and then thrusting his hand forward just as Tom Wheeler ran at him.

Whatever Wheeler had been trying to do failed. Duncan's knife penetrated his body, driven deep by Wheeler's own momentum. Duncan pulled the blade out, admiring the look of shock on Wheeler's face and the slick of red blood on the blade. He thrust it forward again and again, stabbing Tom

Wheeler several times. Wheeler fell after the first few thrusts, and Duncan fell to his knees and kept the assault going.

He stabbed Wheeler so many times he lost count. Once he was done, Duncan stood up, heaving for breath as the red fury in his vision started to clear. He looked down at Wheeler – lifeless, bloody and pathetic – and felt like a god. He'd come here to kill Wheeler quietly and quickly, but had been sucked into a street fight. He'd wanted to prove he was the more powerful of the two of them, and that Wheeler was pathetic.

He'd done it. The man who'd married, fucked and impregnated Ashley Wheeler was dead.

Duncan turned his back on Wheeler, done with the man. He unzipped the jacket he'd been wearing and tossed it to the floor, then checked himself in the mirror. There was a lot of blood on the jacket, but not much left on him. Duncan didn't mind. There were no cameras, and he'd be gone before anyone found Wheeler.

As he prepared to leave the bathroom, Duncan smiled. Now that he'd taken away Ashley's ex-husband, it was almost inevitable she'd get her daughter back. He'd give her back the most important thing in her world, then he'd take it away again.

Duncan exited the bathroom, climbed the stairs and left the diner with a wide smile on his face. His smile vanished entirely when he saw her. "No!"

It was Ashley Wheeler. With her daughter, and a police officer alongside her.

Duncan froze. They weren't meant to be here. His pleasure at Wheeler's execution vanished and his mind was overcome with a haze. He knew he should get away from there, but he was frozen, in disbelief and anger.

His indecision cost him dearly. As Ashley and her

daughter drew closer, it was too late for him to move. He locked eyes with her.

He saw recognition hit her like a lightning bolt. She had already looked stressed, but the look on her face changed to pure terror. Despite his beard, her eyes seemed to bore right through to his identity. He wasn't ready for her to know yet. He was supposed to be destroying her from the shadows, but here she was, shining a light in his face. She knew who he was and what he was.

He hadn't planned for things to go this way, but he had no choice but to adapt. He was good at that. He smiled at her, turned, and walked away.

48

CHRIS

C hris flashed his FBI badge at the cop posted on the door, who took a second too long in checking his identification. It made him nervous. "Is there a problem?"

"No problem." The officer was an older man with a heavy paunch and the look of someone who'd seen too much. "I just need to check my list."

Chris took a step back, letting the officer go through his process. He should be on the list, but even if there'd been some error, he was sure he could talk his way inside. He'd driven from Omaha to Wallingford, Connecticut after getting a call from Ashley Wheeler begging him to come and see her. He wasn't sure it was a good idea to be here, but here he was.

It wasn't like he had anything else to do. He'd thought he was in the clear after dropping Hopkins in hot water, but his superiors had concocted some story about him engaging in improper conduct. As a result, the Bureau had placed Chris on paid leave. He'd called the union. They'd advised him to sit on the bench voluntarily and that it would take some time for him to be reinstated.

He'd decided to go all in, committing himself fully to finding the killer. He'd catch his man or be ruined trying.

"You're good to go, sir." The officer stepped aside from the door and gestured for him to enter.

"Thanks." Chris smiled at the officer and then stepped inside. When he saw Ashley, he held out a plastic bag. "I got you some stuff."

She nodded her thanks and glanced into the bag, taking in the treats he'd brought her, as well as bread, milk, and necessities. It was a small gesture that he hoped might pay a larger dividend later. She looked like she needed it. She looked devastated.

"Lucy is asleep." Ashley sat on the sofa with a sigh, gesturing for Chris to sit beside her. "Thanks for coming. I feel like you're the only person listening to me right now."

Chris sat. "It's fine, honestly. I've got plenty of time all of a sudden, and I'm happy to help. Tell me what happened."

Ashley frowned, clearly wondering whether to ask about his troubles, but she left it alone. "I was here with Lucy, my daughter, when a cake arrived. It had been couriered from the restaurant where I saw Laverri murder the other guy. My old name was written on the cake, the one I had prior to entering witness protection."

Chris didn't like where this was heading. "I—"

"There's more." She tensed up. "I thought it was Laverri. I was convinced. I told myself Lucy had to go back to New York with her father while I figured it out. I took Lucy to meet my ex-husband at a diner. There was a cop with us. That's when I saw him."

Chris frowned. "Saw who? Your ex-husband?"

"Duncan Rowe." She locked eyes on him. They were full of fear and grief. "The man in the photo. The man who attacked me in California, the one who you think is a killer."

Chris's eyes widened. He didn't want to ask the next question, but he had no choice. "Are you sure? You've had a lot on your plate recently, so it'd be quite easy for your mind to play tricks."

"I'm sure, Chris!" Ashley pounded her fist against the arm of the sofa. "I was totally convinced it was the mob – my boss, the fire, the cake – and then I saw that man for the first time in a decade. The mob might still be after me for all I know, but your killer is definitely in Wallingford."

Chris did his best to keep his composure, though his mind was swimming. If Ashley was right and Duncan Rowe was in town, it was only a matter of time before he struck. Though the attacks on her life had been explained away as mob-related, Chris was sure the killer was behind everything Ashley had endured recently. It fit the pattern – dismantle her life before ending it – but he had no proof, other than the pattern he'd seen before.

The pattern that had resulted in twelve dead women.

"It wasn't the mob. It was all him." Ashley sobbed. "I remembered what you said about him attacking people in strange ways. It makes sense."

"I—"

"That's when they found Tom, my ex-husband." Ashley put her face in her hands. "He'd been beaten and stabbed to death in that same diner."

"Ashley, I..." Chris sighed and ran his hand through his hair. "This guy won't stop at that, though. You and your daughter won't be safe until we catch him."

"I know that." She sobbed. "I don't want Lucy to get hurt."

"She won't. Trust me." Chris placed a hand on her shoulder. "I'll do whatever it takes to catch this killer. You can rely on me."

"How can I trust you?" Ashley shook her head, still sobbing, then stood and walked to the window.

Chris watched her clench her fists by her sides and imagined the thoughts that must be rushing through her head. He was always intrigued by the psychology of victims, people who'd had their ordinary lives interrupted by extraordinary events, but this was quite different. This was a woman who had the choice to run or to fight for her life. The only way she was going to fight was if she had a guarantee that it would be over.

It would be finished.

Chris stood and walked to the window, standing a few steps back from her. "Ashley, this guy killed my girlfriend. Tamara. I've given up my whole life and my career to find him. If you help me, I promise you that I'll catch him. I'll end him. No matter what it takes, this will be finished."

She didn't respond for a long time, then she clenched her fists tighter. "It's the only way my daughter will be safe, isn't it?"

"Yes."

"Okay." Ashley nodded. "Only if he ends up dead, though. I don't trust the justice system."

Chris should have seen that coming, given her history with the courts and law enforcement. She was forcing a choice he'd probably already made. "I will kill him."

When she nodded, Chris felt a wave of relief wash over him, but it was quickly replaced by a burning shame. He knew he was using her to catch the killer, to avenge Tamara's death and salve his own wounds. If he made a mistake, she could end up dead, but that seemed to be a risk he was willing to take. He wondered, briefly, if there was anything he wouldn't do in order to catch the man who'd cost so many so much. Who'd cost *him* so much.

He didn't think there was.

ACT III

Act III

49

ASHLEY

A shley sat on the bed, clasping her hands tightly together to stop them shaking. She knew Chris Horan was watching her, leaning against the wall with his arms crossed, but she didn't care. She needed a moment to compose herself. There was so much in her head – grief, fear, regret – she couldn't process it all.

"It's going to be okay." Horan spoke softly, staying where he was. "We're going to get him, then you'll be safe."

Ashley squeezed her eyes shut and nodded. The deal with Horan was her only hope now. She'd agreed to act as bait to catch the killer. They both knew what they were doing was risky, but Ashley didn't care. She'd already lost too much. At least this way she was gambling to win a life and a future for herself and her daughter. It'd be a future free of fear. That prize was worth any risk.

Horan had assured her that Lucy would be looked after by two police officers he'd roped in to protect her. She was assured they both had kids and that Lucy would be looked after. Ashley wasn't totally convinced, but the killer's attack on Tom had been the final straw. He knew how to find her, wherever she went. She had to find a way to keep Lucy safe.

"You can trust them." Horan seemed to read her mind. "They think I'm here representing the FBI. I had to forge some papers, but they think it's a legitimate operation."

Ashley looked away. She didn't care about the hoops Horan had to jump through to make this happen, she just wanted it done. "Okay. I need to know how it's all going to work, though. Can we go through everything again?"

"Okay, that's fair." Horan pushed himself off the wall, moved slowly across the room and sat down beside her. "It's just like we rehearsed it. From the moment he calls you, there'll be bubble wrap around you. You'll be entirely safe from start to finish."

"Okay." Ashley nodded. "What happens then?"

Horan smiled. "After the call, we acquire him. There'll be plain-clothes officers all around this location. I'm confident we can grab him."

Ashley wasn't as confident. Having armed officers protecting her was nice, but there was still a chance she'd end up face to face with the man who'd attacked her a decade ago. She'd escaped him then, but there was no guarantee she'd have the same luck twice. He could end her life in seconds. The prospect of Lucy being orphaned terrified her.

"Don't worry." Horan smiled. "I'm going to do everything I can to make sure he never gets near you. But if he does, we'll have assets ready to swoop in."

Ashley turned her head and looked Horan in the eye. "I've heard all of this before – guarantees of safety and protection. I've been burned before."

"I understand. You're smart to be skeptical." He reached

behind his back and held out a pistol. "This is your guarantee."

Ashley looked down at the weapon. She'd only seen a gun once in her life, when she'd seen Laverri use it in front of her. The idea of holding one terrified her, but it also intrigued her. If she couldn't count on others to help her, she had to help herself. She'd be ready. "Okay."

Horan nodded and pointed at the pistol. "Safety. Flick it if you need to use it."

"Okay."

He then pointed at the trigger. "Point with two hands and pull this."

"Okay." Ashley took hold of the pistol. It was heavier than she had expected.

Horan's voice was grave now. "Once we start on this path there's no turning back. We'll be exposing you to a very dangerous man. You need to be sure."

"I'm sure." Ashley looked up at him. "I'm ready."

After one final, long look at Ashley, Horan nodded and walked to the dining table. He picked up the sign he'd prepared and placed it in the window. As soon as he did so, the cop who'd been guarding her got in his car and drove off.

The sign invited Duncan Rowe to make contact with her. They hoped the lack of a cop on the door would encourage him to reach out.

"Now we wait." Horan slumped onto the sofa and flicked open a magazine. "It might be a while, but I think he'll call."

Ashley nodded and sat in silence, watching the phone that sat on the coffee table. Minutes passed, then hours, until Ashley started to wonder if Rowe was watching her at all. Even if he was, would he be bold enough to call her? Chris had been sure he would, yet Ashley had no idea how long this fake operation could be sustained while they waited.

Finally, the phone rang. It had been five hours. Ashley stared at it, watching it ring. On the third ring, she swallowed hard and answered it. "Hello?"

"Hello, Ashley." Rowe's voice wasn't evil. He sounded just like so many other men she'd spoken to. Somehow, that made him scarier.

"Hi. Thanks for calling." Ashley didn't know what else to say. She wanted to scream at him for killing Tom, and for putting her daughter's life in danger. But she didn't. That wasn't the plan.

"I'm coming for you, Ashley." Rowe's voice was cold, slow, and calculated. "You humiliated me. You belittled me. I've thought about that night for ten years. When I saw you again in that clothing store, the countdown to justice began."

Ashley didn't speak. She was terrified. She'd completely forgotten what Chris had told her to say. She was completely thrown by of the way he recalled that evening. They'd gone on a date. He'd sexually assaulted her. Ashley had managed to escape. That he could blame her was amazing.

"Please." Ashley's voice was soft, barely a whisper as she remembered the words Horan had told her to speak. "I'll make it up to you. Duncan, I'm sorry. Let's meet."

50

DUNCAN

"One night?" Duncan paused for a second, checking his watch to make sure a trace couldn't have found him yet. He still had thirty seconds. "You're kidding."

"One night." Ashley Wheeler's voice was frightened and unsure, but her words were clear. "And you can do anything you want."

Duncan scoffed. He'd been driving past her motel room when he'd seen the sign in her window. He'd sat in his car, looking at the sign, for several minutes. The cops were nowhere to be seen, there was just a simple piece of cardboard with large black writing that invited him to call her. It had taken him a moment to snap out of it, to get over his surprise and drive away from her motel. Only then had he been able to think straight.

He'd returned to his trailer and called her right away. Since she'd recognized him at the diner, he'd been torn up inside. His brain wanted to keep to his plan, destroying her bit by bit, until finally he ended her. But his heart quickened every time he thought about her. Now that she knew he was around, everything had changed. He didn't know why she wanted to speak with him. He knew the invitation was a trap, but he didn't care. He just wanted to be close to her, to see her bleed and to watch her die.

He played along. "All I ever wanted was to have you. I wanted more than just to fuck you. I was in love with you, Ashley. You ruined me."

"I know, Duncan." Her voice quivered. "My offer is sincere. I want to meet with you and have the night we should've had years ago."

"You don't know how much damage you caused." Duncan spat the words bitterly. "What's the catch?"

"You don't kill me and, at the end of it, you leave me and my daughter alone forever. You disappear out of our lives and we never see you again."

He couldn't help wondering if it was a trap. He kept silent for a long few moments, his mind racing with possibilities. In so many years of fantasizing about what he wanted to do to her, he'd never expected to have her as a willing participant.

His mind cycled through a whole range of ideas, ways to cause her pain, ways he'd like to use her body, and have her use his, things he'd like to hear her say to him. As his imagination worked its magic, he felt himself grow hard. His hunger for her was insatiable. Though her offer was almost certainly a trap, it was also too good not to pursue. He could back away at any time, after all.

He smiled. "Okay, where?"

"It can't be my motel." Her voice was firm. "We need to meet away from my daughter."

Duncan wrote down the address she gave him, savoring the fear he could hear in her voice. He'd check the place out thoroughly first, to make sure it wasn't full of cops or some other trap. He still had his revolver, which would be enough to kill her in the event that it was a set-up. Even if she wasn't trying to fool him, he had no intention of honoring the deal. There was no way she'd be alive at the end of the night.

If it was a trap, he'd find some way to flip it. It'd just be another thing to take away from her – hope. He smiled at the thought.

"I'll meet you there. Be ready for a busy night. If there are any tricks, you're a dead woman. Your daughter, too."

Duncan terminated the call. After a quick glance at his watch, he stood. There was no time to waste. This was the offer of a lifetime, assuming she wasn't trying to trick him.

He raced to the small bathroom in his trailer. He filled the washbasin with cold water and, after applying some shaving foam, hacked at his beard with a razor. There was no reason to hide now. He wanted Ashley to see him exactly as he'd been the moment she'd broken him. The moment she'd set him on a path of righteous vengeance that led right back to her. When he was finished, he summed up his handiwork.

He looked like himself again.

The shave taken care of, he gathered the things he'd need. He put on leather gloves, sunglasses and a cap. Next, he grabbed his backpack. Finally, he grabbed the revolver, which he loaded and stuffed down the back of his jeans.

He didn't think he'd need the gun. He wasn't going to shoot her. That would be too simple. Still, he was glad to have it for protection. There was a high chance this was all a ruse, but he'd evaded the cops for ten years. Ashley had been tarred as a chicken little. She'd run to them too many times. He wasn't sure they'd listen to her anymore. They thought it was the mob after her, not someone like him.

He hefted the backpack over his shoulder and stuffed the address into his pocket. As he left his trailer, he smiled. He was going to make her night hell. At the end of it, he'd have achieved something that had eluded him for so long.

He wasn't sure what would come next in his life. He didn't think targeting any other woman would be the same after this, but he'd cross that bridge when he came to it.

For now, he was content to find his muse, the woman who'd haunted him for the last decade. To find her, and kill her.

51

CHRIS

C hris grabbed his pistol from the table and pulled back the slide. He held it there for a moment, inspecting the weapon, then released the slide. A round was now locked and loaded, ready in case he needed to put it into Duncan Rowe's skull. He rotated the pistol in his hand, hefted it, then stuffed it into his shoulder holster. The next time he pulled it out, there was a chance he'd have one of the most dangerous men in America in his sights.

They'd received a radio report from one of the police cars placed around the city. The driver had spotted Duncan Rowe in a rental car driving toward the target location. Chris had ordered the car to follow him. He'd also checked the rental car details himself. He now had Rowe's financial details, and the trap was one step closer to being sprung.

He'd wanted to move on Rowe straight away, but knew he had to be patient. While he was at the wheel of a car, there was a chance he could get away. Chris needed to wait until the killer reached his destination, was on foot and vulnerable.

Only then would he order the net pulled tight. Rowe would be surrounded by officers and wouldn't get anywhere near Ashley Wheeler.

Chris couldn't think of anything sweeter than stopping Rowe mere inches from the thing he wanted most of all.

"You guys ready to move?" Chris looked up at the four Wallingford Police Department officers in the room with him.

"No performance anxiety here." Sergeant Mike Devereaux slapped the barrel of his shotgun against his hand. "Now he's stuck his head up, we'll take it off."

Chris nodded, and there were smiles from the other officers. It wasn't hard to understand their enthusiasm. Wallingford wasn't exactly the crime capital of America. Cases that would be routine for the NYPD or the LAPD actually created a ripple here, another reason why it had been so easy for Chris to falsely requisition the help he needed to track down his man. He felt a little guilty about using them like that, but they'd be fine. He was the one who'd eat the consequences.

Right after Duncan Rowe ate a bullet or two.

Chris had forged the documents to get the help of the local department. It hadn't taken much. They were already on edge. They'd already had two brutal murders and an arson attack they'd thought was the work of the mob. Chris had them convinced Rowe was the guy from the mob who was gunning for Ashley. Now he was relying on them to keep Ashley and her daughter safe while he worked.

Chris was confident about catching his killer. He had a good plan, and a tail in place. He just had to do make sure Ashley Wheeler and her daughter remained bubble-wrapped, and that measures were in place to deal with the killer. Chris was confident in both of those things, which meant the only thing left to do was hope Rowe took the bait.

He couldn't make Ashley completely safe. She was the bait dangling on the line. But he'd surrounded her with so much protection, there was almost no chance of Rowe getting close enough to harm her. To keep Lucy safe, he'd put her in a police station. She had two armed guards looking over her and another twenty cops nearby. She was completely safe.

He needed to check, though. He picked up his phone and called Dean Remmers, one of the two cops assigned to protect Lucy.

"It's Chris Horan. We're confirming final preparations here."

"Good to hear from you, Agent Horan. Sandra is in with her now and we're taking it in turns to look out for her. You don't have to worry about the girl, she's fine."

"Keep it that way." Chris put as much strength in his voice as he could. He had no authority to conduct this operation, but no one had questioned it so far. "We've got a tail on our guy, so it should be wrapped up soon. Keeping Ashley and Lucy Wheeler safe is the priority."

"Understood."

"Thanks. I'll keep you posted."

Chris hung up the phone, feeling a momentary pang of guilt. He'd pulled off the scam of the century, gaining access to all the assets of the Wallingford PD – manpower, technology, and weaponry.

The deception had been shockingly easy. He had officers covering Ashley and her daughter, some ready to conduct traces, others on the lookout throughout the city, and a ready response team. He'd taken every possible precaution to make sure that, this time, the killer wouldn't escape him.

"Hey, Chris?" Sergeant Devereaux shouted from across the room. "We just heard from the chase car. They've still got a lock on Rowe. He's heading toward the target motel. We better get the assets ready."

"Let's go."

52

ASHLEY

"Have they found him yet?" Ashley asked the female police officer, her companion in the motel room. Chris had assigned the woman to be Ashley's closest support, a final protection in case Duncan slipped through all the layers of protection and made it to the motel. "We were supposed to have him by now."

"No, not yet." The officer's voice was calm, and almost reassuring. "You just need to be patient. We've a whole network of protection around you."

Ashley struggled to trust the police officer. She'd been burned by the authorities enough times before. "Okay, I just thi—"

"Hang on." The officer interrupted Ashley as her radio crackled. Then she grimaced. "He's on his way here, Ashley."

Ashley tried to swallow, but her mouth was dry. "What do you need from me? What should I do?"

"Nothing." The officer smiled and placed a hand on

Ashley's arm. "We'll get him. You're protected here. I just wanted to let you know."

Ashley nodded and kept silent. The officer kept smiling until her radio crackled again, stealing her attention. Ashley couldn't hear what was said, but she saw the other woman tense. Without another word of explanation to Ashley, she left the room and moved back to her assigned point. Ashley had no idea how many other officers were there to protect her, but she hoped it was enough to stop Duncan Rowe from getting near her. Though she'd promised him a night with no holds barred, she had no intention of giving him that.

After her stomach-curdling phone conversation with Rowe, Ashley had expected things to get dangerous very quickly. Instead, she'd been bottled up inside a motel room for hours while she waited for Horan and his team to catch the bad guy. It was horribly anticlimactic, and didn't help Ashley feel any safer. She wished she knew what was happening.

Instead, she was alone again, with nothing but her thoughts. She knew there was at least one police officer close by, and many more enacting the plan that Chris was so sure would work. After looking around the room, silent and still, Ashley walked over to the bed and put the pistol down on it. She needed it close. It offered a final chance at life if everything else failed.

She sat down with a sigh and reached for the photo album she'd left on the bed. It was the only one she'd managed to find in the remains of her house, safe inside a metal cabinet that had been scorched and warped, but not breached by the fire. It was also the only thing she'd brought from her motel room to this one. As she flicked through the album, she reached out to touch the photos of Lucy's face, the photos of Tom and her together, smiling, and a hundred other memories from better times. Happier times. She wanted that feeling again.

She turned the page and saw the photo of Lucy that always made her heart melt. It was the best photo of the best thing she'd ever achieved in her life – a beautiful, smart, and curious little girl. As she stared at it, Ashley's thoughts hardened and she felt for the pistol again. Gripping the weapon, she turned it in her hand and studied it. She felt a strange comfort when she held it. It felt like power, something she'd had so little of for so long.

Her eyes flicked back and forth between the photograph and the pistol, until Ashley felt her jaw clench tight. She'd done so much to keep Lucy safe, including some things she was proud of and plenty she wasn't. It had all been done with a good heart and good intentions. She hoped Horan's plan would work, but she couldn't count on it. She had to assume such a calculating killer could outsmart them all. If that happened, it'd almost certainly mean Ashley was faced with death.

She swore under no circumstances would she let him win. If he made it as far as the motel, she'd kill him herself, or die trying. Ashley wasn't prepared to contemplate even one second in the hands of such a beast. There'd be consequences, she was sure of it, but Ashley wasn't taking any chances. Not with so much on the line.

The more she looked at the photo, the more the decision made sense. It meant Lucy would be safe. The female officer had assured her everything would be okay, but Ashley didn't believe her. She'd also said there was nothing for Ashley to do, and she didn't believe that either. Her finger grazed the trigger. She wasn't counting on anything or anyone.

Not anymore.

53

DUNCAN

Duncan let down the window of his rental car and tossed the 'fresh pine' scented air freshener out of it. It wasn't a scent he enjoyed. Satisfied, he started to whistle along with the song on the radio, which was vaguely familiar, his head bopping with the beat. He was just a few minutes away from the address he'd been given, and his excitement was growing.

He was feeling upbeat. He'd been on the lookout for a trap, but after driving around aimlessly for ninety minutes he hadn't seen anything out of the ordinary. He'd driven around trying to spot a tail, stopped for a juice and scanned for officers as he waited, and he'd even googled his name to see if there was anything online. None of his efforts had turned up anything. That didn't make it safe, but it increased his chances.

As he tapped the steering wheel in time with the song, the GPS told him to take the next left. Duncan signaled to turn, checked his mirrors, and then turned down the street. He glanced at his mirror again, realizing the car behind him had turned the same corner he had. Duncan frowned. It seemed odd for two vehicles to be going down the same quiet back street. His eyes flicked between the road and the car as he thought about what to do. He signaled again, turned, and just like before, the same car followed him.

"Fucking hell." Duncan hissed.

As the car's GPS started telling him he'd taken the wrong turn, Duncan summed up his options. He now knew it was a trap. His first reaction was anger: he'd been betrayed by Ashley Wheeler again. Then came regret, because he'd lost the chance to have a night with her as his willing plaything. Finally came fear. The police were onto him.

The only saving grace was that his precautions had paid off. He'd spotted the tail. That gave him the chance to decide what to do about this new development. With a sigh, he reprogrammed the GPS to find the nearest parking garage, a plan forming in his head. Duncan drove the few minutes to the garage without incident, signaled, and turned in.

The car didn't follow. It kept on driving straight past him. He was pleased, but just because nobody had followed didn't mean he was in the clear.

Duncan parked the car in the first available bay and climbed out. He grabbed his bag, locked the car and threw the keys into a trashcan. He thought about doing the same with his cell phone, but decided against it. He doubted the cops could be tracking it. The car and his credit cards were a different matter. He hadn't wanted to use his normal car, so he'd rented one using a credit card. Given they'd found the car, it wouldn't be long before they had his financial details as well. That was fine, he could deal with it.

The only thing that worried him was missing out on an evening with Ashley. He'd hoped she'd learned, but she hadn't. She'd been baiting him, beckoning him closer with soothing words while holding a knife behind her back. A stupid man would have been lured right in by her, with the cops ready to pounce. But as Ashley and the cops were about to find out, he wasn't a stupid man. She'd led him on for the last time.

The first thing he needed to do was get away. The car had kept driving, but that didn't mean he was in the clear. There might be others looking to resume the tail. Or worse, there could be officers on their way to the garage, ready to arrest him. Either way, Duncan was better off elsewhere. He walked to the exit of the parking garage and looked around. He saw no obvious signs that someone was there to pick up the tail, no army of cops ready to take him down.

He took a deep breath, crossed the street, and walked for several blocks, until he found what he was looking for: a group of teenagers leaning against a fence, chatting loudly. Duncan smiled and walked closer to them. As he approached, their conversation stalled, then stopped entirely as they turned to stare at him. Raised eyebrows and muttered comments made it clear what they thought about him.

"Hey, kids." Duncan pulled up about six feet short of the group and raised a hand in greeting. "Want to earn some money?"

Their eyes lit up at that. One of them took up the offer. "You some sort of pedophile or something?"

Duncan sighed as he pulled out his wallet. "No. It's simple, I've got six credit cards here. I'll give you all the PIN numbers and then you can go buy what you want."

The same kid scoffed. "And why would you do that? You think we're stupid and can't spot a cop?"

Duncan figured honesty was the best policy. "The cops are after me. They're tracing these cards. Find a store, buy what you want and move on quickly, before the cops can track you down. This is the best deal you're ever going to get. Take it or leave it. I can easily find another group of kids."

"We're not kids." The boy reached out and snatched for Duncan's wallet, but Duncan held it back.

"One condition." Duncan smiled, then held out his wallet and let the boy take it. "You each go in different directions."

54

CHRIS

C hris pressed the phone closer to his ear. "Please confirm, there have been no hits on the target's cards?"

The Wallingford PD officer on the other end of the line took a second to respond. "There's been no activity on any cards since he rented the car."

Chris hung up his cell phone and slammed his fist into the back of the driver's seat. "Fuck it! We've lost him. Anyone have anything?"

The officers in the vehicle with him shook their heads. Chris and his team had been racing toward Duncan Rowe's location when a disastrous radio call had come through. In short, crackled bursts the officer who'd picked up the tail had told Chris's team that Rowe had driven into a multi-story parking garage. Chris had shouted at him to follow, even if it meant exposure, but it was too late. Rowe had escaped. Now they were pulled over on the side of the road, frantically working the radio and their cell phones, trying to locate Duncan Rowe.

This wouldn't have happened on any Bureau operation, or even a local police operation run by a half-decent force, but Chris hadn't been impressed by the Wallingford Police Department. Given the choice, he'd have had multiple tails on Rowe, switching back and forth between them to remove suspicion. Better still, he'd have been able to switch the vehicles' headlights. But Chris didn't have those things. He had a half-rate bunch of half-rate cops he'd managed to commandeer into helping him through deceit. It was like dealing with recruits right out of the academy.

"Desperation time." Chris started to dial another number as he spoke. "Speak to anyone you can think of, call in favors, do some magic tricks... Just find him!"

Chris put the phone to his ear. As he waited for the person to pick up, he clenched his teeth hard. It couldn't happen again. Chris had lucked across the killer, the man he now knew to be Duncan Rowe. He'd failed to stop him in New York. He couldn't let that happen again. He thought he'd laid a perfect trap, luring the killer toward Ashley Wheeler with plenty of officers ready to pounce.

Rowe was further from their grasp, getting closer to Ashley with each passing second. Nothing would stop him. Though he had measures in place to protect her, Chris knew Rowe was an intelligent man capable of striking hard and fast.

Chris had every asset under his command working frantically to make sure that didn't happen. He had units at the motel, on foot, patrolling in cars and working the phones. It still felt hopeless. There was only one man Chris could think of turning to, the man who'd broken this whole thing open.

"Hello?" James Miles' voice was heavy with sleep, which was strange given the hour. "Who am I speaking with?"

"James?" Chris sighed with relief. "It's Agent Horan. I need your help. I'm close to capturing Duncan Rowe – my killer – but he's escaped my net."

"I gave you everything I had on him, Agent Horan." Miles sounded more alert now. "You said we were square. I shouldn't even be talking to you."

"I don't have time for that. Your information led us here. I just need to know what our killer is likely to do now that he knows we're onto him." Chris paused, and there was silence on the other end. "This is urgent, James. If you don't help me, our deal is off and I'll expose you. Lives are at stake."

"He'll seek to flip the situation, Agent Horan." Miles sounded certain. "I think you've missed your chance."

Chris sighed. He felt like he wanted to cry for the first time since Tamara was murdered. "At least he won't get to Ashley Wheeler."

"What was that?" Miles' voice was sharp. He was clearly angry about Chris' threat.

Chris frowned. "I said Ashley Wheeler is safe."

"No she isn't." Miles spoke slowly, with measured words, his tone serious. "I said he'd seek to flip the situation, not run. If he's as obsessed with her as we think, he'll burn the world down around him if it means getting to her. He'll recalculate, but he's not done. You might've just sped up his clock."

Chris felt a chill run down his spine. "I—"

"Wherever she is and whatever she's doing, you need to get her somewhere else and protect her. You need to put as many guns as you can between Ashley Wheeler and Duncan Rowe, because he's coming for her. It might be five minutes from now, or five weeks, but he's coming. Now that he knows you're onto him, he just got much more dangerous."

"Thanks, James." Chris hung up the phone. He had only a moment to decide. He hated giving up the initiative, but there was no choice. Chris spoke to the other officers. "We need to move Ashley Wheeler. Pull back all units except this vehicle and those defending Lucy to cover the move."

The others nodded and started to make the calls. Within moments, all the resources searching for Rowe would be sacrificed. In their place would be a far more rigorous shield around Ashley. Chris sighed and watched them work. He now had no confidence at all that he'd achieve what had eluded him for so many years. But if he could protect Ashley, he could try again another day. That was the only thing Chris could think to do. He closed his eyes, despite the work that had to be done.

"Hey, Chris?" Devereaux gave Chris's shoulder a shove. "We just got a call from Janice, who's running the financial traces. She's got a hit. Five blocks away."

"Let's get over there." Chris's eyes shot open as the vehicle's engine roared. "This might be the last lead we get."

55

ASHLEY

Ashley looked at her watch and frowned. The cop had told her they'd tracked down Duncan Rowe almost an hour ago, which meant he should've been killed, captured, or at her doorstep by now. The fact that she'd heard nothing worried her. It meant things hadn't gone to plan. Chris Horan had been convinced his plan would work, but Ashley had heard nothing since the female police officer had left the room.

She gripped the pistol tight and rocked back and forth on the bed. All her earlier conviction, her trust in Horan's promises, had evaporated, replaced by fear and uncertainty. She never should have agreed to this. She'd reached out to Horan and asked for his help, and in doing so let herself be duped. Now she was sitting here, like bait, waiting for one of the most dangerous men in America to swallow her.

She reached for her purse to get her cell phone. There were no messages or missed calls from Chris. She found his number in her recent call list, then dialed. It rang for a few seconds then he finally picked up. In the second it took for Chris to speak she heard traffic noises and frantic voices in the background. She wondered what was happening.

"Hello?" He sounded stressed and in a hurry. "What do you need, Ashley? We're a little busy right now."

"Something's wrong." Her words formed into a statement, not a question. "I want to know what's going on."

"It's fine, Ashley." Horan's words were clipped and terse. "You need to let me work."

"I just need to know—"

The line went dead. Ashley lowered her phone and stared at it. She was furious he'd cut her off so swiftly, after all his platitudes about her being part of the team and a key part of the plan. She was nervous and scared, and he hadn't even taken the time to listen to her concerns. She'd thought he was on her side, but he was just like the rest of them.

After one long breath, she made her decision. She stood, grabbed the photo album and her purse, held the pistol by her side and strode toward the front door. She opened the door and walked with long strides to the car, her head held high. She unlocked it, surprised she'd gotten that far, then paused. "Don't try to stop me."

"Ashley, you need to go back inside." The female police officer's voice was calm, but firm. "You're risking the entire operation."

"There is no operation!" Ashley turned to face the other woman. "I'm done."

"It's not that simple." The officer held a hand out, trying to grab Ashley's arm. "I—"

"No!" Ashley stepped back and raised the pistol. She pointed it at the officer, who'd been so kind. "Please! Back off! My boss is dead! My ex-husband is dead! My house is gone! I was promised you'd catch the man responsible, but now I'm being lied to!"

The cop wouldn't let up, though she did stop her advance. "I need you to calm down and think about what you're doing. You're putting yourself in danger."

"I am calm!" Ashley's voice was louder than she had intended and, despite her conviction, she felt her arm wavering. She kept the pistol trained on the officer as she reached for the car door, her eyes flicking between the car and the officer. "Please, just leave me the hell alone!"

"I can't do that Ashley." The officer's voice was calm, despite the pistol being pointed at her. "You need to think. There's no way you win if you leave here on your own."

"Drop the weapon, Ms Wheeler!" another officer shouted. "I need you to put it down very, very slowly."

Ashley glanced around. Two police officers had weapons trained on her, standing a long way apart. She was surrounded. When she turned back, the female officer was still looking straight at Ashley as more cops ran in their direction. There was shouting and pleading and so much noise. Ashley froze for a moment, not wanting to lower the pistol but wanting all of them to go away.

"Please!" She was shouting now, but she looked only at the female officer. "I just want to leave!"

"That's not going to happen, Ashley." The female cop spoke over the others. "I need you to lower the pistol or this is going to end badly."

Ashley squeezed the pistol so tight her knuckles went white. There was no way out. She loosened her grip on the pistol and started to lower it. "Okay."

The cops swarmed. One of them went straight for the pistol, scooping it up and moving it away from her. Two others grabbed her arms. The female cop simply stepped in front of Ashley, a look of concern painted all over her face. She stood there, still and silent, for several moments. Only when Ashley calmed down did she nod at the other cops to let her go.

"Ashley, I understand you're under a lot of stress." The officer smiled, kindly, but with more caution this time. "But you can't point a weapon at a cop."

"I know that, I—" Ashley sobbed.

"I get it. You're scared and it's taking too long. But Agent Horan has it all under control." The officer placed a hand on Ashley's shoulder. "You need to trust the process. We're going to catch this bastard. In the meantime, you need to go back to the motel room and trust that we'll get this guy. You're fine. Your daughter is fine."

56

DUNCAN

Duncan pulled up short, his eyes narrowing as he slowed to a complete stop. "Motherfucker."

Those same eyes widened again as he realized what was in front of him, the car that had been following him and the cop who'd been at the wheel. The officer was in plain clothes, leaning against his car and speaking into his radio. Duncan stood frozen in place as he watched the officer run a hand through his hair. After a few moments, Duncan decided what he had to do.

The man had interrupted his plans, and had confirmed to Duncan that Ashley's promise was nothing but air. She was the bait in the middle of a complicated trap that he'd nearly walked right into. His pain at being denied his night alone with her was acute. Now, through a stroke of luck, he could begin to turn the tables once again.

Duncan never took his eyes off the cop as he shrugged off his backpack, unzipped it and rummaged around inside. Though he had the revolver stuffed into his jeans, it was far too noisy to use in public. Once his hand was wrapped around the handle of the knife, Duncan slowly approached the cop, who was completely oblivious to the threat from behind. Duncan waited, a few steps away, until the cop put down his radio.

Then, as quickly as a rattlesnake, Duncan leapt forward. He grabbed the cop in a headlock and brought the knife up to the man's throat. "Be calm."

The cop tensed and froze, but to his credit he didn't shout, or do anything stupid. "Hey buddy, let's talk."

"My name is Duncan Rowe." Duncan didn't see any harm in admitting it. The cop would die soon. "I want to know why you were following me."

The cop scoffed. "Because I was told to, pal. I was doing my job. I'm assisting a federal investigation, I hope you know? Kill me and they kill you."

"Who's in charge?" Duncan pressed the knife deeper and felt a small trickle of blood run down his hand. The cop clearly felt it too, because he tensed. "Next I take out an artery," Duncan warned him.

"Chris Horan. He's an FBI agent." The cop made the smart decision, his voice revealing fear for the first time. "Please, buddy. I've got kids."

Duncan was silent as he processed the information. The involvement of the FBI wasn't a good sign, but the cop's mention of his kids gave Duncan an idea. The last time he'd seen Ashley Wheeler, her daughter had been close. She couldn't have gone far with her father in the morgue. "I wonder if you know where the girl is? The little girl?"

The cop paused. Duncan knew the man was weighing up his own life – his own kids – versus Lucy Wheeler. "She's in a police station not far from here."

"Where?"

The cop gave Duncan the address. It really was close by, even in a city as small as Wallingford. "Will you let me go now?"

Duncan smiled and pulled the knife across the cop's throat. The man gargled and Duncan kept him in the headlock until he stopped writhing and became a dead weight. Duncan let go as the other man slumped to the ground. As a precaution, Duncan checked for a pulse. There was none.

A quick search of the cop's body produced another pistol, a badge, and a wallet with some cash. Most useful of all were the keys to the car the officer had been leaning against. Duncan unlocked it and was pleased to find a spare uniform in the trunk. He pulled out the clothing, threw it in the back seat along with his backpack, and then hefted the officer's body into the trunk and closed it.

In the time it took to change hastily into the uniform, drive to the police station, and walk inside with the takeaway coffee that he'd found inside the car, Duncan could think of nothing but revenge. He'd intended to go after Lucy Wheeler all along – at least until Ashley had made her offer. That prospect had distracted him. The irony was that, in deceiving him, Ashley had put her daughter in greater danger.

Once inside the station, Duncan avoided clusters of other people and moved away from anyone looking at him too closely. Though he was dressed like a cop, with the badge and the gun to prove it, he assumed that wouldn't hold up to any real scrutiny. He wasn't even sure his plan was a smart one, but it offered a tantalizing way to steal back the initiative. He'd show Ashley Wheeler there were consequences for her dishonesty.

He made his way to the reception counter and smiled at the desk sergeant, who was on the phone and looked frantic. "Chris Horan sent me to take over the watch on Lucy Wheeler."

"Fucking Bureau." The sergeant held his hand over the phone, shook his head and looked down at his notes. "He told us Dean and Sandra were to stay on her."

Duncan laughed and took in the scene around him. Cops were running back and forth and the whole scene was chaos. "Is any of this shit planned? Looks like everything has gone to hell with this big shot's operation. I'm just doing what I'm told. Nobody bothers to tell me why."

"Isn't that the truth? I'll tell them." The sergeant sighed and finished his call, then dialed another number. Duncan watched in silence, enjoying the obvious confusion his appearance had caused.

Based on what he was hearing, Duncan was sure the officer on the other end of the line – one of those guarding Lucy Wheeler – was resisting. Finally, with a sigh, the sergeant placed a hand over his mike.

"Something wrong?" Duncan smiled and took a sip of the coffee. It was cold, but it fit the part.

Another sigh. "Dean Remmers insists his orders were that nobody else is to be allowed near the daughter."

"Fair enough. I'll give Chris Horan a call." Duncan pulled the dead officer's phone out of his pocket and pretended to search through the address book, then put the phone to his ear.

"No. That'll just make us look like shit." The sergeant sighed, then removed his hand from the phone and spoke to the other officer again. "It checks out. I'll escort him back."

Duncan smiled as the sergeant stood, removed his headset

and started down the hall. Duncan followed in silence, then made some small talk with the cop he was relieving, and before he knew it was alone with a tired-looking girl with red hair and dimples. She looked at him with glazed over eyes, clearly regarding him as one more cop among the many she'd seen in the last few days.

Duncan smiled at her. "You need to come with me, Lucy."

The girl frowned. "Why?"

He held out a hand. "We're going to see your mother."

Duncan waited as her eyes scanned his for a moment, then relished the look of relief that washed over Lucy's face. She nodded. With Lucy's consent, he was home free. It had been a close call, but he'd turned the tables on their trap, and now he was going to take Ashley's daughter away from her.

Lucy gripped his hand tightly, and Duncan clamped his own hand around hers.

"Let's go for a ride!"

57

CHRIS

Chris gripped the overhead handle as the SUV's engine roared and he was pushed back into his seat. The inside of the vehicle was silent, a contrast to the external sounds of blaring sirens and the strain of an engine reaching its limit. They were nearing the McDonald's where Rowe's credit card had been used. There was no need for words. They'd all checked their weapons and devised a plan. All that remained was for them to find Rowe.

"We're a minute out." Mike Devereaux broke the silence from the front seat, where he rested his shotgun in between his legs, the barrel pointed at the floor.

"Remember, if he won't surrender then we take him down." Chris didn't mention that he had every intention of taking Rowe down, even if he did surrender. He looked around. There were nods from everyone else in the vehicle. They understood how serious the situation was. "Under no circumstances do we let Rowe get away. We may never get another chance."

Chris was glad the others were on board. Though they all thought they were chasing after the mob, it didn't matter. He had them convinced that Duncan Rowe was a threat that needed to be dealt with. Though they'd prefer to arrest him, Chris wanted him dead and in the ground. There was no other way to end this, and he'd never felt so desperate to do so.

Chris swallowed hard. The phone call from Ashley had him spooked. He just hoped she wasn't wavering. He didn't doubt she wanted to see Duncan Rowe dead, but Ashley was also committed to keeping her daughter safe. It seemed that, in her mind, the best way to do that oscillated between fighting and running – only one of which worked for Chris.

More worrying was the report that Ashley had run from the motel and tried to escape. In the process she'd pulled a gun on a cop and almost got herself blown away, which would have destroyed Chris's operation. He was thankful that the officers had detained her, but it increased the sense of urgency he felt. At any moment, his bait could slip the hook. Chris had to reel in his catch.

"Thirty seconds." Devereaux broke Chris's reverie just as a voice came over the radio.

"Stalker Seven, be advised, we've had three additional hits on the financial trace on Duncan Rowe in the last two minutes." The voice rattled off some addresses, which Chris wrote down.

Chris cursed. How could Duncan Rowe be in so many places at the same time? "That makes four now."

"Each from a different part of the city." Devereaux spat the words. "It doesn't add up. He can't be in all those places at once. What now?"

Chris thought for a second. They were headed to the location where one of Rowe's cards had first been used, only a few minutes earlier. There weren't enough units to cover all the sites while still keeping Ashley Wheeler under close guard. The next decision he made might be the difference between killing Rowe and him getting away.

He made his decision just as their vehicle pulled up at the McDonald's. "Devereaux and I will get out here. The rest of you keep moving. Scramble any available units to the other locations. We'll see what the situation looks like at that point."

The others nodded. Chris gripped his pistol and climbed out of the car, slammed the door shut and watched as it sped on to the next location. He scanned the McDonald's, but nothing looked awry. It was full of families sucking down burgers and soda. It looked as calm and normal as the apartment building in New York City, where he'd disturbed Duncan Rowe in a deadly act.

Chris waved Devereaux forward and they moved fast and low through the parking lot. As Chris approached the main doors, Devereaux moved to cover the only other exit. They paused and locked eyes on each other, then Chris nodded. They entered the restaurant at the same time.

"FBI!" Chris shouted as he swept his weapon around the restaurant, looking for Duncan Rowe. "Stay where you are!"

While Devereaux covered both exits, it took Chris a minute to sweep the restaurant. He checked the dining room, the playground, the kitchen, and the drive-through window. He even looked in the cool room. Duncan Rowe wasn't inside. He cursed, and hoped the officers at the other locations had turned up Rowe. The failure to get his man felt like a punch to the kidney.

Chris lowered his pistol but kept it drawn as he returned to the front of the restaurant and approached a kid behind the register. "You in charge?"

"Yes, sir. I'm Simon Johnson, the shift manager." The kid's voice wavered as he spoke. He looked scared.

"I need to know which of your customers used this Visa card in the last ten minutes." Chris handed over a slip of paper with the number on it. "Quickly."

"I can check." The boy's hands came down from over his head and he punched commands into the point of sale system in front of him. "It'll be a minute."

Chris nodded and took a step back. There was no point intimidating the kid further. As he waited, Chris eyeballed every customer he could see, but none of them looked anything like Duncan Rowe. Then he looked at his phone. None of the other officers had called him, meaning there'd been no progress in finding Rowe at the other sites. He was still hoping there was an obvious answer for the multiple pings.

"Sir?" The boy looked up from his terminal. "I've got the record. I served a customer who presented a Visa card with the same first and last four digits as the card you're interested in. He purchased a large cheeseburger meal eleven minutes ago and it was given to him nine minutes ago."

Chris's eyes widened. "Is he still here?"

"The customer dined in." The boy raised his hand and pointed behind Chris. "It's that kid over there."

Chris turned and looked where the staff member was pointing, straight at a teenager who was sitting on his own. The boy looked confused by the attention, especially when Chris marched over to him. Though he didn't have any legal right to do so, Chris snatched the boy's wallet up off the table and rifled through it until he found one of the Visa cards inside, the same card used to hire the vehicle they'd been tailing.

"Care to explain this?" Chris tossed the wallet down in front of the stunned teenager. He waved the credit card in the kid's face. "You've got 10 seconds."

"Some dude gave it to me. He was giving them out to all the guys, saying to spend up big." The kid shrugged. "Why? Am I in some sort of trouble?"

Chris cursed and turned his back on the kid. He ran back out to the parking lot, waving for Devereaux to follow. As he stepped outside, Chris realized they had no wheels. He'd sent the other cops on to another location, where they'd find another kid with a card and a smile. As the realization sank in, Chris holstered his pistol and dug through his pockets for his cell phone.

"Call the others." Chris was already dialing Ashley's number, but speaking to Devereaux as he did. "I want everyone to head for the motel. And get one car here to pick us up. I—"

Chris was interrupted by the ring of his cell phone. He answered. "Hello?"

"Agent Horan? It's Dean Remmers, I—"

Chris's eyes widened. Remmers was meant to be looking after Lucy. "Do you have her."

There was a pause. "Well—"

"Lucy Wheeler, where is she?"

"Gone, Agent Horan. She's been taken."

58

ASHLEY

Ashley heard the sirens first. They started as a faint whisper in the far distance, but grew louder as several police vehicles converged on her location. She heard the screeching of tires and the slamming of car doors, all in a row. Then came the shouts. Lots of them.

She could have opened the door to see what was happening, or take a peek out the window, but instead she just lay on the bed waiting for the bad news. Already confused about why Duncan Rowe hadn't shown up at her motel, with each passing minute her confidence in the plan to capture and kill him had receded. She was waiting for the inevitable moment when the police admitted they'd failed.

When Chris Horan admitted he'd failed.

She stared at the ceiling and waited. As the sirens cut out and she could hear people talking outside, she waited. Only when there was a pounding on her door did she bother to do anything. She let out a sigh, climbed off the bed, and shuffled toward the door. When her hand gripped the knob, she thought momentarily about asking who it was, but figured that with that many sirens, it was unlikely Duncan Rowe was at her front door.

She opened the door to see Horan, his face as dark as a thundercloud. She made no move to let him in. "You lost him."

"I thought we had him." Horan spoke slowly, as if he'd rehearsed every word. "He killed one officer. I'm afraid there's some more bad news."

Ashley felt her heart quicken. "What is it?"

"Let me come inside and we'll talk, I—"

"No! I want to know!"

Horan's eyes narrowed as he seemed to weigh up her resistance versus the merits of telling her. Finally, he sighed. "Ashley, Lucy is missing. I think he's got her."

Ashley felt her knees give way and she started to fall. She felt herself rushing toward the floor, until something stopped her. She blinked a few times. Horan had stepped forward and caught her. She snarled and sobbed and squealed as she processed what he'd told her. As he supported her weight, she pounded his chest with her fists, futilely trying to translate her fury into violence.

"Ashley, I'm sorry." Horan didn't strike back or defend himself, he just let the blows rain down on him as he eased her slowly to the floor. "I'm very, very sorry."

"You fucking bastard." She hissed the words at him, her breaths coming in ragged, heaving chunks as she continued to strike at him. "I trusted you!"

"I know." Horan's voice was full of regret, but it was a thread of regret in an entire tapestry of misery. "We almost had him."

"You were supposed to help us! Now that bastard has my daughter and is doing God knows what to her!" Ashley locked eyes with Horan, who held her gaze for a moment and then looked down. "You were using me and you were using her. You never cared if anything happened to us, as long as you got your man."

"That's fair." Horan's voice trailed off, as if he was about to say more but thought better of it.

Ashley wriggled free of his grip as she moved back inside the motel room. She closed her eyes. She needed to think. She needed to figure out how to get Lucy back.

She needed to contact Duncan Rowe and beg him to spare her daughter in return for the right to do anything he wanted to her. She knew he wanted her. It'd work.

Ashley heard fresh shouting from outside the motel room. Her eyes shot open. It confused her, until Horan fled inside the room and closed the door. When he drew his pistol, she knew something was wrong. She finally found her voice. "What're you doing?"

"Giving you a choice." Horan locked the door and turned his gaze on her. "But you need to make it."

Ashley frowned. She didn't want to hear any more of his shit. "I'm done with your stunts, Chris."

"You're not listening! Those cops are here to bust us. You and me!" Horan hissed. "I think they've figured out I had no authorization to run this operation."

"So I let them take you down." Ashley's voice was louder than she'd intended. "I just want to find my daughter before he tortures her, rapes her, or kills her."

"You're not getting out of here without me and vice versa." Horan shrugged. "She's been taken, I know that much, but I don't know where. I don't have any leads, but you can bet I've got a much greater chance of finding Rowe than the local police department. Do you really think he'll have any trouble outwitting them?"

"Why should I trust you, after all this?" Ashley brought her face an inch from his, her eyes wide. "He's got my daughter because of you!"

"I know." Horan held her gaze. "I didn't do a good enough job, but I'm probably the only shot you have of finding your daughter."

Ashley's mind raced. She wanted to tell him to go fuck himself, to try her luck with Rowe and hope Lucy would be spared. But a voice in the back of her head told her that was unlikely. Rowe tortured his victims by cutting away the things that were important to them. No bargain with him would lead to Lucy being freed. He was just as likely to cut Ashley's daughter up in front of her. Horan was the one shot she had.

"Agent Horan, this is the Wallingford Police Department," a voice boomed over a megaphone. "Come out with your weapon holstered and your hands above your head."

Chris spoke softly, calmly. "Time to decide, Ashley."

She thought for another second, then gritted her teeth and nodded. "Okay, I'll double down, but I owe you nothing."

"Fair enough." He sighed with relief, then raised the gun and pointed it at her. "You're my hostage."

Ashley felt a moment of fright, until she realized this was their means of escape. "Is that really necessary?"

"More than necessary." Horan smiled sadly. "It's the only way out of here that doesn't involve me wearing a nice new metal bracelet."

Ashley nodded and gasped when Chris moved behind her and pressed his pistol against her head. He gestured toward the door, and they moved there together. The minute she opened it, her senses exploded with shouts and flashing lights.

She held up a hand to shield her eyes, but didn't get a chance to take it all in, because Chris was already pressing her forward. They made it to an SUV and climbed in, with nobody taking a shot.

As Chris started the vehicle, his weapon still pointed at her, the cops made no move to stop them. Ashley hoped she'd made the right decision. She owed him nothing, because his failings had delivered Lucy into the hands of a madman. On the other hand, he was the best chance she had of finding her daughter.

Once they were on the road, Ashley looked at Horan. He had the look of a madman. She realized he was as obsessed with the killer as the killer was with Ashley. Like it or not, he was the last chance she had, her only chance of finding her daughter and getting her back. She didn't trust him, but she'd ride him as far as she had to.

There was nobody left to trust. She was on her own.

59

DUNCAN

Duncan smiled as he tapped the steering wheel in time with a country music song he didn't know. As he sped along at 80 miles per hour, the road ahead of him was clear and so were his mirrors. It had been like that for at least the last hour, with only the occasional car to keep him company. He'd made it out of Wallingford and the trap that had been laid for him, and seized some of the most precious loot in the city – Lucy Wheeler.

Though the little girl hadn't been his target, capturing her was a good result. Ashley's deceit meant he now had the thing that mattered most to her, the thing she'd do anything to protect. He was counting on it. He was going to show her exactly what lies and false promises led to.

"Going okay back there, kiddo?" Duncan turned his head to glance into the back seat of the car. When there was no reply, he scoffed and spoke again. "Suit yourself."

He'd cuffed Lucy to the inside handle of the door, so there was no chance of escape. She'd tried struggling, for a while, until she'd worn herself out and simply sat there sobbing gently, her head downcast. She was still awake, Duncan was sure of that, but she'd given up trying to fight the situation.

He didn't like to target children. He might separate his targets from their kids, but he'd never harm them. Usually.

This was a special case.

Ashley had given him no choice.

Duncan tuned back in to the music, ignoring the girl in the back seat. He didn't know where they were headed, but it needed to be far enough away from the net that he'd nearly been caught in. He'd dumped the car he'd stolen from the dead cop and then stolen another. He planned to find a quiet location and then contact Ashley Wheeler again. Right after he dealt with the light that had just started flashing on the car dash.

He sighed and pressed the button that fired up the in-car commands. "Take me to the nearest gas station."

The GPS took a moment, but soon Duncan was following the map to a gas station. He couldn't chance finding another one with only 20 miles of gas left. He drove to the station, got out of the car and filled it up, whistling a soft tune as he did. He kept his eyes locked onto Lucy Wheeler to make sure she did nothing to expose him, but she kept as still and as silent as she'd been for the last hour.

Duncan walked inside and made his way to the cashier. He fumbled for his wallet and opened it, then realized he didn't have enough cash for the full tank of gas he'd purchased. Worse, he'd handed out all his cards to those kids to get the police off his ass. He waved an apology to the gas station attendant, said he was going back to the car for more cash, then climbed inside his vehicle. Only when he started the engine did the cashier rush outside.

He made it a few minutes down the road before a cop car that had been travelling in the other direction turned around, its light bar flashing. He could pull over or make a run for it. While he had a lot of skills, high-speed driving wasn't among them. It seemed like the best option was to hope the cop was lazy and that he'd get away with a fine. Duncan pulled over and waited.

When the officer reached the car, Duncan had already wound down the window. The officer leaned inside. "License and registration, please."

"Is there a problem, officer?" As he spoke the phrase, Duncan wondered how many times it was uttered across America each day.

"You tell me." The cop's features offered no explanation, and his eyes were hidden behind dark glasses. "License and registration."

Duncan had no answer for the officer. He had no license and no idea where the owner of the car had stashed the registration. "I—"

"Help me! Please!" Lucy chose that moment to make the plea for help that Duncan had been expecting. She was screaming and crying.

The cop features hardened. His eyes flickered between Lucy and Duncan, then he took a step back and placed one hand on his pistol. "I need you to step out of the car, sir. Keep your hands in my sight, move slowly as you exit the vehicle and then stand facing away from the vehicle. I want the child to stay in the car."

Duncan nodded and did as he was told. He kept his eyes on the officer as the cop leaned away and spoke into the radio secured on his right shoulder. In the split second the cop took his eyes off Duncan, he moved his hands quickly, then resumed his slow movement out of the car. As Duncan opened the door, the cop stepped back. Duncan climbed out and waited for the cop to finish talking on the radio.

"Is there anything you need to tell me, sir?" The cop stayed a few steps back, one hand hovering over the pistol holstered on his hip. "I'm just running your plates."

"Sure." Duncan sighed. It was time to confess. "I stole some gas back there. I didn't have the money to pay and I need to get my little girl back home."

The cop's eyes narrowed. "Turn around for me, sir, and place your hands on the car."

Duncan turned around, spread his legs and placed his hands high on the car. As he waited, he listened to the cop speaking into the radio again, and the response. Duncan also watched Lucy Wheeler. The girl had lifted her head and ended her hopeless, static wait. She looked at him through wide eyes, clearly hoping her ordeal was over. He smiled at her and Lucy's eyes flickered between him and the cop.

Duncan swallowed hard when the cop started to describe his appearance. He took his hands off the car and started to turn. "Officer?"

"Stay still!" The cop's voice was raised now. He turned his attention back to the radio. "Dispatch, suspect also has a young, red-haired girl with him."

"Patrol seven, detain the suspect on suspicion of kidnapping and motor vehicle theft. We think he kidnapped the girl from Wallingford."

Duncan had already started to move as the words were spoken, even as he heard Lucy cry out from the car. As he turned, he flicked the knife he'd stashed up his sleeve into his hand. The cop's eyes were wide as he fumbled for his pistol, but he was too late. Duncan took a step and then put all his strength into the blow. The knife went hilt-deep into the cop's stomach.

Duncan dug the blade in several times, pushing the cop over. On the ground, Duncan kept stabbing into his stomach and throat and face, until he was sure the cop was no longer a threat. He was getting tired of these close calls. The attack on the cop was an outlet for his fury. After twenty or thirty blows he stopped, panting, and increasingly aware of the voice still coming from the radio.

Duncan looked down at the knife, shook his head and then glanced at the cop. There was no point hiding this body, the cop's dispatch would know exactly where he was. The only chance Duncan had was to get away quickly. He wiped the knife on the dead cop's uniform and then laughed as he looked down at his own clothes, which were also covered with blood.

Duncan turned back to the car, his heart racing. The fear in Lucy Wheeler's eyes was delicious. She looked at him, her hands and face pressed against the window and tears streaking down her cheeks. Her eyes were red and snot trickled out of her nose. He had a flashback to her mother, ten years ago, terrified as she ran from the car.

All he'd wanted then was to love Ashley.

All he wanted now was to kill her.

60

CHRIS

C hris kept his foot to the floor, glad the undercover vehicle he'd stolen had some balls. He'd used the grunt to get a decent head start on the cops he knew were pursuing them. The fact that they had made a clean escape gave them options.

"We're just going to stop at my hotel for a minute." Chris turned briefly to look at her. "It's possible they'll be there already. If they are, you surrender. Got it?"

Ashley scoffed. "You don't have to worry about me. The minute I'm in danger, you're getting cut loose. You've used up all your credit with me."

Chris started to say something, paused, then let it out. "Ashley, I'm sorry. I failed to protect your family and catch Rowe. I'm going to try my best to fix things, but if we're caught, you need to play along. I'm fucked, whatever happens, but you helped me pull this off – you're implicated too. If both of us get locked up, Rowe wins and Lucy loses."

Her eyes narrowed, but she seemed to accept his advice.

She sat back in her seat and crossed her arms. "Fine. I just want to get my daughter back."

"We will."

Chris slowed the car to take the final turn before his hotel. There was stuff he needed to grab before the cops did, incriminating stuff that would prove he had no authority to launch the operation. It was possible they could still do that, but without the evidence it would take them longer. They knew he'd fooled them and would be keen to prove it, Chris just wanted to make it as difficult as possible. It'd give him more time to catch and kill Duncan Rowe.

Chris pulled the car into the front driveway of the hotel. If it were a decent place, more than three stars or so, there might've been a valet offering to park his car. But given he was travelling on his own dime, there was nobody to bother him. Without a word, Chris popped the trunk, left the car idling and rushed to his hotel room.

Once inside, he scooped up the folders full of documents he'd compiled on Duncan Rowe and stuffed them under his left arm, then he moved to his case and grabbed that as well. He returned to the car, struggling with the documents as he wheeled the case behind him, and threw it all into the trunk. Paperwork spilled everywhere, but he didn't care. The important thing was that the cops didn't get it all.

It had been less than three minutes since they'd pulled in to the hotel. Chris couldn't hear any sirens, and hoped their luck would hold until they were out of the city. He wasn't sure what came after that. There were no leads detailing where Rowe had taken Lucy, though he did know they had to get out of the city. He kept on driving.

"What do we do now?" Ashley broke the silence after a few blocks. "I need to know what the plan is."

"I don't have one." Chris didn't want to lie to her. She'd taken massive risks and was struggling to trust him.

"Okay." It sounded like she was going to say more, when her cell phone beeped.

Chris looked sideways at her as she glanced down at the phone. "What is it? You shouldn't answer any—"

"Oh my God." Ashley's squeal was like nails down a blackboard. The phone fell out of her hand and clattered to the floor. Ashley howled and pounded the dash.

Chris drove on for a moment, then pulled the car over. Although he wasn't sure what was on the phone, he had a sense it involved Lucy. He reached down for it as Ashley continued to sob uncontrollably. The phone was still unlocked, and the photo Ashley had been so traumatized by was still on the screen. Chris felt his heart sink as he stared at Lucy Wheeler, a knife held to her throat, holding up a piece of paper with a location scribbled on it.

"Fucking hell." Chris shook his head. "We're going to get him, I promise. We'll get Lucy back."

Ashley didn't speak or look at him. She just stared into space, her body racked with sobs, tears running down her face. Chris didn't know what to do, except to keep on going. He wasn't sure if the location in the photo was really where they'd find Rowe and Lucy, but he had nothing else to go on. He started driving again, but kept quiet.

It was his fault. He'd failed to catch Duncan Rowe twice now. Ashley and her daughter had paid the price. He'd played his hand, gone all in and lost. He punched the location into the GPS. They were headed in the right direction, and it wasn't far. As far as Chris was concerned, it was a one-way trip. He'd end Duncan Rowe's life or die trying. There was no other result that'd satisfy his guilt.

"Can you hear that?" Her voice was uneven, still emotional and laced with sobs. "I can hear a siren."

Chris heard the slightest hint of it. Distant and pathetic at first, it grew steadily in volume. They were coming for him. Their car was faster than his. Chris gritted his teeth and tried to push the car on, but it was no good. The siren grew louder and after a few more moments he could see the cop car in his rearview mirror.

His obsession had cost him everything – his partner, Hopkins' friendship, his career – but it had cost Ashley Wheeler far more. It was Chris who'd flushed Rowe out of New York City. Though he'd had good intentions, that single act had brought the devil into the house of this poor woman. Her life had been thrown into disarray, and now a madman was holding a knife to her daughter's throat. In comparison, whatever Chris had thought important wasn't.

"You need to let me out, Chris." Ashley suddenly spoke, surprising him. "You have too much heat on you. It's going to get us caught, and Lucy killed."

Chris frowned. "I—"

"No. I've made my decision." Ashley's features were hard. She had no intention of taking him with her any further. "Let me out of the car."

Chris wanted to argue, but he knew he had no right to get in her way. He'd blown their shot at catching Rowe, and his actions had put both Ashley and her daughter in danger. He wanted to get Rowe more than anything, to end all of this, but not as much as the woman sitting next to him. With a sigh, Chris signaled and pulled the car over, then reached into his shoulder holster for his pistol.

"What are you doing?" Ashley frowned at him, then looked down at the pistol.

Chris smiled sadly as he handed it to her. "I'm sorry I didn't get him, Ashley."

Ashley looked at the pistol for several moments, the sound of the siren growing ever closer. She'd made a decision and he had no doubt she'd stick to it. If there was one thing he'd seen in the time he'd known her, it was that she had the strength of her convictions. Finally, she gripped the pistol, looked up at him and exited the vehicle.

A second after she slammed the door shut, Chris floored the accelerator. He'd take the cops on the longest chase he could, to give Ashley as much time as possible. He owed her that much, and it would give her the best chance of killing Rowe. For Chris, that had been all that mattered, now Ashley Wheeler would be the one to end him. She had a much greater stake in this terrible battle than Chris ever had.

She always had.

61

ASHLEY

Ashley finally breathed as the last cop car disappeared from sight, tearing down the highway after Chris. She looked around, pushed herself off her stomach and brushed off the dirt. Nothing was around her except silence and warm sunshine, a far cry from the chaos that had engulfed her right up until a few moments ago. She tucked the pistol down the back of her jeans, covered it with her T-shirt and then started to walk down the road.

She'd hidden low in some high grass beside the road as a fleet of cop cars went past. It left her in no doubt about how much trouble Chris was in, which made her feel better about the choice she'd made. There was no way they'd have been able to avoid the cops. She'd had to shed him. Now there was nobody left to help her. She was on her own.

It was a strange feeling. From the moment she'd watched Laverri shoot a man to the moment she'd told Chris Horan she wanted to get out of the car, she had looked to people in positions of power to help her – her counselor, law enforcement officers and legal professionals. Now all that was over. Now she was walking, alone and desperate, to a showdown with the psycho who had her daughter.

Ashley gritted her teeth and ran, covering the mile to a small satellite town on the outskirts of Wallingford as quickly as she could. By the time she reached the center of the town, her forehead was covered in a thin sheen of sweat and her clothes had that awful damp feel. She wasn't the fittest woman in the world, but fear and urgency had propelled her on. For just a second, though, she needed to pause and prepare.

She put some money into a vending machine to buy a bottle of water. As she sucked it down, she reviewed the decisions she'd made as she ran. The time had helped her solidify what she needed to do, and Ashley knew she had the courage to do it. She finished the water then crossed the street. Just before she walked into a grocery store, she checked that the pistol was in place.

It took her a few minutes to walk the aisles collecting items: some food, bottles of water, a small first-aid kit, a kitchen knife, some rope, and a backpack to put it all in. She wasn't sure exactly what she'd need, so she tried to get a bunch of things that might be useful. After one more quick survey, she took the items to the checkout and placed them on the counter. Only when she was done did she look at the cashier who was scanning her items.

"Going camping?" The girl smiled as she ran a tin of tuna past the scanner. She had red hair and was about sixteen years old, probably working her first job.

"Something like that." Ashley spoke on autopilot as her eyes scanned the store and the street outside.

"Sounds fun." The girl scanned the last item, then looked up at Ashley again. "Seventeen bucks, thanks."

Ashley paid and then spent a moment loading her items into the backpack. She hefted the bag, which was heavy but manageable, and left the store. There was one more thing she had to do. She didn't like the idea, but there was nothing she wouldn't do to protect Lucy. She needed to get to her.

Ashley scanned both sides of the street ahead of her as she walked, waiting for the right opportunity. A couple of times she considered making a move, then thought better of it. She walked a few hundred yards until she found the right opportunity – an older man, but not elderly, struggling to load a bike into the trunk of his car. Ashley looked left and right to make sure there was nobody else around, then moved closer.

"Need some help?" She flashed her best smile at the man as he turned to face her. "Looks like you've got a bit of a struggle on your hands there."

"I'll say." He laughed, running a hand through his hair. "It'll be okay though. It fits, it's just a tight squeeze."

Ashley kept her smile as in one swift motion, she reached behind her back, grabbed the pistol and pointed it at the man. She hated seeing the change on his face – from a friendly smile to a frown of surprise, to an eyes-wide look of fear and loathing. He let go of the bike. It clattered loudly to the ground as he raised his hands slowly.

"What's the problem?" He took a slight step back. "Do you want the bike? The car? Take whatever you like. I don't want any trouble."

"Just the car and any cash you have." Ashley didn't move the pistol, too scared to give him an opening. "Leave the keys and the cash on the ground and ride away."

He nodded frantically. Slowly, he dug into his pocket and tossed the keys onto the road. Another pocket produced a wallet, from which he pulled a small handful of notes. He laid them carefully on the road, using the keys to weigh them down. With one final look of disgust, he climbed onto his bike and started to ride away from her. Ashley stuffed the pistol back into her pants and collected the treasures he'd left.

She closed the trunk of the car and climbed inside. She hated how low she'd had to sink, but her preparations were complete. As she started the car she clenched her jaw and nodded, ready to face the challenge ahead of her. She'd prepared as much as she could, now she had to enter the monster's lair.

He'd told her if anyone else showed up, or there were any tricks, Lucy would die. He'd also told her if she wasn't at the specified location by the specified time, he'd start taking pieces out of Lucy. The thought terrified her. It fueled her with the courage she needed to stop him once and for all.

She put the car into gear and drove.

62

DUNCAN

Duncan looked out of one of the farmhouse windows as he took a gulp from the bottle of orange juice he'd found in the fridge. It was past its best, but there was no way for him to restock. He had to make do with whatever the owners had left in the fridge when they'd gone on vacation. Judging by how much mail had been stuffed into the box and how much food had gone bad in the fridge, they'd been gone a while.

With a sigh, Duncan wiped his mouth with the back of his sleeve and turned away from the window. He glanced at Lucy, sitting on the sofa, her hands tied with rope in front of her, and held out the bottle. Her eyes widened, but Duncan refused to give her any of the juice until she spoke. He was sick of the silent act. The girl would die, but before she did, he wanted to learn as much from her as he could.

"Can I have some?" She finally spoke, her voice soft and frightened. "Please. I'm really thirsty."

Duncan smiled as he stepped closer and handed her the

bottle. She took it with both hands and drank greedily. As she did, he turned back to the window and glanced out again, watching for Ashley. He was growing impatient. He'd expected to see either her or an army of police by now. His message had been clear: show up alone by 7:00 pm, or he'd start cutting pieces off Lucy.

"That's enough." Duncan snatched the bottle from the girl, his tone revealing more of his frustration than intended. "Do you think your mom is coming?"

"She'll come for me." Lucy held his gaze for a second, then looked down. "She always tries to get me."

"I hope so." Duncan smiled at the girl, walked to the kitchen and came back with a large chef's knife. He held it in front of the girl. "You know what this is?"

The girl nodded. "A knife."

Duncan pointed at the clock on the wall. "And you know what that is, right? You're a smart little girl. What's it say?"

"6:57." She looked at the clock, then up at him. She clearly didn't understand the point of his little game.

"Do you know why that's important?" Duncan sat down beside the girl, leaving her some space as he looked up at the clock, the knife beside him.

"No."

"Because when that clock strikes 7:00 pm, your mother will have forced me to do a terrible thing, Lucy."

"What?" Her voice was more frightened now. Her eyes locked onto the clock and her lip curled up.

"You'll find out."

Duncan walked to the window and peered out again. There was no activity outside the house, despite his instructions. He thought he'd made himself clear.

He'd foiled her game, now she had to play his.

Or so he'd thought. He couldn't believe she hadn't come yet. Though he was alert for any sirens or trickery, there was simply nothing happening outside the house. The sun had disappeared over the horizon, bringing darkness, both outside the window and inside Duncan's thoughts. Was she really stupid enough to try and dupe him again?

He didn't want to cut Lucy. He might be willing to kill her in front of her mother, but he wasn't a monster. He'd only do it to wound Ashley, not because he enjoyed hurting children. But if his instructions weren't adhered to, what choice did he have? If Ashley had followed his orders, he'd have ended Lucy Wheeler's life quickly and painlessly. But she hadn't, so now Duncan had to prove a point.

He glanced at the clock again and sighed. After one final look outside, he pulled out his cell phone and sat back down next to the girl. He opened the camera application and framed Lucy into the shot. He reached out and touched the knife against her leg, running it slowly and very gently back toward him, then paused. Her eyes tracked the blade, her breathing heavy and coming in panicked, shallow bursts. She looked up at him with wide eyes.

"Please, don't hurt me," she sobbed, her bottom lip quivering. "Please. I haven't done anything wrong."

"No, you haven't." Duncan's voice was somber. He didn't want to have to do this. "But your mother has hurt me very badly, many times, and now she's hurt you."

"Please, I—"

Duncan shook his head, cutting her off. "Lucy, look at the clock and tell me what time it is."

"7:00." She sobbed again.

The intensity of her scream was something to behold, even before the knife bit into her flesh.

63

ASHLEY

"Damn it!" Ashley pounded the steering wheel over and over as the time on the dashboard clock ticked over to 7:01 pm. "Damn it! Damn it!"

Though she kept driving, way too fast, she was too late. She'd been delayed by road works and that had cost her twenty minutes. She'd been speeding the whole way toward the remote farmhouse, but it wasn't enough. It didn't matter that she was less than two minutes away. His instructions had been clear: be on time or Lucy would get hurt.

Missing Rowe's deadline felt like an explosion in her heart. She'd thought she could handle this, but she'd stumbled at the first hurdle. As the countryside raced past, lit only by the vehicle's headlights, she hoped Rowe would cut her some slack. He was a monster, but all of his victims had been grown women, not children. She hoped desperately that he wouldn't take out his anger on Lucy.

Her phone beeped, and Ashley knew what it would be even before she opened the message. She gasped, and the car swerved. The photo was dark, but it showed a blade slicing into Lucy's thigh, crimson blood spilling over her creamy white skin. Ashley howled with pain and rage. This was all Ashley's fault.

After another minute, sobbing furiously as she sped along, she turned off the main road and into the driveway of the farm. Gravel crunched under the wheels of the car and she took in every detail that was illuminated by the headlights. She was frightened, but she had no choice but to keep pushing on. She now knew Duncan would take out his frustration on Lucy, and Ashley would do anything to prevent that from happening.

Ashley pulled the car to a stop about 50 yards back from the homestead. All the lights were out, and she couldn't see any movement inside. But somewhere in there was her little girl, in desperate fear and pain. Despite her own fear, Ashley was going to end this and protect her little girl.

Not taking her eyes off the house, she wound down all the electric windows and cranked the radio as loud as it would go. She rummaged through the pack on the seat next to her, finding the things she needed. Then she reached for the pistol, took a deep breath, and killed the car headlights.

"I can do this." Her voice was barely a whisper as Ashley stared out of the car into total darkness.

The car beeped as Ashley opened the door, but that sound was masked by the thrashing rock music. The vehicle stayed dark, because she'd turned off the interior light. Darkness was her friend as she crouched low and moved away from the car. She doubted she had more than a few moments until Rowe grew impatient watching from inside. She was counting on it.

She wanted to rescue her daughter, but she wasn't going to walk right into his trap. She had no doubt he'd kill Lucy in front of her, then move on to her. The only way to stop him was to mess with those plans. He knew Lucy was the only bait that would lure her in. Ashley hated thinking of Lucy like that, but she had to.

Gripping the pistol and the kitchen knife, she stalked toward the house. He'd tormented her for long enough. She was going to put him in the ground.

64

DUNCAN

D uncan snarled as the rock music switched to another song, the third since the car had parked and the headlights had gone out. He wasn't sure what game Ashley was playing, but he wasn't enjoying it. On the plus side, there were no sirens. Ashley hadn't told the cops about his message. She had made other mistakes, though.

"Your mother is a very stupid woman, Lucy." Duncan turned to the little girl, who was sobbing hysterically. "What's she playing at?"

He waited for the little girl to talk, but she didn't say a word. With a sigh, Duncan turned back to the car. He was sure he'd be able to see if the car door had opened and Ashley had climbed out. For some reason, she was staying in the vehicle. Duncan watched for several more minutes, waiting for movement, but there was none. As the music changed again, he finally lost the last of his patience and turned away from the window.

"You're going to wait here," Duncan told Lucy as he tied her tightly to the leg of a table. "I'm going to kill your mother."

As the girl wailed, Duncan scooped up the property owner's shotgun and stalked toward the front door. When he reached it, he removed the keys, stepped outside and locked the door behind him. Short of smashing a window and making a bunch of noise, there was now no way for Ashley Wheeler to get inside. He was standing between her and her daughter, far more capable of violence than she was.

"Your delaying will cost you dearly!" His shouts probably couldn't be heard over the music, but with each step he took toward the car he brought the shotgun up slightly more. The message should be clear. He paused a few feet away and then shouted again. "Get the fuck out of the car, Ashley!"

He stood, the shotgun pointed at the windshield in the pale moonlight, his muscles tensed. The longer he waited, the more doubt crept into his mind. He couldn't understand why she'd deliberately antagonize him, not when he had her daughter. With a snarl, he lowered the barrel and fired a shot at the front grill. The shotgun blast drowned out the music for just a second, but still Ashley stayed in the car.

"Last chance!" He pumped the shotgun and roared with rage. "Keep me waiting any longer and I'll stick a blade in Lucy's stomach."

Still nothing. Duncan stepped closer to the car. He pulled open the door and blinked several times. She wasn't inside. In the dim moonlight he could see nothing in the front except a rucksack on the passenger seat. He turned around quickly. He didn't need her sneaking up on him.

He took a step back and looked around. Ashley was nowhere to be seen. He couldn't sense any movement anywhere. He started to walk back to the house, enraged. He couldn't believe the woman would be so callous with her daughter's life. She'd been as cruel to her own daughter as she had been to him a decade ago.

He wasn't concerned about Ashley getting to Lucy. Even if she had the means to get inside the house, there was no way she'd be able to untie her daughter. The knot was tight, and he had no intention of untying the little girl, either before or after he killed her.

All she had done was make him mad.

He raised the shotgun and fired it into the air. The hunt was on.

65

ASHLEY

Ashley gripped the pistol tightly as she heard the boom of the shotgun. She'd continued her long run around the property to the back of the house. The shot told her Duncan had discovered her simple ruse and was coming for her. She'd swallowed her fear when she'd exited the car, but now fear himself was coming for her.

She only had a moment to act. She pulled up short for a second, staring at the back of the small family homestead. The owners must be either dead or out of town. She couldn't think about that right now. Her daughter was inside and her tormenter was outside. The time she'd bought herself was almost up.

Ashley felt, at this moment, exactly how she'd felt back when he'd attacked her and stalked her. She was being hunted by a predator, but hidden. She could stay hidden, as she had so many years ago, but this time she had a whole lot more to lose. She thought of Lucy, terrified and in pain. She wouldn't let her daughter be subjected to this man's insanity, wouldn't let him use her to get what he really wanted.

This time, she had to emerge from the shadows and fight him.

She tried to open the back door, but it was locked. Ashley cursed softly and peered into the window next to the door. The house was totally dark. Her plan relied on quickly being able to get in and then out of the house with Lucy in tow. The darkness meant she was going in blind, with no advantage.

That wouldn't stop her. She gripped the pistol and smashed the window in front of her. It broke loudly, shattering into large shards, some of which fell onto her. Stealth was no longer an option. She used the butt of the pistol to chip away the last of the glass, then took off her sweater and draped it over the window.

"Mommy?" The voice was soft, a whisper, but it was unmistakable. "Mommy?"

Ashley's voice caught in her throat before she had a chance to reply. She didn't know exactly where Lucy was, but she could tell she was close. Ashley started to climb inside the window. She had one leg inside and the other halfway over when something in her pocket began to vibrate, and a split second later started to ring. She froze, then cursed, realizing her phone wasn't on silent. She fumbled for it, still straddling the window, and cut the call.

"Too late." Rowe's voice was molten fury. "You're not half as smart as you think you are, Ashley."

Her eyes widened at the sound of his voice. She turned and saw him, a cell phone lit up in his hand and a shotgun pointed at her. "I—"

The butt of the shotgun rushed toward her face and slammed into it hard.

66

DUNCAN

"Finally!" Duncan let his arms fall away from under Ashley, dropping her in an unceremonious, unconscious heap onto the bed. "Together again!"

Duncan took a step back and admired his handiwork. Ashley was sprawled on the bed and her daughter was tied up next to her, screaming as she tried desperately to rouse her mother. Duncan smiled. Though he didn't want to torment the girl, Ashley had pissed Duncan off with her constant attempts to trick him. He'd been quite clear: turn up, alone and on time, or the girl gets hurt.

Instead, she'd been late, tried to sneak into the house, and failed.

Slamming the butt of the shotgun into her face hadn't been the subtlest move, but it had been the easiest way to subdue her and regain his dominance after so much fucking around. Now he had both Ashley and Lucy Wheeler exactly where he wanted them – subdued, restrained, and under his guard.

"Mom? Mommy?"

Duncan smiled at the sound of Lucy Wheeler's voice, the girl crying for her mother. He leaned in close. "Is she awake?"

"It's okay, baby." Ashley's voice was groggy as her arm moved slowly and pulled her daughter into a cuddle. "I'm here now. It's going to be fine."

"No, it's not." Duncan's voice interrupted the tender moment, and he enjoyed seeing Ashley tense and pull her daughter closer. He still had something of value to take away from her, a way to punish her for all she'd put him through. "It's really not."

Ashley started to speak. "Duncan, I—"

"No!" His shout was far louder than he'd intended. "I've had enough of your apologies, your promises, your bargains, your lies."

Duncan looked down at Lucy Wheeler. Ashley tried to pull her closer, to shield her daughter from his gaze, but Duncan leaned in further, until he was just inches from the girl's face. In the dim light of the single lamp he'd turned on, he enjoyed seeing the terror that washed across Lucy's face. He wondered if a child seeing the devil himself would be more terrified. She started to cry.

"Leave her alone, you bastard!" Ashley's spittle sprayed him as she shrieked. "It's me you want. She's just a little girl!"

"She would have remained that, if you had cooperated." He didn't take his gaze off Lucy as he spoke. "It's time for a lesson, Lucy, about mommy. You see, ten years ago, years before you were born, your mom and I had a lovely relationship. We dated. I wanted more."

"It wasn't a relationship, you sick fuck!" Ashley started to sob. "It was one fucking date, after which you tried to rape me."

"I. Do. Not. Want. To. Hear. It." Duncan was inches from her face now, close enough to see her fear and smell her breath. "You led me on and then broke my heart!"

"You're delusional, Duncan," she hissed, when he finally paused. "I agreed to go on a date with you because I felt sorry for you."

"I would've looked after you. I would've been good to you, not like that scumbag ex-husband of yours." Duncan glared at her, then turned to Lucy. "You could have been my daughter, Lucy. We could have been happy. But your mother had other ideas. She ran from me, so I had to punish those other women on her behalf."

Duncan sighed. Things could have been so much better.

67

ASHLEY

"Now the consequences must be greater."

Rowe's words chilled Ashley. She'd underestimated the degree of pain his delusions about her had caused. Now he was scolding her for breaking their deal, then for her amateurish rescue attempt. Finally, in a cold, quiet voice, he promised them pain.

Then again, he'd been promising pain for several minutes now. When Ashley had decided to break Lucy out herself, she'd done it knowing full well that if she were caught, the consequences would be immediate and severe. That he'd delayed so much, talked so much, had caused her to doubt that assumption. It was almost like he was building up to something, preparing to unleash whatever he'd had planned for so many years.

His pacing, his fast talking, his sweating and shaking showed her that, far from the calculating killer Horan had painted him to be, Duncan Rowe was actually just crazy. She watched him shifting the shotgun from hand to hand, speaking to himself as much as to Ashley and Lucy, as if he was building up to something or didn't want to get started.

The second he did, she was determined to act. She had to protect her daughter. She'd lunge at Duncan, hoping to take him down in the struggle. She'd do anything to stop him. She knew the plan had almost no chance of working – he was bigger, stronger, had a gun, and wasn't concussed – but the only alternative was to watch him destroy Lucy. She'd gladly sacrifice herself if it meant crippling or killing him. That was the only way she could save Lucy.

Before that, she'd try to talk to him one more time. "Duncan, please. You don't need to do this. I know you've killed others, but you can walk away, and we will too."

He laughed. "Why would I do that? I was prepared to make deals with you, but you shat all over that."

"Because there are cops and FBI agents on their way here right now," she lied. Nobody was coming. Rowe probably knew that.

"No deal." He stopped pacing for a moment and smiled at her. It was like glimpsing pure evil. "I think it's time to get started."

Before she could speak, he turned and left the room. Ashley didn't move off the bed. She edged closer to Lucy and wrapped her in a hug. Her daughter cried as she cuddled into Ashley's chest, like she had so many times before Ashley had lost custody. Ashley clenched her jaw, hoping to ward off her own emotions as she heard Duncan's footsteps growing louder as he returned.

"I've got something special for you, Ashley." Rowe peered inside the room with a smile on his face, then stepped inside.

Ashley flinched when she saw the knife in his hand. It looked razor sharp, something the homeowners took pride in.

He started to pace again, back and forth, the knife in one hand and the shotgun in the other. She hugged Lucy tighter to her chest as she watched him, pacing and shaking his head. Suddenly something changed. He nodded to himself, as though he'd made a decision, then turned to her sharply and stared.

Her plan to stop him amounted to nothing. He lunged at her faster than she could untangle herself from Lucy. She'd only just started to turn when the knife bit into her. She cried out and squeezed Lucy tighter, the pain in her shoulder burning like fire. Her scream was drowned out by the pained bellow that Duncan Rowe unleashed. It was a sound from the bowels of hell, the sound of venom spewing forth after brewing for ten years.

Though the knife was out of her a second later, Ashley knew it wasn't over.

68

DUNCAN

"Fucking hell." Duncan's voice was high pitched, unable to believe what was happening as he drew in closer to Ashley Wheeler.

She was a bloody mess. He'd cut her plenty and then stabbed her in the back as she'd tried to move away from him. He hadn't meant to. He didn't want it to end yet. He'd just wanted to cause her some pain before killing her daughter. He'd wanted this moment to last for hours, but now it looked like it'd be less than a few minutes. Her blood was flowing onto the carpet, causing her life to ebb away.

"Why'd you make me do this?" He curled up alongside her, his face twisted in anguish as he hissed the words. "Why couldn't you do what you were supposed to?"

"Kill me." Ashley ignored his question and pleaded with him instead, her whisper barely a kiss of air against his ear. "Kill me, but spare Lucy. Please."

Duncan pulled away from her and howled, climbing to his feet. He threw the knife against the wall and started to pace again. He wanted to take things back, to fix things, to make her see how badly she'd hurt him. He wanted her to see that they should've been together, that everything that'd happened since had occurred because she'd rejected him.

"You stupid woman!" Duncan's sobs were coming thick and fast now. "Things could have been so different!"

Ashley didn't respond, she just wrapped Lucy up into a hug. The little girl was crying uncontrollably. As Duncan watched them, curled up together, he felt jealousy unlike any he'd felt before. No matter how much pain he caused Ashley, he knew he could never take away the bond she shared with her daughter. He wanted her to feel like that about him. She was as fixated on Lucy as he was on Ashley.

"It could have been so different." He fell onto the bed again, crawling over to where they were cuddling. "This could have been mine."

"No!" Lucy's scream was broken by her sobs, but the pain and the hatred in her words were clear.

"You could have been mine!" Duncan shouted into her face, feeling something switch in his head. "But now you need to go away!"

"Lucy, run!" Ashley screamed.

As Duncan was about to reply, he felt something grip his leg. He turned to look down, feeling like he was moving in slow motion. Ashley had locked both her arms around his ankle while Lucy sprang up from the bed and ran out of the room. Confusion overwhelmed him. How was she free of the ropes? It felt like he lost the initiative in a split second. He needed to wrench it back.

Duncan brought his fist around in an arc and slammed it into the side of Ashley's head. He rained blows on her until he felt her grip on his ankle slacken. He was surprised it took so long, a testament to the pain Ashley was willing to endure to give her daughter a chance to escape. Duncan turned to chase after the girl, feeling as if a simmering pot had been turned back up to full boil.

He'd been stupid and soft and sentimental. He'd taken his eyes off the prize he'd lusted after for ten years. He hadn't wanted Ashley Wheeler, not since she'd left his car all those years ago. No, what he wanted was to destroy everything important to her. Nothing else would satisfy the pain she'd caused him. His own stupid weakness had nearly cost him that opportunity.

He paused only to grab the shotgun, then chased Lucy into the night.

69

ASHLEY

A shley groaned as she pushed herself off the bed. She wasn't sure how many wounds she'd sustained, but she did know Lucy was alone and afraid, being pursued by a maniac. She'd engineered Lucy's escape, untying the rope binding her legs while she hugged her. Now she had to help. She fell to the floor, landing hard. She felt lightheaded, and her eyes were heavy. It'd be all too easy to lie there, close her eyes and fall asleep. But she had to move.

Fear and panic at what Duncan might already be doing to Lucy pushed her on. She placed both hands on the side of the bed and pulled herself up, staggering awkwardly but managing to stay upright. Stumbling toward the door, Ashley was careful to keep hold of something as she moved. She was certain if she fell she wouldn't get back up again.

She picked up the knife and stumbled through the house toward the open front door. With each step she felt herself growing weaker, her injuries making her a desperate mess, but she pushed on into the night. Somewhere out there in the darkness, he was stalking her daughter.

"Lucy!" Ashley screamed as loud as she could.

The boom of the shotgun was her only response. It wasn't far away. Ashley paused when she heard it, the fading remnants of the blast enough to increase her heart rate, but she couldn't stop. She gripped the knife and struggled into a strange jog, the movements of a desperate woman with only one thing left to do before she died. She had no idea if she was even moving in the right direction. All she could do was take a gamble and hope it paid off.

It did. After struggling forward for a few minutes, she heard a squeal. It was Lucy. She clenched the knife and continued on in the direction of the squeal and the shouts of Duncan Rowe. The darkness was unrelenting, the chill night air stung her lungs, but she felt no pain. Adrenaline was taking care of that. Yet still Ashley felt her strength draining and her body failing with every step.

Then she saw him. Ten steps away, standing over Lucy. He had the shotgun raised and pointed at her daughter, the person who kept her going, the only thing she cared about or was proud of. Ashley clenched her jaw and felt her mind cloud over with rage. She stalked forward. Duncan was berating Lucy, but Ashley couldn't hear the words, only the threat in the tone of his voice.

He was a predator. And now, so was she.

The faint sound of sirens off in the distance did nothing to reassure her or slow her actions, because she had no faith they'd get here in time. She needed to do this herself. There was nothing on the whole planet more important to Ashley than protecting her daughter.

"Duncan!" Ashley put all her remaining energy into

drawing his attention away from Lucy and toward her. Her voice was hoarse and full of emotion. "You're a dead man!"

He laughed, turned his back on Lucy and came face to face with Ashley. "This is your doing. I was going to drag Lucy back and dismember her in front of you, but here will do just fine."

As he began to raise the shotgun, Ashley lunged forward. Both her feet left the ground and she speared the kitchen knife into his chest. Her dead weight was an advantage as her momentum pushed him onto his back. She landed on top of him, hard, forcing the knife in deeper. He grunted and immediately reached up for the blade.

"Lucy! Look away!" Ashley shouted as she plunged the knife into his chest several more times, then collapsed on top of him. "Don't look baby."

She lay there, sobbing, spent. Struggling to move, she rolled off of him and Lucy crept up alongside her. The sound of sirens approaching rapidly filled her ears and Lucy stared down at her

Ashley looked up at Lucy and smiled.

ABOUT THE AUTHOR

Steve P. Vincent is the USA Today Bestselling Author of the Jack Emery and Mitch Herron conspiracy thriller series.

Steve has a degree in political science, a thesis on global terrorism, a decade as a policy advisor and training from the FBI and Australian Army in his conspiracy kit bag.

When he's not writing, Steve enjoys whisky, sports and travel.

You can contact Steve at all the usual places:
stevepvincent.com
steve@stevepvincent.com

ACKNOWLEDGMENTS

This book would never have seen the light of day without the love and support of my wife, Vanessa Pratt.

My trusty team of beta readers help me mop up the messes and untangle the wires before they embarrass me. Thanks to Gerard Burg, Dave Sinclair, Andrew McLaughlin, Janice Harris.

Amanda Pillar smashed the cover for this one. You should read her books. She's a talented woman.

Vanessa Lanaway applied the editorial scalpel and became my second favourite Vanessa.

Readers, friends, family - thanks to you all.

www.ingramcontent.com/pod-product-compliance
Lightning Source LLC
Chambersburg PA
CBHW030045130726
47901CB00007BA/1985